NEUTRAL ZONE

TEAGAN HUNTER

Editing by Editing by C. Marie

Proofreading by Judy's Proofreading & Julia Griffis

For you, you badass bitch.

CHAPTER 1

"Here! Here!" I tap my stick against the ice, begging for the pass.

The defenseman slides the puck my way from behind the net, and I take off at full speed, keeping my head up and making sure I'm in the clear.

"Wheels, wheels, wheels!" someone yells from the bench. I'm not sure who it is, maybe Greer? He's not in the net tonight, but I know he's sitting there watching the game with sharp eyes. Either way, I listen, charging up the ice, spinning around one LA player, then another. I lock eyes with the goalie as I let the puck fly off the toe of my blade.

All twenty thousand people in the sold-out arena explode in cheers when it hits the back of the net.

"FUCK YES!" I shout as the rest of the Comets empty the bench, crowding around me, knocking my helmet with their own, and shoving at me.

"Now, *that's* an OT win, baby!" Rhodes says, tapping his bucket against mine.

1

"That was all you," I tell him as Wright, another defenseman, grabs me and gives me an excited shake.

Rhodes gives me a look like I'm full of shit, but I'm not. If he hadn't read that pass the way he did, I wouldn't have been able to take off like that. He set it up, and I followed through on it.

The team bumps heads with the goalie, a tradition we have when we win, then we make our way off the ice, feeding off the cheers from the home crowd. I barely hold back a groan when I'm stopped in the tunnel and told to get my smile ready. I'm about to be bombarded by the media; I know it.

"Tonight's first star of the game, with the game-winning overtime goal, is Ivan FIIIIIITZGERALD!"

I hop onto the ice, skate a few quick circles, and toss the t-shirt in my hands into the crowd before taking a seat next to our commentator, J.P.

"Heck of a game there, Ivan! How does it feel to have the overtime winner?"

I grin. "Good. Really good."

"I heard you tap your stick for Beast to pass the puck to you. You saw that opening from a mile away, didn't ya, big guy?"

I did. I saw it playing out in my head before I begged for the puck, but I can't tell him that. I'll come off as too cocky, and that's not who I am, especially not in front of the cameras.

"I saw something that might work, so I took the shot."

"Good shot, too." He laughs. "Well, we'll let you get going, go celebrate with the guys. Thanks for taking the time to talk, and hey, thanks for that winning goal. Congrats on a great game, Fitzy."

"Yeah, thanks, J.P."

I shake his hand, give the still-roaring crowd another wave, and then head down the tunnel to the locker room, more than ready to hit the showers and go home for the night. We have tomorrow off before we continue our three-game homestand, and I'm looking forward to it.

"A couple of us are hitting up Slapshots. You game?" Hayes asks as soon as I walk into the dressing room.

"Nah, man. I'm going to head home." I yank my sweater over my head and toss it into the laundry bin, then drop down into my cubby.

"You sure? Guaranteed to find some willing pussy there." He lifts his dark brows up and down.

"Don't talk about women like that, idiot." Miller, a forward with some hot hands, slaps Hayes across the back of his head as he walks by.

I can't help but laugh because I'm pretty sure Miller was Hayes at one point before he settled down with Scout, the donut truck owner turned romance novelist. Now, he's wrapped around her finger and follows her like a lost puppy.

Looking at Hayes, I point at Miller. "For the record, I'm with him."

"You are?" Miller asks, his mouth ajar. He snaps it

3

shut quickly, then puffs his chest out. "I mean, yeah—of course I'm right and you agree with me."

I do my best to hide my laugh.

Hayes lifts his eyes skyward. "Fine. We're guaranteed to find some ladies who would love to be ravaged."

I shake my head. "While that's slightly better, no, thank you."

"You're no fun," Hayes complains, but thankfully, he drops it.

I don't feel like explaining that I don't want to go out because I *hate* going out. It's not my scene, and it never will be my scene. The few times I've been out with the guys haven't really been my idea. I only did it for team bonding and shit when I was first brought on. In fact, the last time I went to Slapshots was with Greer and Hayes, and that night ended up changing the direction of Greer's life.

That's not something I'm looking for now.

I'm content with what I have—hockey, hockey, and more hockey. It's all I've ever needed to be happy. It's not that I don't want to settle down someday; I don't hate the idea like some guys, but I'm not actively pursuing it either. If it happens, it happens, but for now, I'm happy playing the best game ever to exist and getting paid damn well to do it.

And none of that has anything to do with the fact that I'm horrible at putting myself out there. No. That's not it at all. I just like being alone.

"Fitz! Media!" Coach Heller yells, and I try to keep my eyes from rolling.

I *hate* talking to the media. They all ask the same questions, forcing me to give the same answers creatively. They must get together and coordinate this attack on players. There's no way they don't.

I finish stripping off all my gear, then toss on a pair of shorts and a navy Comets t-shirt before heading off to fulfill my duty. As I predicted, it's a bunch of the same old bullshit.

"How did it feel to get the overtime winner?" *Just terrible. I hate winning.*

"What about that pass from Rhodes? Incredible, huh? Did you practice that?" *No. Not at all. We never practice. It's purely natural talent.*

"You guys struggled a bit during the second period. Any reason for that?" *Because we sucked. No real reason other than simply playing bad hockey when we should have been playing hockier hockey than the other team.*

While those aren't the answers I give, they're the ones screaming loudest in my head.

"Fuck, this shit is hard sometimes," I mutter as I head back to the locker room, feeling completely exhausted after being forced in front of the camera. Sure, it was probably only five whole minutes of my life, but it felt like years. I am not cut out for this part of playing professional sports, that's for damn sure.

"I fucking feel that," Rhodes says as he slings his bag

5

over his shoulder. "I'm pretty sure I'm getting fined for my interview."

I laugh. "Did you shove the microphones out of your face again?"

"You're damn right I did. I could *smell* the spit on one." He wrinkles his nose. "And tobacco. I hate when they do that. It's bullshit."

It really is.

"I might have also given them an earful of my opinion on that crap call in the second. But, hey, they asked."

I shake my head. "They'll never learn."

"Nope. Sure won't." He claps me on the shoulder. "I'm heading home to the wife. Great game out there tonight. Later, man."

"Yeah, later," I say as he walks out of the room.

There are a few stragglers, a couple of guys I'm not close with, so I finish stuffing my bag and hit the road too. I manage to make it to my old 1971 forest green Chevy truck without being bothered again—a miracle, really—and the first thing I do is stop at Smoothie Town for my late-night strawberry fix. It's a little tradition of mine after home games. Win or lose, I get a smoothie for the drive home.

I shove the truck into park and check my phone for the first time since before the game. I'm unsurprised to find a few texts waiting for me.

. . .

Mom: MY BABY BOY!

Mom: Before you yell at me, I know you're not a baby, but you'll always be MY baby.

Mom: I'm so proud of you, son. I love you. Call in the morning, okay?

If you looked up "hockey mom" in the dictionary, the name Anya Fitzgerald would be right next to it because that's exactly what my mother is—a hockey mom through and through. She's been my biggest cheerleader since I first stepped foot on the ice, and that dedication has never waned. Hell, she's more into my hockey career than my father, and I think it strengthens our bond.

Don't get me wrong—my dad loves and supports the hell out of me, but football is where his heart lies; he even coaches it at the college level. So, while he appreciates that I'm an athlete and greatly respects my work ethic, he doesn't understand why I couldn't put that devotion toward football rather than hockey. It was always a sore subject between us, and my mother was excited to get a break from all things football and focus on something else.

So, yeah, I fully expected to be hearing from her after that game.

I shoot her a few texts, a grin on my face as I type.

Me: I promise to call first thing in the AM.

Me: Well, maybe not the FIRST thing. Time difference and all that.

Me: And I'll always be your baby boy…just don't tell any of the guys I said that. Deal? I love you, too.

Satisfied, I turn off my truck and hop out, heading toward one of my favorite things about playing home games.

"Hey, Fitz. That was a great goal tonight," Dirk, the kid behind the window, says when I walk up.

"Thanks, man. It was all Rhodes, though."

"Really? Because I didn't see it go off his stick into the net. Pretty sure that was all you."

My cheeks grow hot under the attention, and I clear my throat. "Can I—"

"Get a twenty-ounce strawberry smoothie?"

I chuckle. "That predictable?"

He shrugs. "I prefer to call you a regular instead of predictable."

"I appreciate that."

He's full of shit, though. I *am* predictable. I know it, and he does too. Hell, even my teammates know it. The only place I'm not predictable is on the ice, which I suppose is good because I keep the goalies on their toes.

Outside of the rink, though, everything about me is consistent. I get up at five every morning, go for a quick three-mile jog, then head back to my apartment for the same breakfast I have every day: oatmeal mixed with strawberries and a slice of toast topped with peanut butter and even more strawberries because my strawberry obsession is alive and well.

After breakfast, I set my coffee to brew and hit the shower while the machine does its thing. After that, I do what I do every other day—hockey. It takes over my whole afternoon and evening during the season and, truthfully, the rest of the year too.

My life is pretty boring, except for that one thing I don't ever talk about with anyone.

"Here you go," Dirk says, pulling me from my own head as he slides my drink across the counter. The kid shakes his head at me when I try to hand over my card. "On me. My way of saying thanks for getting those two points for us."

Points we needed, especially after starting our season with a three-game losing streak. We were still reeling from losing in the Playoffs after Greer's injury kept him out of the lineup, so we tanked our first three games. We're already in an uphill battle, and the season has just begun.

"Thanks, Dirk. Have a good night." I slip a fifty-dollar bill into his tip cup, returning to my truck before he can complain.

I swing myself up and into the driver's seat, then head home. It's a quick five-minute drive, and I'm parking my big beast before I know it. I wave to the doorman as I hustle past him to the elevators. I hit sixteen and sip on my drink as the car takes me up.

I grin when the elevator doors open because I can hear her from here.

I unlock my door and push it open just wide enough for me to shimmy through, moving quickly so she can't slip out. She's done that too many times for my liking, especially with Miss Drake living down the hall and feeding her too many treats any chance she gets. I got a reaming from the vet last time I took her in, and I'm not looking for a repeat of that.

"Hey, Carl," I say, scooping the fluffy brown and white cat into my arms. "How was your night?"

Meow.

"That good, huh?" I scratch under her chin. "You hungry?"

Meow.

"Come on, let's get you something."

I let her leap down to the floor, then make my way to my kitchen, pulling her food out from her designated cabinet and filling her bowl with a small scoop. I add a little treat on top just because I can. Carl rubs against my legs as a thank-you, then dives right into her second dinner like I didn't leave her a first one before I left.

Carl does her thing, and I make my way to my bedroom, stripping out of my clothes. It's been a long day, and I'm more than ready to relax. I pull on a pair of sweatpants, skipping a t-shirt, then pad back to the poorly decorated spare bedroom I use as my office, where I flop down into my desk chair. I don't even bother pretending I'm going to do anything productive. I know exactly what I'm sitting here for.

Her.

I shake the mouse to wake up my computer, then navigate to my favorite streaming site. As I expected, she's already on.

RoPlaying is online. Would you like to watch?

Not join. *Watch.*

Because that's what I like to do—I enjoy watching.

I didn't realize it's something I'm into until a few years ago when I was more into watching the woman I was seeing than I was into actually having sex with her. It's not that I don't enjoy sex, because I definitely do, but just sitting back and watching is perfectly fine by me. The sounds, the lighting, the outfits…it does more for me than the actual act of having sex. It's not just about the physical aspect of it; it's everything.

I asked her one night if I could just watch, and she allowed it. She thought it was weird but agreed. I asked her to go to a bar and flirt with another guy, told her I'd sit in the corner and let it play out. Again, weird for her, but she did it. We had some great sex that night, but when I asked her if I could sit *outside* her house while she had the curtains drawn open and watch…well, it crossed the line for her. She informed me I was a pervert and the only reason she was dating a "toothless loser" like me was because I played pro hockey.

After that, I backed off the dating scene. I didn't want this newfound thing of mine to get out, especially not to the media. The last thing I needed was a headline calling me a Peeping Tom.

It's been me, my hand, and porn sites since. That's how I found this particular stream I can't seem to get enough of, by surfing the web. I figured I like to watch, so what better way than watching a cam girl?

I click join, then settle into my chair as her image fills the screen.

As usual, she's wearing a mask. It's a black and gold Venetian style that doesn't cover her entire face, but it's enough to hide her real identity. She has on heavy makeup that makes her green eyes extra bright and a light pink wig that ensures she could walk down the street next to you and you'd have no clue you're standing beside her.

She keeps her voice low as she talks about her day, all while painting her toenails. She's fully clothed but wearing lingerie that doesn't leave a whole lot to the imagination, especially not with her legs bent and the bottoms of the tiny shorts she's wearing flirting with flashing the parts of her I'm dying to see.

That's all she's doing—painting her toes and talking.

And I'm absolutely fucking addicted to it.

I have no idea why. I'm not sure if it means there's something wrong with me that I find this so damn hot, but I do. I love every minute of it, and my cock is already beginning to swell behind my sweats.

It's been two months since I found her channel, and it took me all of one night to get hooked on it. Now, if I miss a stream, I feel off. It's sad, I know, but here we are anyway.

Watching her isn't why I didn't want to go to Slapshots tonight. Okay, so watching her *is* part of it, but no matter what, I still would have told Hayes no, not only because I'd rather be sitting right here but because I don't have any interest in hitting up a bar. I have no desire to pretend to be one of the guys who only worry about getting laid. I'm happy staying home and doing my own thing. I learned long ago I don't crave the attention some other guys on the team do.

My gaze is pulled back to the screen when she jostles around, and I don't miss how her tits spill out of her top even more. She's wearing a black bra that barely covers anything, showing that she's well aware of who her audience is and what they're there for...myself included, as much as I hate to admit it.

I press against my cock that's now hard as a rock, trying to relieve some of the growing ache. I promised myself when I started tuning in for this that I would never, ever touch myself while I watch, and so far, I've kept that promise.

I should feel ashamed for doing this, for watching her and enjoying it so much, but she wouldn't be on this camera if she didn't *want* people watching, right?

At least that's what I tell myself to feel better.

She dips her brush back into the bottle—a deep orange—and her tongue pokes out of the corner of her mouth as she concentrates on what she's doing. After she's done with her toes, she moves to her hands, and I watch diligently as she paints each one twice.

That's the weirdest part of all of this. She doesn't talk much, but it doesn't make watching her any less appealing. It should, but it doesn't. I'm still here, showing up nearly nightly even though there's never much said other than a few low sighs. Sometimes she'll talk about her day, like tonight, but others she's silent. It doesn't make it any less thrilling to watch her.

It's pathetic.

I'm pathetic. I gave up a night out with my teammates to watch someone online do the most mundane things.

"And done," she says softly in that raspy voice of hers. She looks down at the task she's completed and smiles, then shimmies her hips, making her tits jiggle once more. I watch with rapt attention like the pervert I am.

My eyes drift over to the button that's been taunting me for months now.

Request Private Video.

I want to click it. I want to click it so fucking badly my hands actually tingle with need.

But I don't. I never do. That's crossing a line I can't uncross.

I try not to think about the times she's accepted that request from other people, the things she could be doing in those chats. I want to pretend she doesn't, want to pretend it's just me and her and nobody else is watching.

She looks over at the clock that's hanging on the wall of the background that's one of her favorites to use and sinks her teeth into her bottom lip when she looks back at the camera.

Oh yeah. She totally knows what she's doing.

"It's getting late," she says in a husky whisper. "I have an early morning. Thanks for tuning in this evening."

Her eyes move to the camera, and it feels like she's staring into my soul. Like it's just *us* in this room. Like there aren't other people watching her.

Some nights, like tonight, she'll have her comments turned on, and her eyes flit over them as they roll in. Nearly all are respectful, but some make me want to reach through the screen and punch whoever is on the other side.

So, I do what I always do at the end of every stream I watch. I sit forward, hands on my keyboard, and I write her a message.

.   .   .

15

ShootsAndScores: I'm glad you chose orange. It's my favorite color. Hope your day was amazing, Ro.

A slight smile plays on her lips as she reads over the messages, and I tell myself it's because of mine, though I highly doubt that.

"Good night," she says.

When she covers the camera with her hand and the screen goes black, I pretend her words were just for me.

"Good night, Rosie," I reply.

CHAPTER 2

ROSIE

"Son of a…"

I glower down at the mess all over the floor of the donut truck I've practically been running on my own for the last six months or so. This isn't the first time I've dropped a container of sprinkles and I'm sure it won't be the last, but this whole situation would be much better if I hadn't dropped an entire pitcher of cold brew too.

Why did I think grabbing ten things from the fridge at once was a good idea? Oh, right—because I'm running behind on getting ready to open and doing several things at once is completely necessary because if I don't, there is no way I will get this truck open on time, and Scout will *kill* me if that happens.

Setting my hands on my hips, I close my eyes, suck in a deep breath, and then exhale.

In. Out.

In. Out.

Breathe, Rosie. You've got this. You're off your game today, but you can fix this.

When my heart rate finds a natural rhythm and I don't feel like the next thing out of my mouth will be a curse word, I peel my eyes open, then get to work cleaning up the mess I made.

It's a Monday morning, and by morning, I mean *morning*. It's currently 4:45 AM, I'm supposed to open at six, and I still have about ten things on my to-do list. Big things. Important-to-running-this-truck kind of things. I mean, it's *Monday*, for crying out loud. There is no way we won't have a line forming five minutes before we open, and there's no way it will not be stretched out to the parking lot at one point.

This place is a hotspot for the players of the Carolina Comets, our local NHL team. I guarantee at least half the team will roll through here like they do nearly every morning. The last thing I want to do is upset Scout by making their experience here bad. They bring in big crowds, and if they think this place has gone to the crapper…well, it won't be good, that's for sure.

"I'm screwed," I mutter to nobody else but myself since I'm the only one here for another fifteen minutes at least.

Stevie, the older sister of the truck's owner, should be here soon to help prep for the day. She usually comes in before she drops her daughter off at school, then pops back in for the lunch rush we always seem to have. Who knew donuts and coffee would be such a hit at noon?

I let out a big yawn as I towel up the rest of the

sprinkles-and-coffee mess, then dump the soaking wet rag into the wash bin.

"Real rude of you," I say to the now-cracked coffee pitcher as I pick it up off the counter. "I was really looking forward to you this morning."

I'm running on about four hours of sleep, so the beautiful pitcher of jitter juice was just what I needed to add a pep to my step, but that's not happening now.

"Guess I'll have to settle for hot coffee." I sneer at the pot that's currently being filled. "You're gross, but you'll do."

"Are you talking to yourself again?"

I spin around to find Stevie walking in through the door at the other end of the truck. Her dark brown hair is pulled into a high, sleek bun, and she's dressed in cute jeans and a form-fitting long-sleeve green sweater.

I look like a damn trash goblin standing next to her. My blonde hair is tied up in a messy bun, and I'm pretty sure the clothes I'm wearing—a pair of jeans and a simple long-sleeve striped shirt—are the same ones I wore two days ago. I didn't even have the chance to swipe on some mascara this morning or do anything to my eyebrows.

I'm a wreck.

And an uncaffeinated wreck at that.

"You're early," I say by way of greeting.

She lifts a shoulder. "Greer woke me up early when he went out for his run, so I figured I'd get a jump on the day. He's going to take Macie to school for me since she doesn't like riding in my 'lame' SUV."

I wrinkle my nose. "Running is so gross."

I've never understood why people find it enjoyable, but to each their own. I'd much rather get my activity in by doing something more exciting like rollerblading or playing volleyball on a beach. Oh man, the beach sounds really nice right about now. Well, maybe not *now* now because it's October, but still.

"Right? It should be outlawed unless you're running from Michael Myers or something. Then I'll allow it."

"You'd run *away* from him? I'd run *to* him."

"But he's a total psycho killer, Rosie—why would you run to him?"

"A psycho killer, sure, but in a *hot* way. He's just misunderstood."

Stevie laughs. "You really need to stay away from Harper. You two together would be dangerous in the same room."

Harper, the wife of one of the many Carolina Comets players who frequent Scout's Sweets, is known for being obsessed with all things horror. She loves it so much she's built a successful business making props for horror movies and creepy dolls.

Hmm. Maybe I can get her to make me something for my streaming setup.

"So, what's going on here?" Stevie's eyes wander around the chaotic state the place is currently in.

"I dropped the sprinkles."

She grimaces. "Oh no."

"Oh yes. It was extra unfortunate because I also dropped the cold brew." I gesture to the busted pitcher. "It's broken."

"Oh no," Stevie mutters again. "We open in..."

"Less than an hour? I know." I exhale heavily, then give myself a shake. "Okay, here's what's happening: you're going to the store and grabbing sprinkles. We need a mix of red, white, and blue, the biggest tub you can find. Hell, grab two. Then we need four things of cold brew, unsweetened, dark roast. And of course, another pitcher. But it *has* to be the forty-eight-ounce one or it's not going to work." I clap my hands together. "Annnd go!"

Stevie doesn't move. She just stands there, brows raised. That's when I realize...

"Oh god. You're the boss' sister, so you're basically my boss and I totally just overstepped. I—"

Stevie's laugh cuts off my words, and she waves her hand. "No, it's not that. It's just you remind me so much of Scout, taking charge and kicking ass. I love it. No wonder she trusts you with her baby so much."

Phew. "Thank you. Truly. I promise I'll have everything cleaned up and ready to go before you get back."

"Oh, I know you will, you little badass." She throws me a wink, then grabs her purse off the hook and pulls it over her shoulder.

"Has anyone told you lately how amazing you are?"

A saccharine smile curves her lips, and her eyes glaze over like she's remembering someone saying that very thing only recently. "Only Greer."

I want to be annoyed by her answer. I want to think, *Ew, gross. Stop being so in love.*

But I can't find it in me, not after everything Stevie's been through, not just in her life but with Greer, the goalie for the Carolina Comets who she started dating earlier this year. They deserve each other, and more than that, they deserve to be happy.

I wish I had that too.

"I still can't believe you're together."

She laughs. "You're telling me. Especially since I swore I hated him."

"You hated how hot he made you, maybe, but you never hated him."

Her cheeks pinken. "Hush or I'll send *you* to run errands, and I'll inevitably mess up the morning prep. Then, when Scout is freaking out about all the one-star reviews we'll get bombed with, I'll tell her it's all your fault."

I gasp. "You'd never!"

She lifts a perfectly shaped brow. "Want to bet?"

She wouldn't, not really—but that doesn't mean it doesn't scare me.

"Fine." I mimic zipping my lips and throwing away the key.

Stevie chuckles. "Smart move. I'll be back in a bit. Try not to break anything else, and text me if you do!"

I gasp. "Too soon, Stevie! Too soon!"

She laughs her way out of the truck, jogging toward her car parked at the back of the lot next to mine, and I begin prepping the one thing everyone will be lining up for—donuts. I knead the dough, then move on to forming the donuts. Having done this for the last however many mornings, I move quickly, blazing through my to-make list like it's nothing.

I glance at the clock: roughly twenty minutes to go until we open.

"I got this. I can do this."

A throat clears behind me, and I nearly drop *another* container of sprinkles at the sudden intrusion.

When I see who it is, I narrow my eyes. "What the hell is wrong with you, just sneaking up on people like that? I could have had a heart attack, and then I'd be really pissed."

"You'd probably also be dead, so would there really be anything to be mad about?"

"Yes!"

He grins at my answer. "Morning, Rosie." That soft, velvety-smooth voice of his slides over me, tickling in all the best places.

I swear I feel my knees start to buckle, and I catch myself from falling at the last second. I've already had a bad morning; I'd rather not add to that by making a complete fool of myself in front of one of the star forwards on the Carolina Comets.

"How's it going?" he asks.

"Fine," I tell him, even though this morning has been anything but fine. "We'll be ready to open in a few minutes."

"No problem. I know I'm a bit early, and I'm in no rush. I'm early for everything today."

I nod. "Stevie ran out to grab some coffee and sprinkles. We're out. I dropped them. I dropped the sprinkles all over the floor and made a mess, and then I dropped coffee on top of it and broke the pitcher, and I—"

Am rambling. I'm rambling like a damn fool in front of Ivan fucking Fitzgerald, a professional hockey player who is by far the most attractive man I've ever seen in person. And on my television screen, because, yes, I do watch all of his games.

Man, I really wish I'd gone to sleep earlier last night. I truly am a mess today because rambling is *so* not me. Well, not anymore.

"Rough morning, then?" Fitz asks.

I huff out a contrived laugh. "You could say that."

"I know how you feel. I'm that guy who always wakes up at five AM on the dot, and this morning, I was up at four thirty like some psycho, *and* I'm ninety percent sure I stepped in gum on my way here." He scrapes his shoe against the gravel like he's still trying to get it off.

"I was up at four thirty."

I would have been up at four if my alarm had gone off. Apparently, that extra half hour really does make a difference for my sanity.

His cheeks turn a deep shade of red. "I…I didn't mean…"

I wave him off. "I'm kidding. I mean, not about being up because I totally was, but I'm just playing with you. If I weren't getting up for work at that hour, I'd also think getting up at four thirty is for psychos."

"It should be outlawed."

"Like running."

He tips his head to the side, that run-your-fingers-through-it-worthy brown hair falling over with the movement. "Running should be outlawed?"

"Unless that hottie with the babysitter obsession is chasing you, then yes."

He mouths *babysitter obsession* like he's trying to figure out what I'm going on about. He shakes his head. "I was just running, and not because I was being chased."

"So, you got up, got dressed, and decided to go for a run?"

"Three miles."

"Three miles?! Like, *on purpose?*"

He laughs. "On purpose every day."

"Even Sundays?"

"Even Sundays."

I clutch my chest and gasp. "Sundays are meant for being lazy! That's, like, a rule!"

He points at his chest. "Hockey player in the middle of hockey season."

"So you don't run during the offseason?"

The color on his cheeks deepens again. "Well, yes, I still run then too."

"So you're just a psycho year-round?"

"Yeah, I guess so."

I shake my head. "I always knew there was a secret naughty streak behind your cute toothless smile."

The second the words leave my mouth, I realize what I've done. I smack my hand against my traitorous lips, eyes wide with fear as what I said registers for Fitz.

His usually bright and cheerful hazel eyes darken a smidge, and that grin on his lips falters slightly. His cheeks turn a deep red.

I've embarrassed him.

Hell, I've embarrassed *me*.

I'm an idiot. A complete dumbass.

Why would I say that? Why? This is Fitz. Fitz! He comes here damn near daily. I have to see him all. The. Time. Why did I have to go and make things completely awkward between us by saying he's *cute*? And using the word *naughty*?

What. Is. Wrong. With. Me.

The worst part? I can't take it back, because that would make me look even worse. Complimenting him and then walking back the compliment? No. That's tacky.

God, I need more sleep.

Fitz clears his throat, and I rush to say something —*anything*—before he can call me out on what a complete dumbass I am.

26

"Coffee will be a minute. You can wait over there." I point to the picnic benches.

Fitz peeks over his shoulder to where my finger indicates, then looks back at me. His brows are raised, and his lips are rolled tightly together like he's barely holding back whatever is sitting on the tip of his tongue.

But, to my complete shock, he doesn't say anything. Instead, he spins on his heel and heads for an empty bench, sliding onto it, folding his hands on the table, and just...sitting there. He doesn't pull his phone from his pocket and play on it or try to talk to me.

He just...sits. It's weird and comforting all at the same time.

And like the well-mannered and not-at-all-awkward human I am, I turn my back to him and get back to work, pretending he isn't even there.

Though that's impossible because he *is* here.

He's here, and I can *feel* his eyes on me, can feel his hazel stare boring into me as he rakes his gaze over my body while I finish prepping the donuts for the morning rush. It makes it hard to focus on the task at hand, especially when I can't stop thinking about what I said to him.

"I always knew there was a secret naughty streak behind your cute toothless smile."

Who says that?!

And who then sends the person away?

I'm horrible at customer service. Horrible! Scout should fire me. I don't deserve to work here.

"You're being dramatic, Rosie," I mutter to myself. "It's not a big deal. Fitz knows you didn't mean anything by it. It's fine. *You're* fine."

But I'm not fine. I'm anything *but* fine. I'm a sleepy mess who just made things awkward with a pro hockey player.

"Um, Rosie?" I turn to find Stevie walking into the food truck, several bags in each hand. She hoists and sets them on the counter before turning to me, then she drops her head toward mine. "Why is Fitz sitting out there looking like someone just told him he'll never win the Stanley Cup?"

"Because I sent him away."

"You what?!"

The words are shouted, and I swat her, trying to get her to be quiet.

"Shh!" I say. "Not so loud."

"Sorry," she mutters. "I'm just trying to figure out why you *sent him away*. And why is he here so early?"

I shrug. "He said something about being up early and running."

"What is it with these damn hockey players and their running? It's so gross. Except for when they come home all sweaty—that part is kind of hot."

I roll my eyes. "We aren't all blessed with that."

"True," she says dreamily. She shakes her head, bringing herself back to reality from whatever dreamland she just drifted off to. "So, what happened?"

I slide my eyes in Fitz's direction. He's still just...

sitting there. And staring. I wish I hated it, wish it made my skin crawl, but the way I feel is neither of those things. It's the exact opposite, really.

I grab Stevie by the arm and tug her to the side of the truck that's not visible from the lot.

"I told him he's naughty and cute."

Stevie's jaw slackens, and I swear her eyes grow to twice their normal size.

"I'm sorry…" she says slowly. "You said *what* to him?"

"I told him he's naughty and cute," I rush out again, this time covering my face with my hands, again not caring about the mess. I'm already a wreck this morning; what's a little icing in my hair after everything else?

"How? I mean, how *exactly* did you say those things to him? What was the context? What led up to that? *Why?*"

"Okay, that's a lot of questions all at once, but what I *believe* I said to him was, *I always knew there was a secret naughty streak behind your cute toothless smile.*"

I don't *believe* I said that to him. I know for a fact I did, mostly because those words are going to be permanently seared into my brain.

"Okay…and why did you say this again?"

"Because I called him a psycho?"

"Wait, wait." Stevie holds her hands up. "You called him a naughty cute toothless psycho?"

"Sort of?" I wince. "It sounds so bad when you say it."

"Yes, because I'm sure it didn't sound bad *at all* when you said it."

"Well, you're taking it out of context, so yes, it's worse coming from you."

"Rosie!"

"Stevie!"

She laughs, then shakes her head. "I'm sure it wasn't *that* bad. I mean, he's still here. That's something, right?"

"I guess. But I did tell him to go sit over there, so maybe he's just a good listener?"

"We could say that. Or maybe—and this could be a stretch, it's just a guess—he thinks you're insane?"

"That's plausible." I grimace at the thought of Fitz never coming to the donut truck again because I scared him away. "I'm the worst."

"No, you're not. You're…well, you."

"Is that a good thing or a bad thing?"

"Good thing. I think. Most days. But maybe not today because something is totally off with you."

I wince, then turn away from her, tugging my gloves off and swapping them out for fresh ones. I fit them over my hands, then dive back into getting the donuts ready. "I know. It's… I'm just tired."

"Late night?" she asks, reaching into the grocery bags and pulling out a fresh tub of red, white, and blue sprinkles for our Stars, Stripes, and Sprinkles donuts and a new pitcher to replace the broken one.

"That's an understatement," I mumble.

I want to say I was up late for a good reason, like

studying for the bachelor's degree I'm currently working toward or brainstorming an amazing new donut for the truck that'll bring in even more customers. Something important. Something my parents would be proud of.

But it wasn't any of that.

"Your usual?" I nod. "And? How'd it go?"

"Well, RoPlaying brought in a bunch of cash last night, all while painting her fingernails." I pull off a glove and hold my hand up to show off my fresh manicure.

"Oh, I love that color!" Stevie grabs my hand, looking at it closer. "I wish I was talented enough to paint my own nails, but I can't do anything with my damn left hand. It always looks like I let a toddler loose with a paintbrush."

I laugh, because I used to be the same way, but I trained myself to get better at it.

"You know we have no problems with the streaming, but these late nights…" Stevie starts in that mom tone of hers.

"I know, I know," I say, understanding what she's getting at. "I promise to get to bed earlier tonight and triple-check my alarm."

When I started my account on MyFans, I was just uploading photos. I wasn't completely nude in them, but they weren't tame either. I was shocked when people began purchasing them, though I didn't really want to think about *why* they were purchasing them. It was fun, and it made me feel good. Appreciated. *Desired.*

I loved the feeling so much that, after a few months

of selling pics, I gave streaming a try. If people were paying that much for photos, what would they pay to see me live?

At first, it was strange having a camera trained on me while I went about my normal routine, but after a while, it felt weird to *not* have eyes on me. I liked it—*a lot*. Being watched was…exhilarating. It made me feel like I could do anything. Made me feel *sexy*, something I had never felt before.

I also enjoyed bringing pleasure to other people. I'm not doing anything overtly sexual, mostly just stroking my body in suggestive ways and posing to show off just enough skin to leave them wanting more. It's just enough to get your mind and heart racing. I've been asked to do a few private videos, but I always decline them. Being on camera and chatting is one thing, but I'm not sure I'm ready for more just yet. I don't plan on doing this forever, but it's fun for now and a great way to pay for my classes.

When I started working here, I was upfront with Scout about my late-night activities. My confession was met with nothing but support, and I knew I'd found the perfect place for me to work.

"I would never be brave enough to put myself out there like that, so I'm proud of you," Stevie says with a warm smile.

Unease slithers through me. I haven't told Scout and Stevie about *why* I'm doing this—money.

Don't get me wrong, Scout pays me well, but college isn't cheap. When I got my bill for my tuition this semester, I wanted to puke, but I didn't let it stop me because I *need* this degree and knowledge if I ever want to make my dream come true—opening my own bakery.

But how do I tell the people who gave me everything I want to branch out on my own? I'm scared, something I promised I'd stop being a long time ago. I guess old habits and all that...

"Thanks," I reply quietly before peeking at the clock. We're down to only a few minutes before opening, and I'm almost ready. "Want to tell Fitz he can come grab his donut and coffee before the chaos begins?"

"Why should he get special treatment?"

Stevie and I both spin around at the new voice.

"Greer!" my co-worker squeals excitedly like she didn't just see him this morning. She crosses the truck and stretches over the counter, puckering her lips. Her boyfriend happily meets her for a kiss, and I avert my gaze.

Only I'm not so smart because instead of looking *literally anywhere else*, I turn my attention straight to Fitz.

He's looking at me too.

There's a moment when all we do is stare at one another. His hazel eyes are locked on to my own green ones, and I'm trapped in a damn staring contest with a hot-as-hell hockey player.

It would be great if I hadn't already embarrassed myself in front of him several times today.

Just the reminder of it has me tearing my eyes away. I

grab the nearest towel, smacking it against Stevie's ass, which is practically through the window at this point.

"That's enough."

She pulls her lips from Greer's and sends me a pout. "But kisses."

Greer, the grumpy asshole he typically is, sends me a glare. "Yeah, Rosie, *kisses*."

I shake my head. "You're both ridiculous and we need to open, so finish up or I'll be the one telling Scout *you* ruined the day," I tell Stevie with a pointed look.

She sighs, presses another quick kiss to her boyfriend's lips, and slides back over the counter and into the truck. "Fine. But only because angry Scout scares me a little bit."

"Based on what I've heard from Miller, that's a fair statement," Greer comments.

"I'm pretty sure you can't take anything Miller says seriously. He still plugs in a night-light when we go on the road." Fitz chuckles lightly, his eyes drifting to mine only briefly before he turns to Stevie. "Think I could get a cold brew and two of the Strawber-licious donuts?"

"Sure thing, Fitzy Baby," she says, heading for the donut rack where several fresh strawberry donuts are cooling.

"Baby?" Greer practically growls.

Stevie ignores him, and I can't help laughing. Everyone on social media calls him Fitzy Baby, and I know Stevie is just doing it to screw with Greer. She loves getting him all wound up.

I get to work on making Fitz's coffee for him. He's been coming here since he was traded from Vancouver last season, so I know his order by heart at this point: cold brew with a pump of vanilla, a splash of half-and-half, and two pink packet sugars. Then, depending on the day, he'll get one or two strawberry donuts. He'll eat one sitting at the picnic bench he just abandoned, then he'll take the other to go. He's definitely a creature of habit, something I've come to learn about all the hockey players who stop by here.

I finish his drink, then slide it over the counter his way. He reaches for it before I can remove my hand, and when our fingers brush, I swear I feel it right down to my toes. A spark of something I can't quite figure out rushes through me.

If he notices it too, I can't tell. His face gives nothing away.

"Thanks, Rosie," he says quietly, retracting his hand as well as all the warmth that just flowed through me. "I like the color you chose."

I glance down at my hand and my newly painted nails, the one I chose because a subscriber suggested it because it's his favorite color. I don't tell him that because then I'd have to admit to what I do on the side. It's not that I'm ashamed, because I'm not, but I'm also not ready to announce it.

When I look up, Fitz is gone, taking the rest of the concentration I had right along with him.

This is going to be a long day.

CHAPTER 3

FITZ

I get it. I'm a complete fucking asshole.

I've been watching Rosie stream for two months now, knowing full fucking well who is behind that black and gold mask, knowing I see her every day at the donut truck.

Hell, it's what kept me glued to her videos in the first place. When I happened upon her selfies, even though she was wearing a wig and heavy makeup, I knew it was her. Those green eyes I can't ever seem to stop looking at were a dead giveaway.

I tried. I tried really fucking hard to pretend I never stumbled upon her account. Hell, I went an entire week without seeking her out, but I couldn't stay away any longer.

So, I caved. I caved, and now I spend entirely too much fucking money a month to watch her parade around her apartment in lingerie. I'm a sick fucking man in a fucked-up situation, and it's all my fault.

I even skipped out on the donut truck today because I

didn't want to face her after what happened yesterday. She was frazzled in a way I'd never seen her be before, and it got even worse after she let her *naughty* and *cute* comment slip. I wasn't expecting it, and based on her reaction, she wasn't expecting to say it either. But she did, and suddenly, it was out there hanging between us and making things awkward. I haven't been able to stop thinking about it since.

The moment the word *naughty* left her lips, a wave of embarrassment flooded me because she has no clue just how naughty I really am, watching her nearly every night, knowing damn well she doesn't know I'm on the other side of the screen.

Sure, she coupled it with calling my toothless smile *cute*, something I'm sure nobody has ever said to me before, but I'm too focused on the other part.

I should just tell her I found her account. What's the worst that could happen? Besides, maybe she'll think it's sweet that I support her and won't think I'm a total creep.

Yeah, like that'll happen.

That's not my luck with women. It's *never* been my luck with women. Why would that change now, especially with Rosie, someone who is completely out of my league? I mean, fuck, she's brave enough to post sexy photos and strut around for strangers while I can barely even talk to her without stumbling over my words. We're completely different people.

"Incoming!"

I lift my head just in time. A puck goes sailing by, and judging by the wind that comes off it and brushes against my face, it was damn close to hitting me.

"Holy shit!" Miller yells as he strides across the ice. "Fuck, man. Sorry about that. I thought you'd see it."

"It's fine," I tell him.

Though, really, it's *not* fine. I could have been seriously hurt, and it's all my fault. I'm totally distracted out here.

We sat through a couple of hours of video reviews and went over our upcoming schedule, and I'm positive I only retained about fifty percent of everything we covered. Hell, even Miller was taking notes, and I was just sitting there like a sleep-deprived zombie.

Now, we're out on the ice, and my mind is still racing. I'm not focused on my drills like I need to be, even though I *really* need to be focused because we're facing Vancouver tomorrow, and I'd rather not make a fool of myself against my former club.

"You good?" Miller asks.

I nod. "I'm good."

"You sure? You look a little lost in thought there."

"Just tired. Late night."

"You? Mr. Stays at Home Like a Lame Old Man?"

I grin. "That's quite a mouthful of a name."

"How about Mr. Boring Old Man?"

"Why am I always an old man? Aren't we close to the same age?"

"Yes, but you're still older, and I'm still a spring damn chicken." He points to me. "Old man."

"I'm like ninety-five percent sure every guy on this team would kick your ass if they heard you talking about how old they are."

He puffs his chest out. "Pfft. I could take them."

"Drop the gloves, then."

We spin around to find Adrian "Beast" Rhodes glaring at Miller with a challenge in his gaze. I swear I can *hear* Miller's asshole pucker from here, and I can't help but laugh when his eyes expand to roughly double their normal diameter.

"Y-You don't want this smoke," Miller says, trying his damnedest to sound tough, but there's no mistaking the tremble in his voice.

Rhodes grins, and though I'm sure he doesn't intend for it to look menacing, that jagged scar that runs down his face makes it appear that way. "That's what I thought."

What's even funnier is that despite the fact that Rhodes looks scary and definitely throws his weight around on the ice like nobody's business, he's probably one of the nicest, most loyal guys you'll ever meet.

He looks at me. "What's up with you today? You seem off. Everything good?"

"He had a late night," Miller answers for me, an obnoxious grin on his face.

Beast's brows rise high. "That so? Special overnight guest?"

"Only if you count Carl."

He frowns at my answer. "It's so weird that you named your female cat Carl."

"I didn't name her. She named herself."

"Right." He rolls his eyes. "Just keep your head up. There are idiots out here all over this ice just whipping pucks around."

He strides backward toward his own set of drills he's been running all morning.

"Hey!" Miller protests at the insult a full thirty seconds after he skates away, finally catching on to the fact that Rhodes was talking about him. "How rude," he says, putting his hands on his hips a la Stephanie Tanner.

This time it's me who rolls his eyes. "Get back to work."

"Fine," he grumbles. "But keep your head up—I don't need my ass beat today. I'm pretty sure Scout wouldn't appreciate it if I came home with a black eye." He tips his head, then a slow grin spreads across his lips. "On second thought, hit me. I want to test this theory. Maybe she'll think it's hot and jump my bones."

I shove him. "Go away, Miller."

"I'm going, I'm going. Nobody is any fun today. Everyone is boring—*and* moving slow as fuck, which I really don't like to see."

I thought it was just me, but as I stand here looking out at the ice, all the guys are a little sluggish. I'd be fine with it if so much wasn't riding on this season. The Comets have taken several first-round Playoff exits in the years since the team last won the Cup. Everyone is on thin ice, especially our coaching staff. Not a single person on this team wants to see anything happen to our head coach, Heller.

Coach Heller, or Coach Hell as we sometimes call him because the dude can make life a living hell, is the best there ever was, and it would be a damn shame to see him go down because of our mistakes. We all know it's the nature of the business when a team isn't performing the way it should be, but in some way, it will be on all our shoulders too.

This season, we need to win. We *have* to win. For Coach, for ourselves.

There's no other choice.

An idea hits me, and I'm shocked I'm even thinking about it because when I say I hate going out, I mean it. It's my least favorite thing ever, especially since I'm usually stuck babysitting all the rookies, but maybe that's exactly what this team needs: some bonding time.

"Miller!"

He lifts his head my way, then skates back toward me when I beckon him over.

"'Sup?"

"You're right, we're slow. We should probably do something about it."

His eyes light up. "Oh! I know what we could do— Slapshots. *All* of us."

I try not to laugh because it was entirely too easy to

make him think this was his idea, but that's Miller for you.

I nod. "I think that's a good idea."

"So, you're in, then? Like you'll actually come out with us?"

"I mean, if it's for the team, I guess I could consider it."

He punches my shoulder lightly. "Nine good?"

I nearly balk at his suggestion. Nine at *night*? We probably wouldn't leave until eleven or later...I'll completely miss RoPlaying streaming.

But it's fine. Totally cool. It's for the team, right? And I'd do anything for the team, even miss my favorite late-night activity.

"I'll check my schedule," I tell him dryly.

"As if it's actually full." He laughs, and I'm not even hurt by his comment because it's a fair assessment. "All right, then, it's settled. I'll rally the troops."

I nod, watching him skate away and up to Hayes, who excitedly agrees.

I go back to my drills, trying not to freak out about what I've just gotten myself into.

I won't lie, we just arrived and I'm already itching to pull my phone from my pocket and check to see if RoPlaying is online. This is usually the time she starts her streams, and I'm dying to check in on her.

It's ridiculous. *I'm* ridiculous for this little obsession of mine, but I'm going to chalk it all up to superstition. It hasn't escaped my notice that whenever I catch a stream, I score the next game. Might as well keep that going, right? I'll do whatever it takes to keep us winning games. It's still early in the season, but we need all the points we can get in a tight division like ours.

Yeah, that's what it is, I tell myself.

"First round is on me!" Miller shouts through cupped hands, and everyone in our group cheers, drawing the attention of just about every patron in the bar.

To be fair, we've been drawing attention since the moment we walked through the doors. Sure, Slapshots is known as the Comets' frequent hangout, but that doesn't mean we don't turn heads whenever we walk in. Add in the fact that there are about fifteen or so of us here and that we had to combine three different tables so we could all sit together, and we definitely have the attention of the entire room.

"Water for me," requests Hollis, the fiancée of our team captain, Lowell. She lays a hand on her large belly, a grin playing on her lips.

Since she and Lowell are days away from having their second kid, this may be their last chance to come out for quite a while. It's crazy to me because I can't even imagine having one child while trying to juggle a hockey career, let alone two of them running around. They're brave, that's for damn sure.

Miller sends her a thumbs-up before heading to the

bar to place our orders. We've all been here enough times for Rod, the owner, to know what we want. Sometimes I don't even have to say anything, and he just slides a fresh IPA my way.

"That's a lot of drinks. Should someone go help him?" Wright speaks up. "I mean, it is Miller…"

"Hey!" Scout, Miller's girlfriend, shouts in his defense, but there's no denying the smile on her lips. She's aware Miller is the guy we all love and love to pick on. He's used to it, and so is she.

"Nah. Let him figure it out on his own."

"Adrian!" his wife admonishes, sending him a glare.

He sighs, then shoves away from the table, heading toward the bar to help Miller. It's hilarious to see a man so big and scarred as Rhodes fall at his wife's feet like he does, but he's madly in love with the woman he drunk married in Vegas. I remember sitting in Vancouver when the news broke about it. It was all over every NHL website and social media page, going viral over and over again. I'm not sure anyone thought they'd still be together years later, but it's clear as day that's not changing anytime soon.

"Can't believe I managed to get us all together outside of the rink. I don't think that's happened since…" Smith, a past player on the Comets turned video coach, tips his head as he thinks about it. "Shit, I'm not sure when. Maybe when I was still playing?"

Emilia, his girlfriend, gives him a soft smile at the mention of his old career. Smith used to be known around the league for racking up assists like crazy, and everyone called him Granny Apple Smith. The dude is going down as a legend for making some crazy goals happen.

"Had to have been before Hayes and Fitzy Baby joined the team," Wright says, nodding his head toward our end of the table.

"I think you might be right," Lowell chimes in.

Greer grunts. "That's because nobody wants to be seen in public with Miller."

"Hey!" Scout says again, and we all laugh, including her.

"Be nice," Stevie whispers to her grumpy boyfriend.

The command is quiet, but since I'm sitting right next to her, I don't miss it, which means I don't miss when Greer's cheeks darken with embarrassment. It's such a rare look for him that I can't help but laugh, earning me a nice middle finger from the grumpy goalie himself.

"What'd I miss? Why is Greer flipping people off now?"

The baker who banished me plops down in the empty chair across from me, and I guess that answers the question of if she's streaming.

Her blonde hair that's normally twisted up in a messy bun is hanging loosely around her shoulders. While she's typically hidden behind an apron, there's never been any mistaking that Rosie has a whole lot of curves, and the tight, low-cut, off-the-shoulder black top doesn't do anything to veil them either. This look is a lot closer to what she wears during her streams, and I'm doing all I can to not take notice—to not let my *dick* take notice.

I'm failing because it's *really* hard to ignore her beauty.

Rosie gives Stevie a one-armed hug, then peers around the table, waving and smiling at everyone who already knows her from the donut truck we all frequent. There's no mistaking the moment she realizes I'm here, and this time it's *her* cheeks that darken.

"Oh," she mutters. "You."

A chuckle rumbles out because it's obvious she's thinking about our encounter the other morning.

"Me," I reply.

Stevie snickers, drawing our attention. Her gaze is flitting between me and Rosie, and I have no doubt it's because she knows what happened. It was painfully obvious the two of them were discussing it while I was sitting at the table.

"What's up with you two?" Greer asks, not missing the tension between us.

"Nothing!" Rosie says way too loudly and quickly. Then those jade eyes are on me, narrowed and daring me to say something that challenges her answer.

Like the gentleman my momma raised me to be, I roll my lips together and keep quiet.

"Right," Greer says, not believing anything Rosie says, and I don't blame him. I wouldn't believe us either, not with how fidgety Rosie is acting.

Really, it's for nothing. So she had a slip of the tongue and called me naughty and cute…big deal. No reason to be flustered by it. I mean, I've practically forgotten about it by now.

Okay, no. That's a lie. It's *still* rattling around in my head, but whatever. I'm cool. *We're* cool.

"Hey there, Rosie," Hayes says, sliding his arm across the back of her chair and leaning into her.

She shoots him a megawatt grin, the same one she gives me every morning when I show up for my caffeine fix. "Hey there, Hayes."

He winks at her, and she giggles.

A twinge of annoyance rushes through me at Hayes being so cozy with Rosie. I don't like it because I know how the young forward is with women. He treats them as nothing more than something to play with for a bit, then leaves them in the dust. Rosie deserves better than that.

She also deserves better than me being a creep and watching her streams, but we're not going to get into that now.

"I present to you: alcohol!" Miller shouts at the opposite end of the table from us as he sets down a tray filled with glasses. Rhodes sets another tray down beside us, and I automatically reach for the IPA that's sitting nearest me.

"Hey, Rosie. Glad you could join us. What can I get you to drink?" Rhodes asks. "Miller's buying, so make sure it's something expensive."

"Um…" She taps a perfectly manicured finger against her chin a few times before saying, "Vodka soda?"

"Top-shelf vodka soda—got it. Be right back." He heads off back toward the bar.

I bring my beer to my lips and take a hefty drink, thankful for the delicious hoppy liquid that slides down my throat. I'm starting to feel a little on edge, and I'm not exactly sure why, but I want it to stop. Hopefully, this will help.

I can feel eyes on me, and when I lift my gaze, I'm surprised to find Rosie staring at me intently. Her eyes are flitting over every inch of my face, and it's getting hot under her stare. I hate it and love it all at the same time.

When she realizes I've caught her staring, she doesn't hide it. She simply quirks a brow, like she's begging me to say something.

I don't. Instead, I look away, grinning into my beer like an idiot. She's so feisty, and I fucking love it.

"Oh yeah, I forgot to tell you…" Miller starts as he passes out drinks. "I signed us all up for karaoke."

"What?!"

"How?!"

"They don't even have karaoke here!"

I have no idea who exactly shouts their displeasure, but I agree with all of them. I'd rather pull out another one of my teeth before singing karaoke.

"I brought my machine from home. Rod said it was cool."

"Dammit, Rod!" Lowell hollers toward the bar,

shaking his fist in the air.

The owner-slash-bartender shrugs, then returns to making drinks.

"You have a karaoke machine?" Wright asks Miller.

"That you *brought from home?*" Disgust and disbelief drip off every one of Rhodes' words.

"Scout, how could you let him get a karaoke machine?" Harper asks. "You know that's just asking for trouble."

She holds her hands up. "Hey, that was all on him. I walked into his apartment one day and it was just there, and he was singing Shania Twain. He refuses to return it."

"Because it's awesome! Besides, someone had to bring the fun tonight, and I volunteered myself." Miller points at Rhodes, Smith, and Greer. "You three assholes are grumpy about ninety-nine percent of the time." He moves on to Wright and Lowell. "And you two are just old dudes who are all settled down and shit and never want to do anything fun because of your *ladies*." He looks at Harper and Hollis. "No offense, of course." His eyes land on me next. "Then there's Fitz and Hayes. They're just...well, Fitz and Hayes."

"Hey, I'm fun!" Hayes tries to redeem his image.

"A little *too fun* sometimes." The captain throws daggers toward the forward, probably annoyed because Hayes got in some trouble over the summer and we all had to hear about it from management.

I get it. Hayes can be a handful, but he's still a good

kid. A little immature, but weren't we all at some point?

"He's fun," I say, sticking up for him. "But I take no offense at what's been said about me. I *am* boring, and I'm totally cool with it."

"You're not *boring*," Stevie says softly. "You just prefer your own company."

"More like the company of his hand." Hayes holds his palm up, waiting for someone to slap it.

And someone does—the curvaceous blonde with lime eyes sitting across from me.

Rosie.

I raise a brow at her, surprised by her betrayal.

"What?" She shrugs, not caring what she's just endorsed. "See a hand, smack a hand."

"Gave me cookie, got you cookie," Hayes says before holding his hand up again, and Rosie slaps it once more.

"That one was a bit cheap because I love *New Girl*, but see? You can't deny someone a high five. It's impossible."

I hold my hand up, just to test her theory.

She smacks her palm against mine. "See?" she says excitedly. "It's just the natural reaction."

"All right. I'll allow it." I lean across the table. "But just so you know, that makes the *third* time you've insulted me."

Her eyes flare as she sinks lower in her chair, covering her face, and I swear I hear an "Oh god" come out of her. I laugh, then take another sip of my beer.

Maybe tonight won't be so bad after all.

CHAPTER 4

ROSIE

When Stevie invited me out tonight, I figured it would be fun. I've been out with the players a few times, and there are always lots of laughs to be had.

And fine, maybe a *tiny* part of me was hoping Fitz would be here. I haven't seen him in a few days, and I'm not sure if it's because he's avoiding the donut truck or if it's for a different reason. If he *is* avoiding Scout's Sweets, I don't blame him. I made it plenty awkward the other day; he has no reason to want to come back.

Now that I'm here and sitting across from him...ugh, I wish more than anything I had magical powers and could make myself invisible because I did it again, stuck my whole damn foot in my mouth, and then some.

"Why, why, why..." I chant to myself as I walk out of the bathroom stall, the same one I've been hiding in for the last ten minutes.

Not only did I mess things up with Fitz the other day, I just did it again when I high-fived Hayes for insulting him. I played it cool and shrugged off his comments, but deep down, I'm totally dying inside, and I'm really beginning to believe something is truly wrong with me. It's the only explanation I have for being off my game like I am.

"Are you talking to yourself again?"

I clutch my chest, whirling around to find Stevie leaning against a wall. She shoves off, stalking toward me with a smirk.

"How did you…" I shake my head, moving toward the sink and dispensing soap onto my hands. I run them under the water for the requisite twenty seconds, then grab a few paper towels. I turn, leaning against the counter as I dry my hands off. "What are you doing in here?"

"Checking on you because, no offense, you're kind of a mess this week. That isn't like you at all."

"Yes, you're right. I'm always *super* put together."

We both laugh because that's not true at all. Sure, I'm not usually this big of a mess, but put together? That's not me either.

"Is it okay that Fitz is here?"

"Of course. Why wouldn't it be?"

She gestures noncommittally. "You know…all your nerves. The slip of the tongue. You calling him naughty and cute. Your intense staring session out there. Is it your crush on him?"

I whip my head back. "My…" I sputter out a laugh. "What crush? What are you talking about?"

She lifts a shoulder. "Well, I mean, I kind of figured

you had one. You're always talking about how hot he is."

"Well, duh. You have eyes—you can see how attractive that man is. I mean, those eyelashes alone."

"Ugh, men always have the best eyelashes."

"And that jaw of his? Perfection."

"Greer's is better, but Fitz's isn't so bad."

"And those hazel eyes? Wow. *Wow!* Talk about mesmerizing. Don't even get me started on his missing tooth. It's just…" I sigh. "*So* hot."

Stevie doesn't say anything for several moments, then suddenly, she's doubled over, clutching her stomach as she laughs louder and harder than I've ever seen her laugh before.

"What? Why are you laughing?"

She looks up at me briefly, then drops her head, laughing again. I fold my arms over my chest, staring daggers at her while she continues to laugh. It feels like hours before she finally settles down, but when she does, I am not expecting what she says next.

"You're totally into him. Like full-blown *writing his name and drawing hearts on your notebook* kind of into him."

"What? You're insane!" I retort. "There is no way. Fitz is just…well, he's Fitz. Cute, yes, but a crush? No. That's not… That's not…"

Oh god.

Realization smacks me right in the face.

Ohgodohgodohgod.

I've been a bumbling idiot around him all evening, and I was the other day too. I chalked up the incident at the donut truck to just being tired and exhausted, but now that I'm acting like a fool tonight, maybe it's more than that. Maybe it's…

"Oh no. Oh no no no no." The last time I felt like this was when I realized things about my former best friend. When I realized… "I have a crush on him."

I look up at Stevie, who doesn't look the least bit shocked by my revelation.

"I have a crush on Fitz," I tell her.

"Yes, I know."

"Like a real, true crush."

"I know," she repeats with a grin. "So, what are you going to do about it?"

"Nothing!" I rush out. "Not a thing."

"What? Why not?"

"Because I can't! I'm… I'm…"

"A totally single and available girl?"

"Well, yeah. But—"

"A smokin' hot babe who Fitz would be so lucky to have?"

"Of course, but—"

"No. No buts. You're going to walk out there and—"

"I can't, Stevie."

"Yes, you can."

"No. You don't get it. I *can't*." I wring my hands and begin walking the length of the bathroom, back and forth and back again.

Stevie's brows crash together as she watches me pace around like a nervous lunatic. I'm sure she's wondering

54

what's going on because this isn't me. At least, this isn't the version of me Stevie knows.

I've worked hard over the last few years to not be the timid version of myself I used to be, to not be scared to go after what I want. For the most part, I've done that. I went out and got the baking job I wanted. I've started putting myself out there with friends. I mean, I'm out at a bar with professional hockey players. Hell, strangers pay me to stream in lingerie for crying out loud! Not to mention I'm going to school for my business degree so I can open my own bakery one day.

This me is so different from the woman I was. I overthought everything. I let so much of life pass me by, and after what happened with Levi, I vowed to never, *ever* be that person again.

But here I am—scared once more.

When Stevie gets tired of my pacing, she steps toward me, putting a hand on my arm to stop me.

"I..." I blow out a breath. "I've been in this spot before. With my..." I swallow a lump that's seemed to form in my throat. "With my ex-best friend. We... Well, *I* sort of fell in love with him, and..."

"He didn't love you back," she guesses with a sad smile.

I nod. "Yeah. So as you can see..."

"This is super hard for you."

"Yes."

She sighs. "All right, I get that. I really do, but being scared? That's not the Rosie I know. That's not the

55

woman who dresses like a wet dream and streams for thousands of people every night. That's not the woman who bosses me around on the regular and takes control of every crazy situation like it's nothing. That's not the woman who has been working hard to embrace everything she is. You're a badass who can do whatever she wants. Own it."

The longer she speaks, the more my shoulders press back because Stevie *is* right. I've come so far. Why am I letting some guy set me back now?

"I'm going out there," I tell her confidently.

"Hell yeah you are!" Stevie shouts, hyping me up.

"I'm going to march up to him."

"Yes!" She whoops loudly, clapping her hands together.

"And I'm going to ask him out."

"There's my girl!" She grabs my shoulders, steering me toward the door. "Let's go get him!"

"Yes!"

Only, when I reach for the handle, I pause because all those fears from before start settling into my stomach again. What if Fitz turns me away like Levi did? What if I'm not enough for him? What if he laughs and tells me to get lost? What if...

"What if he doesn't like me?"

"I'm sorry, have you seen your knockers? Of course he'll like you!"

It's just enough to make me laugh, and all my nerves fizzle away.

I shove my shoulders back and pull the door open. My eyes zero in on the table the rest of our party is at. Everyone is lost in conversation, including Fitz, who is currently laughing at something Hayes is saying. He looks so hot with his head thrown back, his eyes screwed tightly shut, and his adorable toothless grin on full display.

"I want to kiss his face."

Stevie laughs from beside me. "Maybe don't lead with that."

We make our way back to the table just in time to hear them start talking about the game they have on Thursday.

"Puh-*lease* tell me you're going to be starting in goal for the next game," I say to Greer, dropping back down into my chair. "Those two points against Nashville after all the bullshit that happened with you getting injured last season would be so damn good."

"Not really up to me," he says. "That's all on Coach."

But I can tell from his eyes that *he* wants to be in goal too, wants to get his revenge on the team that steamrolled him, knocked him out of the game for a few weeks, and then subsequently cost the team a deep Playoff run as they took another first-round exit. Everyone knows it's too many in a row now, which spells trouble across the board.

"For what it's worth, Macie agrees," Stevie says, referring to her hockey-obsessed daughter. Sometimes I think she loves the game more than the guys out there on the ice. "And, of course, she's hoping for a good scrum or two."

"Hell, *I'm* hoping for a good scrum," Rhodes chimes in. "That fucker barreled over Greer on purpose. I know it, and he knows it too. He's got a beating coming."

"Didn't you whoop his ass already?" Hayes asks.

"Sure." Rhodes shrugs, then a vicious grin appears on his face. "Doesn't mean I wouldn't like to do it again."

Ryan, his wife, fans herself. "Ugh, I love it when you get all growly like that."

Several of the guys groan, but I hear no objections from the other wives and girlfriends at the table because I'm sure they feel the same way Ryan does. I know I do.

I'm not one of those people who watch the game just for the fights. Hockey is entertaining in other ways too, but I'd be a damn liar if I said seeing the guys dropping gloves doesn't make my lady bits tingle in all the right ways.

"Can I be the one to go after him? I'm itching to have my first fight this year."

My eyes slide over to Hayes. "You've never been in a fight?"

"Not in the NHL. AHL, a few times."

"You'll get one eventually. We all have to answer the bell at some point," Lowell says. He would know since last season he had his very first fight himself. He came out with a black eye, a bruised knuckle, and a Gordie Howe hat trick. It was amazing.

"I've never been in a fight either," Fitz says from across the table.

Slowly, I turn toward him. "Never?"

He shakes his head. "Not even in juniors."

"Damn." Hayes whistles. "We gotta get our boy in a tussle or two before his career is over."

"How'd you lose your tooth, then? I always figured it was a fight."

"I lost a tooth?" He sits forward, his brows wrinkling in fake concern. "I didn't do inventory this morning, so you'll have to tell me which one." He smiles big, poking his tongue right through the gap in his teeth.

Heat rises in my cheeks for what feels like the fifth time in his presence, and I'm really starting to think this reaction from me is exclusive to Fitz.

He laughs, sitting back in his chair. "I took a stick up high." He points to the faded scar on his chin. "Got me here too. Ten stitches."

I lean across the table to get a good look at it. When I move, so does he.

He's right…there…only a few inches away, and I'm stuck. I can't move. It's not possible, not when he's so near and when he's looking at me like he is.

His eyes are the perfect swirl of green, brown, and amber. Those damn long, dark lashes of his are thick and make the color ten times more potent. Being this close, I can see the dots of freckles under his eyes. It's just a smattering, and I itch to reach over and trace every single one with the tip of my finger.

"Your eyes…" I hear myself say. "They're beautiful."

Said eyes widen, and someone clears their throat, breaking the staring contest we're trapped in. It's Greer, his stare bouncing back and forth between us yet again. It lingers on Fitz for a moment longer than me, which has him falling back in his chair. He reaches for his beer and chugs the entirety of it, then drags the back of his hand over his mouth.

"Going to grab a refill," Fitz mutters before abruptly rising from his chair and making his way across the bar.

"Is anyone else going to say anything about the eye-fucking that just happened?"

"Shut the fuck up, Hayes," Greer mutters through clenched teeth.

I ignore them both, mostly because I'm already out of my chair and following Fitz to the bar. It's clear I've made him uncomfortable, and we both know it's not the first time today. I need to apologize.

"Hey," I say, slipping onto the stool next to him.

He startles a bit, then gives me a tight smile, shifting around on the stool, almost angling himself away from me.

Yep. I totally made things awkward between us. Awesome.

"Hey," he says tentatively. His eyes go to the empty glass in my hand, and he signals for Rod once more. "Vodka soda, too. My tab."

Rod nods, letting us know he heard him.

"You didn't have to do that. Besides, I'm pretty sure it's *me* who owes *you* drinks at this point."

60

Fitz laughs. "True, but it's the gentlemanly thing to do, and I'm pretty sure my momma would whoop my ass if she heard I didn't offer to buy you a drink."

"Are you, a grown man, scared of your mom?"

He lifts both brows. "Damn right I am. She might be a tiny Russian woman, but she's scary as hell."

"Your mother's Russian? That explains your first name."

"Yep, that's from her. My father is Irish. Quite the combo, huh?"

"Do you speak anything other than English?"

He leans into me, and I find myself matching his movements, eager to hear whatever it is he's about to say. Those hazel eyes peer into me, and I swear he's looking right at my soul as he whispers a few things in a language I know nothing about.

Well, fuck me. I swear every word he just spoke— whatever the hell they were—went right between my legs.

"What does that mean?" I ask, hoping he doesn't hear how breathy that came out.

"I have a pet goat."

"Oh."

My cheeks heat yet again, and a laugh bubbles out of me.

"What?" he asks, his lips quirked up in a smile. "What's so funny?"

"Nothing." I shake my head. "I just…I didn't expect that."

Did I just get totally horny from him saying that? Guilty as charged.

Rod sets our refills in front of us, and I reach for mine as if I haven't had anything to drink in days. I drain half the glass, then immediately regret it. I've not had a lot to eat today, and I'm a bit of a lightweight. I already know this is going to go straight to my head.

I set my glass back on the bar top, then turn to Fitz, who is slowly sipping on his beer. "So, do you really?"

"Hm?" He shifts until he's facing me.

"Do you have a pet goat?"

"Oh, no. But there's a guy who is a season ticket holder for the Comets, comes to all the games and spends a shit ton of money at the events, and he has several pet goats—like a whole litter of them."

"A litter?"

Fitz nods. "At least eight, but it could be more by now. Who knows."

"He sounds amazing. I've always wanted a big farm with lots of animals."

"Really?" He tips his head, studying me. "You seem like more of a big-city gal to me."

I shrug. "I mean, sure, I like living in the city, but being somewhere quiet with land would be nice too. And great internet, of course."

He laughs. "A necessity at this point."

"Sometimes I love the internet and sometimes I hate it. It's this great place where everybody can be whoever they want to be, but it's also dangerous for that exact reason."

"A double-edged sword, that's for sure. I don't get on social media often, but sometimes I'll see the comments on the team's pages and…" He shudders. "They're something. And creepy."

"Oh, trust me, I am well aware of how creepy people can be."

During my last live stream, I had no less than ten people tell me they wanted to jizz all over my tits. The saddest part is that's a tame night for me. The messages that fill my inbox… They're downright pornographic.

There are some diamonds in the rough, though, like *ShootsAndScores*. Every time I sign off my streaming videos and he's been watching, he sends me a note that always feels so…genuine compared to the rest, like maybe he's not watching me just for my tits. Like last time when he chose my nail polish color. It wasn't the usual "pink to match the head of my swollen cock" comment. He was one of the few who wasn't a total perv. While that shouldn't be unique enough to make him stand out, it is.

"So, do you know anything else in Russian?"

"Not a damn word."

I bark out a laugh. "You can only say *I have a pet goat?*"

"Much to my grandmother's dismay, yes."

"Does your mother speak Russian?"

"A little. When my grandparents came over to the US,

they tried hard to blend in and only speak Russian at home or whenever they absolutely needed to. So, my mother grew up speaking English and only picked up a little bit of Russian over the years. Whenever she'd read to me and my sister at bedtime, there was this book about this bad goat, Billy B. Bad or something like that. She'd read some parts in Russian and some in English, something her mother would do with her. I don't remember the entire story now, but I still remember how to say *I have a pet goat* in Russian because that was the opening line of the book. My sister knows more and even studied it in college, but I just don't have the knack for picking up other languages."

I don't say anything because I don't know what to say. It's not only the most I've ever heard Fitz say all at once, it's also the most I've ever learned about him. Seeing him open up and talk like this…I'm not used to it, and I wish he would do it more.

"What?" he asks after several seconds of silence.

I shake my head. "It's nothing. It's just…you don't talk very often, so I'm taking it all in."

"Yeah, I'm, uh, I'm not big on talking. I like listening more. I'm more of an observer. A…"

"A loner?"

When his brows shoot up, I realize how awful that came out.

"That sounded so bad, like I was calling you a loser or something. I wasn't. I would *never*. There's nothing wrong with being a loner. Hell, I'm a loner. In fact, if I wasn't out tonight, I'd be at home sitting in front of my co—what? Why are you grinning at me like that?"

"It's nothing. You're just, uh…" His cheeks flush. "I like it when you ramble."

Now it's *my* cheeks that heat up.

He likes it when I ramble? Well, *I* like that he likes it when I ramble. Hell, I'm beginning to suspect I like everything about him. Minus the running, of course. That part is just gross, and you cannot change my mind on that.

"Thank you." I tuck a loose strand of hair behind my ear. "I think."

He chuckles quietly. "You're welcome. It's *cute*."

I cover my face, groaning into my hands at his reference from the other morning, and I hear him laugh. No, I *feel* him laugh, my entire body vibrating from the rumble that leaves him.

Then he does something I'm not expecting. He wraps his hands around my wrists and pulls at my arms. All at once, every fiber of my being is on fire, and if this is what it feels like to burn, I'll do it every day for the rest of forever.

"Come on, no hiding. I didn't hide."

He tugs gently on me again, and this time I let him pull my hands away.

"Because you couldn't. I *banished* you."

Another laugh rolls out of him. "Yeah, you did. That was very *naughty* of you."

There is no doubt in my mind that I look like a

fucking tomato with how red my face feels. I try to hide again, but he doesn't let me. In fact, he doesn't stop touching me at all. He just holds my wrists in his hands and... *Is that his thumb rubbing against me?*

I glance down just in time to see him swipe it over the inside of my wrist twice before he realizes what he's doing and yanks his hands away.

I miss his touch instantly.

"I'm sorry," he says. "I didn't mean to embarrass you."

"And I didn't mean to embarrass *you*. I'm not usually so..."

"Frazzled?"

I nod. "Yeah, that. It was just an...off morning for me."

"I know. That's why I didn't think much of it." He shrugs, then brings his beer up to his lips, taking a healthy sip before setting it back on the counter. How he makes drinking a beer that smells like a skunk's ass so hot, I don't even know, but watching as he swallows...the way he drags his tongue over his lips...it's mesmerizing. I swear I could watch a ten-hour movie on this alone.

Holy crap, my crush on this man is so bad. Like beyond bad. The last time I felt this way about someone was...

I swallow back the lump that's formed in my throat, trying to ignore it, trying to ignore all the old insecurities that are rising. I don't need them. I don't want them. They aren't true.

I'm Rosie Calhoun. I am a badass who goes after what she wants, and right now, I want Fitz.

"Well, now that we've gotten all that out of the way…I was wondering if—"

His cell buzzes against the bar top, drawing both of our attention.

"Sorry," he mutters, grabbing it and turning the screen on. He sits forward, his eyes attached to whatever's happening. A small smile plays at the corners of his lips. "I'm sorry," he says again, completely enamored by whatever is on his screen, which I can't see from my vantage point. "I, uh, I have to go. Someone needs me."

He's up and out of his chair, leaving before I can even ask if everything is okay. He stops to quickly say goodbye to the rest of the raucous crowd we're with, then he's out the door and disappearing into the night.

I'm Rosie Calhoun. I am a badass who goes after what she wants, and right now, what I want just walked out the door to go home to someone else.

Lucky me.

CHAPTER 5

I'm not proud of what happened at Slapshots tonight.

Not the walking-out-of-the-bar part—while I didn't like leaving Rosie, especially when we were having a good conversation, that part was justified.

It was something else.

It was when we were sitting with the rest of the group and she leaned over the table to get a look at my faded scar, and like some idiot, I let her. Hell, I even met her inch for inch.

She was so close and smelled so fucking good, like strawberries, and she was staring me right in the eyes, and then it happened…the thing I'm not proud of.

I got a boner.

I got a fucking *boner*. I'm in my mid-twenties, dammit! I should be able to control my dick a whole lot better than that, but I didn't. I didn't control my dick and I popped a fucking boner *from a staring contest*, then ran away like a scared child.

Only she followed.

She followed me, and I hated it...but I loved it too.

It's not usual for me to get worked up like that, especially not in public, but her sitting there looking at me like she was seconds away from reaching her tongue out and running it along my jaw... *Fuck me.* It did something to me, something I *really* liked...something I wouldn't mind a repeat of.

But I have a feeling I completely blew it tonight, all thanks to fucking Carl.

I glare over at the fluffy white-brown cat who is snoozing away in her tower like she didn't just ruin my entire night. When I initially got a notification on my phone, I laughed when I saw her prancing about the apartment. Sure, she was a little shit for being up on the countertops when she knows I hate it, but it's her place too. Then she had to go and do the one damn thing that drives me nuts and is the whole reason I installed the cameras to begin with: she locked herself in the pantry.

For being smart enough to pull the door open—I really need to get my super to fix that—she sure is dumb when it comes to not locking herself inside. This is the fourth time she's done it. Last time, I was at an away game and had to get my neighbor, Miss Drake, to let her out. I, of course, then saw Miss Drake take her bathrobe off and sit stark naked on my couch. Since I just got those images out of my brain, I really didn't want a repeat of that tonight, so I grabbed an Uber and booked it home to let Carl out.

So now I'm sitting at my computer with a controller

in my hand, trying to work out my frustration because I got cockblocked by my cat.

"Holy fuck, my life is sad," I say to myself.

Carl stirs a bit at my words, and her eyes peek open just enough for her to narrow them at me. So, I do the mature thing and flip her off. She gives me a look that says, *Do it again and I will murder you in your sleep.* I don't doubt her threat for a second.

Ugh, how pathetic am I? Having a pissing contest with my cat? What a sad, sad life I'm leading. I'm even sadder than—

Ping!

My eyes go to the corner of the screen, and my lips part when I see the notification that's bouncing there.

RoPlaying is online. Would you like to watch?

I've never in my life clicked a button faster.

I toss my controller to the side, not caring at all about saving whatever game I was just playing, then give all my attention to the screen as Rosie fills it.

I can tell almost instantly that something is different tonight. For one, she's streaming way later than she typically does, but it's more than that. She looks...off. Still gorgeous, but off. Maybe it's how tightly her brows are drawn together as she lies on her belly on the floor with a coloring book spread out before her. She's pressing so hard on the pages her knuckles are turning white. She's quiet as usual, but it feels like *more* tonight. It's like she's...

"Oh, fuck."

She's upset.

She's upset, and I have no doubt in my mind I'm to blame for it.

I left her sitting at the bar like a total asshat. I didn't give her any sort of explanation. I bolted. I should have explained better, should have told her I wasn't leaving because I didn't want to talk to her anymore. I should have just told her I had to leave because my cat insists on cockblocking me and it had nothing to do with her.

But I didn't say any of that because my social skills when it comes to women are about non-existent. I had the same girlfriend through high school. We broke up when she went off to college, and hockey consumed my life from there. I've had some one-night stands and short flings, like the girl who dumped me for liking to watch, but nothing serious, especially not with women like Rosie, who is so damn strong and fierce. She scares me as much as she turns me on, and I'm not exactly sure what that says about me, but I don't have the time to analyze it now.

I'm too worried about how I've somehow managed to screw up Rosie's night by being an asshole. Albeit unintentionally, but still.

My eyes stay trapped on the screen as she colors for an hour. It's a full hour of nearly complete silence. The only sound she makes is the occasional sigh or groan. Nothing has been said, and yet, I still can't seem to look away. She has that kind of effect on me.

When her eyes flit to the side of the screen of her

laptop, I know she's about to log off, and I swear I've never wanted her to stay more.

I wish I had more courage, wish I were brave enough to reach out and tell her I'm sorry for leaving tonight. But I can't because that would be admitting so much, and I don't want to open that can of worms.

"Sorry I was extra quiet tonight," she says, looking directly into the camera. "It's been a long day, but being here with you all has made it better."

Her eyes go to the chat box that's already filling with mostly disgusting comments from anonymous assholes.

WineDine69: I want to cum all over your titz bby gurl.
EatinP: SHOW US YOUR CANS!
BigDNRGY: I want to motorboat you, then fuck your ass.

I want to find every single one of these idiots and kick their ass.

But I can't. So instead, I do what I do every night—I send her a message.

ShootsAndScores: It sounds like you had a rough day, and I'm sorry about that. I hope tomorrow is much better. You deserve it. Good night, Ro.

. . .

A genuine smile forms on her lips for the first time this evening, and I tell myself it's because of my message.

"Good night," she says, and once again, I pretend it's just for me.

The screen goes black, and I lean back, staring at the void, wishing I'd never gotten myself into this situation and had never found her stream. Maybe then I wouldn't be sitting here with a giant hole in my chest that makes me feel like shit.

I want to make this right with her. Tonight. Now.

But I can't.

Ping!

My eyes find the notification in the corner of the screen, then I'm stumbling out of my chair and away from the computer because *What in the actual fuck?*

RoPlaying has sent you a message.

I read the notification once.

Twice.

Three fucking times.

She messaged me.

She fucking messaged me!

What. The. Fuck.

I drag my hands through my hair repeatedly, like I'm trying to scrub this from my brain because I *am* trying to scrub this from my brain. She can't message me, and we can't talk because she *cannot* know it's me.

I mean, sure, I can be *anyone*. She doesn't *have* to know it's me. Hell, she streams anonymously, so it's the same thing, right?

I shouldn't. I *really* fucking shouldn't. I— *Fuck me.* How did this mouse get into my hand? Why am I clicking *Read?* What the hell am I doing? I exit quickly before I can see what she wrote.

"Fuck, fuck, fuck." I jump out of my chair and toss the mouse anywhere but in my hand so I don't do something stupid like *actually read* the damn thing.

But just like before, I don't know what happens because suddenly I'm not standing anymore. I'm sitting, and the fucking traitorous mouse is back in my hand, and I'm clicking on my inbox.

"I'm possessed. I have to be."

But do possessed people actually *know* they're possessed? And do they say it out loud?

My heart batters inside my chest as the page loads, and I swear I'm about two seconds away from ripping the plug on the computer and hammering this room shut. My super won't like it, but I don't give a shit. I need to walk away, and apparently, I can't be trusted to do it myself.

RoPlaying: Hi.

It's a simple message. Totally normal. Nothing to freak out over.

· · ·

RoPlaying: This is probably totally inappropriate, but I just wanted to let you know your messages always make me smile. And tonight, I REALLY needed it. So, thanks.

RoPlaying: You don't have to respond, by the way. I know this is weird.

I *do* have to respond. She knows I've seen the messages. She knows I'm currently online. I'll look like a complete asshole if I don't reply.

Never mind the fact that I *want* to respond. So fucking badly.

"Keep it simple. Don't fuck this up," I mutter to myself as I put my fingers on the keyboard.

I take a deep breath, then type out a message.

ShootsAndScores: You're welcome.

See? Simple. Easy. Totally not weird.

ShootsAndScores: I'm sorry people are creepy to you in the comments. I hope that's not what upset you tonight.

. . .

"No, no, no. Fucking shit," I curse.

Something is wrong with me. My limbs are operating of their own accord. Maybe it's like *Invasion of the Body Snatchers* or something? I don't know, but I *do* know this is wrong. Wrong, wrong, wrong, and I *have* to stop. This cannot go any further.

"Please don't respond," I whisper, watching the bubbles appear, then disappear in the chat like they're directly tied to my last breath and the next message she sends is going to be all the oxygen I need to survive.

RoPlaying: Unfortunately, I'm used to the creeps at this point. I just ignore them. Tonight, it was something…else.

RoPlaying: I was sort of…ghosted?

"Shit." I drop my head into my hands, crushing my palms against my eyes, trying to delete this whole night from my memory.

I'm the fucking worst.

Is that what she thinks happened? That I ghosted her?

I so badly want to type back: "Hey, it's Fitz. I didn't ghost you. My cat is just a fucking idiot."

But I can't do that.

Another message pops up, and I lift my head to read it.

RoPlaying: Maybe ghosted isn't the right way to put it.

RoPlaying: But let's just say this night didn't go the way I thought it would, and the guy I was talking to isn't the guy I thought he was.

ShootsAndScores: I'm sorry. It's never fun when that happens.

RoPlaying: Do you have experience being ghosted?

ShootsAndScores: Honestly, no.

ShootsAndScores: But that's mostly because I don't do much dating.

RoPlaying: Right. I'm sure you wouldn't be here watching me if you did.

· · ·

RoPlaying: Oh my god. That came out SO wrong and insulting.

ShootsAndScores: It's fine. I understood what you meant.

ShootsAndScores: And you're right. If I were in a relationship, I wouldn't be here. I'm not that kind of guy.

RoPlaying: Well, I suppose that's good to know. It is something I worry about doing this. I don't ever want to be considered "the other woman."

RoPlaying: You were saying you don't date…

ShootsAndScores: I didn't say I don't date, just that I'm not dating currently. My job just keeps me busy. Lots of travel involved.

RoPlaying: Ah, that makes sense.

RoPlaying: So no secret girlfriend in every city?

. . .

"Ha. Hardly," I murmur.

Some guys definitely do that shit and it makes me fucking rage, especially because the assholes who do it are usually wearing a wedding band, but that's not my style at all. I'm a one-woman kind of man. Well, whenever I can find a woman, that is.

As sad as it is to admit, I don't remember the last time I had someone to warm my bed. It's been... Fuck. At least a year?

ShootsAndScores: Not even close.

RoPlaying: Good.

RoPlaying: Not that I have any say in the matter anyway.

RoPlaying: You know what? That was out of line. Ignore me. I'm having an off night.

ShootsAndScores: Because of the guy?

. . .

RoPlaying: Yes.

ShootsAndScores: Whoever he is, he's an idiot.

RoPlaying: Right? Biggest dum-dum alive. I'm a catch!

Oh, she has no idea what a catch she really is.

I itch to tell her that. I want to type so many things, want to tell her she deserves so much in this world. But I can't.

In fact, I need to stop this conversation immediately. It's already gone too far.

My computer pings again with a new message.

RoPlaying: That sounded conceited. I swear I'm not usually this full of myself. In fact, in the past, I NEVER believed I was worth much of anything, but I'm trying not to be that person anymore.

"What the…"

ShootsAndScores: Who the hell told you that you weren't good enough?

. . .

I read my message a few times, hoping like hell I don't come off as some psycho who is entirely too invested in a stranger's life, but I can't help it. Who told her that shit? And did she kick them in the nuts? I sure as fuck hope so.

RoPlaying: Well, nobody SAID it, but it was heavily implied.

RoPlaying: Let's just say striking out tonight isn't the first time I've had a guy blow me off for someone else.

I really hate that she thinks I blew her off for someone else. I look over at the someone else again. Carl is awake now, watching me intently with those damn blue eyes of hers that made me unable to say no to her in the first place. Right now, they're saying, *You love me and you're going to forgive me for tonight.*

"Not a fucking chance," I tell her. "You're a little shit, and I'm withholding treats tonight."

It's an empty threat. I know it, and she does too. She's a spoiled fucking princess. Hell, I left *Rosie* to take care of her ass. She's got me wrapped around her finger.

I'm either a really good cat dad or a complete idiot.

Based on what Rosie is saying to me, I'm leaning toward the latter.

ShootsAndScores: Maybe the guy from tonight has a really good reason for ghosting you.

RoPlaying: Are you defending him?

ShootsAndScores: No? Just playing devil's advocate.

ShootsAndScores: I mean, I clearly don't know the guy, so how could I defend him?

Those damn dots dance on the screen again, and a full minute goes by before she responds.

RoPlaying: That's fair.

RoPlaying: And you're right, maybe he does have a good reason. But why didn't he give it to me when he had the chance?

. . .

ShootsAndScores: He could have been nervous? Or shy? Or just stupid?

"Monumentally stupid." I shake my head at myself.

ShootsAndScores: You're a beautiful woman, so maybe you intimidate him?

RoPlaying: LOL me intimidate someone? Not likely.

RoPlaying: But he is pretty shy…

ShootsAndScores: I know if I saw you out and about, I'd be completely tongue-tied.

RoPlaying: You're going to make me blush.

ShootsAndScores: Sorry. I think.

RoPlaying: Don't be. I like it.

· · ·

RoPlaying: But it is getting late, and I should go. I have an early morning.

RoPlaying: Thank you for chatting with me and letting me vent. I think I needed it, and all my friends are still out at the bar.

ShootsAndScores: Sure. Glad I could help.

RoPlaying: Maybe we can do this again?

No. Never. We can never, ever do this again.

ShootsAndScores: Of course we can.

"God, you're pathetic."

Something tells me I should really stop having conversations with myself, but at this point, it's pretty clear I'm insane, so why stop now?

RoPlaying: Good night. XO

. . .

ShootsAndScores: Good night, Ro.

The green icon next to her name goes red, indicating she's away, and I breathe a sigh of relief.

"I'm fucking screwed."

Meow.

I glare at Carl. "That's enough from you, cockblocker."

Meow.

She doesn't care that I took an already shitty situation and made it even shittier.

I need to fix this. I *have* to fix this. I'll go to Scout's Sweets tomorrow and I'll make this better. I'll set the record straight about why I left tonight. I'll tell her everything and hope like hell she can forgive me.

"I'm going to make this better, Carl. I'll fix it."

Meow.

She sounds like she doesn't believe me, and I'm not sure I do either.

CHAPTER 6

ROSIE

Four years ago, I realized I was madly in love with my best friend, the guy I grew up next door to and had known my entire life.

Three years ago, I was ready to tell him I loved him. I just needed to find the right time. This was big, life-changing. I couldn't just spring it on him. It had to be *right*.

Two and a half years ago, everything fell apart when he told me he'd met the love of *his* life and was moving out of the country and the lease on the apartment we shared wasn't going to be renewed.

And as of yesterday, I have officially blown my shot yet again. Fitz has a girlfriend, or *someone* waiting for him at home. I'm too late *again*.

I should have stayed home. I should have stayed in my little cave of happiness and spent those hours streaming, making money to make my dream of having my own bakery come true. I should have never thought asking him out was a good idea.

But I did think it was a good idea, and I got my hopes up that something might be possible between us. I should have known it would never happen.

I tried to salvage the night by doing some coloring while streaming. I thought zoning out a bit and making some money doing it would make me feel better, but it didn't. I talked less than normal, and by the end of the stream, I was still upset. Even though I promised I wouldn't interact with my subscribers in my DMs, when I saw the message from *ShootsAndScores*, well, I couldn't help myself.

Sure, I could have reached out to Stevie, but I knew she'd still be out with Greer and everyone else. She doesn't get out much without Macie in tow, so I wasn't about to ruin her night away. Besides, what's the point of this new "go-getter" attitude of mine if I'm not willing to make new friends and do bold things?

I was stunned when he read the message and even more surprised when he wrote back, but I think talking to him helped. I felt a little better by the time I went to bed, and then this morning when I got to the truck, I was feeling a lot lighter, maybe even good. I think it has to do with the conversation I had with ShootsAndScores.

"Oooh, you're smiling. Who are you thinking about?" Stevie waggles her brows. "Fitz?"

My smile drops, and she doesn't miss it.

"Oh no." She sets down the box of spice refills and crosses her arms over her chest, leaning against the prep table. "You two left last night right after each other, so I

87

figured you were making a poor attempt at trying to be discreet, but now I'm worried things didn't go as well as I'd hoped."

"Things did not go as well as you hoped."

A frown tugs at the corner of my lips, and Stevie reaches out, squeezing my forearm.

"I'm sorry," she says. "What happened?"

"Well, I *thought* we were hitting it off. We were even joking about what happened the other morning. Hell, I had literally opened my mouth to ask him out when…" I trail off, thinking back to the look on his face. That damn smile. How warm it was, how full of affection…the *love*.

"Did he say something?" Her back goes straight. "*Do* something? Because I swear, I'll call Greer right now and he'll find Fitz and he will gladly take a skate to his di—"

"No, he didn't do anything." I smile. "Though I am very happy to know I have Greer in my corner if that ever did happen."

"Oh, honey. You don't even know. His gruffness is just a front, and when he gets mad, he gets *mad*. He'd do anything to protect the people he cares about, and that includes you."

Warmth spreads through me because I know she means it. This little family they've created here is something special, and I know without a doubt in my mind I'm included in that too. Sure, it might just be because I serve the whole team delicious fried dough, but I'm okay with that. It's still nice to know they have my back if I need it.

"So, you were about to ask him, and then…" Stevie prompts.

I wince. "He got a text or a call. I'm not sure which, but whatever it was, he got this smile on his face and said he had to go. Actually, he said, 'Someone needs me.' Then he left."

Stevie's brows are pulled tightly together, her head tipped to the side as she stares at me. She doesn't say anything for several moments, so I continue.

"I'm guessing it was a girlfriend or something. It just felt so…familiar, you know? Like whoever it was, it was personal."

"Fitz doesn't have a girlfriend."

"Maybe it was a booty call?"

Stevie chuckles. "No, that's not Fitz either. He's not that kind of guy."

"How do you know?"

"Because Greer knows, and that man loves to give me all the good gossip from the locker room. You'd be really surprised what comes out of his mouth when he's lying there in a post-orgasm daze."

Now it's my turn to laugh because I just picture Greer spilling all the dirty secrets of everyone on the team. Stevie's right—he might come off as a grump, but deep down, he's a big softie. Hell, one time, I caught him on a phone call to his mother, and even *I* about swooned when he told her he loved her. Sweetest damn thing I've ever heard.

"Maybe it was something else," Stevie suggests.

"Maybe it was a friend? Or family? I know he has a sister and a few nieces. Could have been something with them?"

"Yeah, maybe." I lift my shoulder. "But whatever it was, it was enough for him to just up and leave with no explanation."

"But maybe it's a good explanation."

"That's what the guy online said too."

"Excuse me? What guy online? Are you talking to someone? Are you cheating on Fitz?"

I glower at her. "First of all, there is *nothing* happening between me and Fitz. Second, no, I'm not *talking* to someone. He's just...a friend. A *new* friend. I just met him last night. Sort of."

Stevie looks completely unconvinced, and I'm not sure I blame her. Don't sound exactly sure of myself at the moment.

"Care to elaborate on that very confusing statement?"

I sigh. "He's a subscriber."

"What? I thought..."

"That I promised to never DM them? I know, but he's not a creep. He *always* leaves the *sweetest* comments. So last night after everything that happened..." I shrug. "I was feeling lonely. I needed someone to talk to."

"Um, hello?" She waves at me. "Am I invisible or something?"

"I know I have you, and I totally love you for that, but I also didn't want to interrupt—"

Stevie holds her hand up. "I swear, if you're about to say something stupid like *interrupt your night with Greer*, I will boob punch you."

I grab said boobs, protecting them because no, thanks. Boob punches are the worst.

"I wasn't going to say that."

She lifts both brows.

I groan. "Fine, I totally was. But"—I step away when she moves toward me—"you guys never get time away to just be you, and when I left, you were making sex eyes at each other. There was no doubt in my mind you were going to end up banging in the bar bathroom."

A slow grin spreads across her face as she gets a faraway look in her eyes, telling me I am right on the money. She shakes her head, pulling herself out of her dirty little reminiscence.

"Who cares!" She pushes a finger into her chest. "Friend. There when you need me, no matter what."

I sigh. "Yes, I know. And I promise next time, I'll totally bother you with my trivial issues." She glares at me but allows me to continue. "Anyway, this guy was online and said basically the same things you are, that maybe Fitz left for a good reason and maybe I should hear him out."

"You totally should. I agree with this dude, whoever he is. What's his name?"

I shrug. "Not sure. We didn't get that far. I just know his username, ShootsAndScores."

Stevie's brows rise. "ShootsAndScores?"

"Yeah? Why are you making that face?"

She shrugs. "No reason. It's just...a little odd, isn't it?"

"No? Should it be? I mean, I just kind of assumed it's because he's a jock or something."

"Huh."

"*Huh* what?"

"Nothing." She waves me off, but I have a feeling it's more than nothing. "So, what'd you two talk about? Anything pervy?"

"It's not *all* pervy stuff, you know." She shrugs when I send her a pointed look. "I just said I was having a bad day and told him a little about why, and he convinced me I should give Fitz another chance. Then I went to bed because I had to be up at four for prep and he had an early morning too."

Stevie nods a few times, her lips pursed, but she doesn't say anything. I'm not sure how to gauge her reaction, thinking maybe she's upset that I'm chatting with some random guy online. So, I ask her that.

"No, no." She shakes her head. "It's not that. Well, I mean, it's a little bit that because I worry about your safety, but it's also so common now I'm not too surprised by it. I just thought...with Fitz and all..."

"I know. I thought with Fitz and all too, but I'm telling you, I think he's seeing someone else."

"Maybe. Maybe not. But I agree with this ShootsAndScores guy—you should give Fitz a chance to explain. He might have a good reason for leaving like he did."

I'm sure she's probably right because it doesn't sound like Fitz to have a secret girlfriend, but who knows?

"I'll talk to him."

"Yeah? Maybe you can do it at the Halloween party."

I groan. She's been trying to get me to agree to this damn party for the last three days.

"You do know Halloween was last week, right?"

"Of course I know. Macie dressed up as Greer, goalie pads and all, and scored a ton of candy that I'm still snacking on. But the guys are gone, so we're celebrating when they're home at an adults-only party. And you're coming." She sends me a sweet smile.

"I'll think about it."

"Don't think. Come. It'll be fun!"

"We'll see." I point a finger at her when she opens her mouth. "That's all you're getting out of me, so zip it."

She nods, a grin tugging at her lips. "Where do you want me to put these extra spices, badass?"

I laugh at the nickname, then direct her to the storage area. We spend the next several hours slinging coffee and donuts and chatting about everything other than what happened last night, and I watch the parking lot the entire time, searching for the hockey player with the missing tooth.

Fitz never shows.

The Comets are on the road and Stevie is driving me nuts complaining about Greer being gone. I want to grab her by the shoulders and shake her and ask her how she thinks *I* feel. The guy I'm totally crushing on might be seeing someone else, and I don't know because I don't have his contact info, so all I can do is sit around and wait for him to show up to get any answers out of him.

It's been a tense few days inside the tiny donut truck, so tonight, I'm turning to my favorite thing to do to take my mind off things: baking. I have my laptop set up in the corner of the room, and I'm wearing my wig and mask as usual. I have my lingerie—a *very* sexy maroon set that shows off almost my entire ass every time I bend over to check the cookies—and a new pair of heels I'm trying out.

I never thought this would be my life, especially having grown up in the household I did. You kept quiet, and you did what all good little girls are supposed to do—study hard, go to a college of your parents' choosing, and marry a man who is going to take care of you. You do everything you're told and you don't ask questions, so that was what I did. I listened and let everyone else make my decisions for me. I was going to go to State, and I was going to find a husband.

The older I got, the less and less I wanted that, but I was too scared to tell them because I didn't want to disappoint them. So, when Levi came to me and told me he was leaving and he'd like me to go with him, I did.

I didn't realize that just a few short years later, he'd leave me too.

I try not to think about that as I pull a fresh batch of sea salt caramel chocolate chip cookies from the oven, making sure to press my ass out as far as I can to give the camera a good shot. Based on the way my notifications go nuts, they love it.

I smile to myself. Who would have thought I'd be doing this? Baking half-naked and getting paid to do it on camera? I sure as hell didn't. I really didn't expect to enjoy it so much, either. Sure, sometimes the pervy comments can be taxing, but overall, it's nice. Most of my subscribers are older single men or widowers who miss having someone around. They don't want me to do anything sexual; they just want someone to spend time with. I like being that comfort to them, and I like having their eyes on me. It's a win-win.

I let the cookies rest as I strut back toward my laptop and grin into the camera.

"How's everyone doing tonight?"

I keep my eye on the comments, knowing exactly what name I'm hoping pops up.

I haven't spoken to ShootsAndScores since the other night, though not for lack of wanting to reach out. I've just been swamped with classes. Who knew going to college and juggling not one, but two jobs would be such a damn struggle? I'm more tired than normal, but I know in the long run when I'm operating my own bakery, this is going to pay off big.

Several answers come through on the chat. Some are polite, and some are not so great. I do my best to ignore those, but one catches my eye.

BallSoH@rd: You're fat but you got some great tits. Show them to us! My cock is aching for you.

I grind my teeth, trying not to let the comment get to me. I mean, this person is literally paying to be here. They must like what they see enough, right?

Another comment pops up.

ShootsAndScores: @BallSoH@rd, your cock is really going to be aching when I knee you in the balls.

I laugh.

"I'm not sure you're supposed to knee your fellow man in the balls, ShootsAndScores."

ShootsAndScores: Two things...

. . .

ShootsAndScores: If he deserves it, fuck yes you can.

ShootsAndScores: And that's no man. A man doesn't treat a woman like that.

His responses get several positive reactions in the chat.

In real life? His words go straight between my legs.

I don't respond to him out loud again, mostly because if I say something, I'm nearly positive there's no way I'll be able to mask the lust in my voice. Ridiculous since I don't know this guy, but still.

I stream for another thirty minutes or so and make another batch of cookies, then decide to call it a night. I have some reading to do for my economics class, and I'm not looking to fall behind when the semester just started.

"Thanks for joining me tonight. I won't be back tomorrow, but I'll be around on Sunday."

I wait for a comment from ShootsAndScores since he always sends one when I end my streams.

A minute goes by.

Then another.

When I finally hit three, I accept that he's not going to say anything, and my shoulders slump in defeat. Maybe things were too weird the other night? I don't know, but now I have two guys ghosting me. Sure, ShootsAndScores is just a client, but it still stings.

I blow the camera a kiss, then cover the lens with my hand as I turn off the stream.

A minute later, a message pops up.

ShootsAndScores: Evening, Ro.

Well, well, well, maybe this night isn't over yet.

Homework can wait.

CHAPTER 7

It's official: I'm the fucking worst.

Practice ran long, I was trapped in the doc's office for thirty minutes, and then I got sent down to press and ended up spending entirely too fucking long standing in front of a camera getting my picture taken about ten billion times.

By the time I got out, the truck was closed for the day, and I knew I was screwed, especially since we left for a road trip bright and early the next morning. We got five out of six possible points, and now we're on the plane back to North Carolina. I'm itching for two things: a strawberry smoothie and to see Rosie so I can fix things between us because I know she must still be upset.

I talked myself out of asking Greer to ask Stevie for Rosie's number about ten different times. The most recent was in the locker room before we boarded the plane. When Greer chucked his helmet across the room after the shootout loss, I figured it probably wasn't the best moment.

Now, he's passed out beside me, and I have my phone out angled away from him, Rosie's stream playing in my ears. She's currently pulling a fresh batch of cookies from the oven, and when she bends over, I can see the edges of her ass cheeks. I have to fight back a moan at the sight.

She hasn't spoken for a half hour, and I wonder if it has anything to do with that asshole's comments. It's not the first time someone's been a dick to her and I'm sure it won't be the last, but I fucking hate that I can't do anything about it. I can't remember the last time I was so fired up about something. Maybe when Greer told me about that piece of shit who cornered Stevie at Slapshots and tried touching her?

I wasn't lying to Hayes when I said I've never been in a fight, but that only extends to the ice. Off it, I've had my fair share of tussles, especially in high school when guys would try to mess around with my sister. Hell, I even missed two weeks of hockey when Richie Johnson slapped her ass in the middle of the cafeteria. It was worth every fucking minute of riding the bench.

Rosie keeps her video going for another few minutes, then signs off for the night. I miss her the second the screen goes black, and I want her to know she has someone in her corner. Before I can overthink it too much, I pull up the chat and shoot her a message.

ShootsAndScores: Evening, Ro.

• • •

RoPlaying: Hey there. :)

RoPlaying: How's your night?

ShootsAndScores: Long and hard.

That's not a lie, but what I don't tell her is that we lost in overtime and I'm kicking myself because it was my fault. I lost my edge and went down, giving Seattle the opportunity for a breakaway in three-on-three hockey. They ripped it past Greer, and that was the end of the game. If I had just kept my stride, we'd have been fine. We lost a point thanks to me.

I'm not sure what it means that when I've had a rough night, she's the first person I want to talk to, but I try not to think about it.

RoPlaying: Well, that sounds like a fun night to me. ;)

ShootsAndScores: Oh god, I didn't mean...

· · ·

ShootsAndScores: Anyway, I meant what I said. That guy deserves a kick in the nuts. I'd be more than happy to do it for you.

RoPlaying: And take away all my fun? Now that's rude. *pouts*

ShootsAndScores: I see those types of comments roll in sometimes. The number of times I've had to bite my tongue so I don't go off on people… Well, it's a lot.

ShootsAndScores: I'm sorry you have to deal with that.

RoPlaying: It's fine. I'm still getting paid either way. I mean, at least they compliment my great cans while being colossal dicks.

ShootsAndScores: You signed up to stream. You didn't sign up to be treated like a piece of fucking meat. Guys are pigs.

RoPlaying: Does that include you?

. . .

Fuck. It includes me in ways she doesn't even know.

ShootsAndScores: Sometimes, yes.

RoPlaying: Wow. I'm surprised by your honest answer. Most guys would pretend they're perfect only to reveal later they were a liar the whole time.

ShootsAndScores: Experience in that?

RoPlaying: Years and years ago. I had an ex in high school who was very…friendly with everyone.

I gnash my teeth, trying my best to hold back all the bad words that want to flow out of me.

ShootsAndScores: Fuck that guy.

RoPlaying: Lots of people did.

. . .

RoPlaying: LOL Sorry. Easy joke.

RoPlaying: But, yeah, fuck that guy. He didn't deserve me then, and he damn sure doesn't deserve me now.

I love that she knows her worth, and I hope she always sticks to her guns on that.

RoPlaying: Thank you, by the way, for saying something in the chat. I think it helps when others comment back about what assholes people can be. I try to block them whenever I see something, but it moves so fast I don't always get the chance.

ShootsAndScores: I'm always there to back you up.

ShootsAndScores: Well, when my schedule allows me to catch a stream, that is.

RoPlaying: You travel for work a lot, then, huh? Do you like it?

.   .   .

ShootsAndScores: I love it. I wouldn't trade the job for anything.

RoPlaying: What do you do?

"Shit. Fuck. Shit."

"Shh!" Hayes says from behind me. "People are trying to sleep, asshole."

I glance over my shoulder to make sure he can't see my screen, but I don't have anything to worry about. He's currently sporting a white eye mask that says *Go Fuck Yourself* and his head is bent at the most uncomfortable angle. Ford, the new guy on the team, is sitting next to him. He's wearing headphones and his face is buried in his iPad, so I don't think I have anything to worry about there either.

I turn my attention back to my phone, where another message is waiting for me.

RoPlaying: Sorry. You don't have to answer that. I didn't mean to pry. It's just, you know so much about me from streaming…

ShootsAndScores: Are you guilt-tripping me?

. . .

RoPlaying: Maybe a little?

ShootsAndScores: That's okay. I'll allow it.

Honestly, I'd allow her to do just about anything she wanted.

ShootsAndScores: I work in sports.

RoPlaying: Hence the name.

RoPlaying: Agent?

ShootsAndScores: Something like that.

RoPlaying: Do you work with hockey players at all?

I sit forward in my seat, my heart hammering so fucking loud I have a feeling it's going to stir more than one guy awake.

Why the hell would she ask me that? I didn't give anything away, did I?

Calm down. She's probably just asking because the team is at the damn truck all the time. She knows hockey players. It's cool. You're cool.

I choose my next words very carefully.

ShootsAndScores: I know a few.

RoPlaying: Me too!

RoPlaying: I mean, not to brag or anything, but I actually know a whole team of them.

RoPlaying: Wow. That sounds like they're running a train on me or something.

My breath gets stuck in my lungs, and I can't breathe. I'm wheezing, my whole body burning with the inability to properly pull in air.

Hayes kicks at the back of my seat. "Dude, if you're going to die, do it quietly, huh?"

I don't even bother responding to him.

. . .

RoPlaying: OH MY GOD. I don't know why I said that. Ignore me.

RoPlaying: I know them from my job. My other job. I bake. I LOVE baking. It's my favorite thing.

ShootsAndScores: Even more than streaming?

RoPlaying: Oh, definitely. I mean, don't get me wrong, I love to stream and do this. It's fun and it allows me to explore myself in ways I never knew I wanted to, so how could I not love it? But it's not my passion. My passion is making delicious sweets. I'd love to open my own bakery someday.

ShootsAndScores: I think that's incredible. You should do it.

RoPlaying: Yeah? I think so too.

RoPlaying: Do you like sweets? What's your favorite kind? I'll bake it next time so you can watch. :)

. . .

My cock aches at the idea of watching Rosie bake my favorite sweet. I can just picture her in nothing but an apron, smears of flour and icing all over her body as she whips up something with strawberries.

I try to wipe the image from my head, not because I don't want to think about it but because if I keep thinking about it, there's a chance I could blow my load without ever touching my cock.

ShootsAndScores: Strawberry donuts.

RoPlaying: Really? That's so strange. That guy from the other night, the one who ghosted me, he's a big strawberry nut too. I know because he ALWAYS orders two strawberry donuts. I don't know where it all goes, though, because the man certainly doesn't look like he eats two donuts every day.

RoPlaying: Sorry. I'm rambling. I do that sometimes.

ShootsAndScores: Don't apologize. It's cute.

RoPlaying: Okay, this is getting weird. HE said that to me too.

. . .

"Fuckfuckfuckfuck." It comes out all one word, and I can't stop chanting it.

Why? Why would I say that? And why would I tell her strawberry donuts are my favorite? I'm being so fucking obvious I might as well just confess who I am right now.

ShootsAndScores: He sounds like a cool guy.

"Fucking really? That's what you come up with?"

Another kick to the back of my chair from Hayes. Beside me, Greer rips his own eye mask off and whirls around in his seat, then smacks Hayes on the side of his head.

Hayes sits up with a glare. "Hey, man. What the fuck?"

"What the fuck is right. He's not even being that loud, and you keep fucking kicking the seat because you're being a little bitch about a tiny amount of noise. Shut up and deal with it like the rest of us or I swear to fucking god, I'm going to break your legs off and beat you with them myself."

"That's quite the vivid image," Ford mumbles.

Greer turns his icy stare to the new guy, who just holds his hands up in the air.

"I'm being quiet," he promises.

"Good. Now stop kicking the seat and go to sleep, Princess."

Hayes doesn't say anything. He just slips the mask back down his face and settles into his seat.

Greer flips around and falls back into his chair, and suddenly *I'm* the one he's scowling at.

"Shut the fuck up or I'll make you sit with Miller next time," he tells me flatly.

"Hey, I heard that!" the guy in question calls from the back of the plane, earning himself a rousing chorus of "Shut up, Miller!" from just about everyone.

Greer smirks and nods toward my phone. "What are you doing over there? Watching porn?"

"I'm minding my own business."

He shrugs. "Fair enough. Just keep it down."

I nod, and he returns to his previous position, eye mask in place. It's not even thirty seconds before he's snoring softly beside me.

RoPlaying: He is when he's not ditching me.

RoPlaying: Anyway, I don't want to talk about him tonight. I'm still upset because he still hasn't explained what happened.

· · ·

ShootsAndScores: I'm sorry. He sounds like a jerk.

RoPlaying: He really isn't.

RoPlaying: At least I don't think so.

RoPlaying: I'm going to give him another chance whenever he gets back.

ShootsAndScores: Back?

RoPlaying: He travels for work a lot too.

RoPlaying: Wow. I just realized the two of you have a lot in common.

ShootsAndScores: Sounds like we're both cool guys.

RoPlaying: That was terribly lame, and I loved it.

. . .

RoPlaying: Anyway, thanks for sticking up for me tonight. I like having you there to have my back.

ShootsAndScores: Happy to be of service.

RoPlaying: If I can ever be of service, just let me know. ;)

Does she mean...
    I shake away the thought.

RoPlaying: Good night. XO

ShootsAndScores: Good night, Ro.

I click my screen off and set my phone against my chest. I close my eyes and am almost asleep when something hits me.
    I pull the streaming site back up and navigate to our chat.

. . .

ShootsAndScores: In a totally non-pervy way, you're gorgeous and worth watching...and not just because of your great cans.

I turn my phone off before I can see if she responds. This time, when I close my eyes, I go right to sleep...and I totally dream of Rosie.

"But, Mom! *Puh*-lease! Pretty, pretty please!"

"No." Stevie shakes her head. "It's a school night. You don't need to be staying the night with Aunt Scout and Uncle Miller on a school night. You basically spent all summer with them. You can survive an entire week at home."

"But they have a puppy!" Macie, Stevie's young daughter, crosses her arms over her chest and sticks her bottom lip out. "I want a puppy."

"You can get a puppy when you learn to not leave your backpack in the middle of the living room every day. Dogs are a big responsibility. How am I supposed to trust you with one when you don't even clean up your own messes?"

"Because a dog is different!" The kid looks over at Greer. "Tell her, Greer!"

He holds his hands up. "I'm not getting in the middle of this." He leans over to me. "Mostly because I'm totally on team Macie, and I'd rather not go without sex for agreeing with the kid over Stevie."

"I heard that." Stevie glares at her boyfriend, then turns back to her daughter. "Tell you what—we'll talk about it when you're twelve, how's that?"

"Twelve? *Twelve?* That's *forever* away!"

It's not, but I'm sure to her, it feels like it. Thing is, I have a feeling Stevie is going to cave well before then, especially if Greer has anything to say about it.

Stevie pinches the bridge of her nose. "Macie…"

"Mom…" she mimics.

"I don't have time for this. I need to go help Rosie," her mother says, cutting her one last glare before turning and walking away, putting a pin in the conversation.

The kid lets out a sigh, then flops down on the picnic bench next to Greer. She looks up at me with sad eyes. "Do *you* have any pets?"

"I do."

"What kind?"

"A shithead cat."

She narrows her eyes. "You can't say shithead, but I promise not to tell my mom."

"Um, *you* just said shithead," Greer points out.

Her eyes widen. "Oh crap."

"You're not supposed to say crap either."

I swear her eyes get even bigger, and I have to tuck my lips together so I don't laugh because she looks like she might cry.

"But if you promise to cool it with the puppy

115

begging, I won't tell your mom."

"Really?"

Greer nods. "Yeah, but mostly because *I* want a puppy too, and if you keep it up, we'll never get one. Your mother is stubborn."

Macie rolls her eyes. "I know. She always tells me I got that from her."

The goalie reaches over and tugs on her braids. "You did, and it's my favorite thing about both of you."

She smiles up at him, then looks over at me. "Can I meet your shithead cat?"

I shrug. "Sure. Why not?"

"Yes!" She fist-pumps the air, then jumps off the bench, racing toward her mother, who is back inside the truck, rushing around with Rosie as they try to placate the line of hungry people. "Mom! Fitz said I could meet his cat!"

Stevie glowers our way, and Greer cowers under her heated stare.

We got in late last night and I crashed as soon as I walked through the door. I didn't even cuddle with Carl like I usually do, something she was apparently very unhappy about this morning based on the fact that she ignored me when I was getting ready.

I was surprised to find Greer pulling into the parking lot of Scout's Sweets at the same time I did. I wanted to beeline right for Rosie and explain to her what happened at Slapshots, but I don't want to do it in front of Greer.

So instead, I've just been sitting here waiting for the

right moment to talk with her.

"So, what's up with you being here this morning?" he asks. "I figured you'd be at home being a loner or something."

"Um, donuts. Obviously."

He nods a few times. "Right. Obviously." He slides his eyes toward the truck where Rosie is currently grinning at a customer, listening intently to whatever they say before throwing her head back on a laugh. "And it has nothing to do with her, right?"

I whip my head back. "Excuse me? Why would you say that?"

"Just a hunch. You two looked awfully cozy at Slapshots right before we left."

"You were watching me at Slapshots? Didn't your mom ever tell you it's not nice to stare?"

"First, leave my beautiful angel of a mother out of this conversation." He glowers at me. "Second, I was paying attention, not staring."

"You know, every day you say something that makes me even more surprised you got Stevie to fall in love with you."

He reaches down and grabs himself between the legs. "It's my huge dick, not my pretty words that did it."

"More like you *are* a huge dick."

He grins. "And proud of it." The smile slips just as quickly as it appeared because of course it did because it's Greer and smiling is *so* not his thing. "Now tell me: do you have a thing for the hot baker or not?"

It's my turn to glare at him, and I'll give him credit because the dude is no fool. He knows why I'm glaring.

"So you do have a thing for her, then. Stevie had a suspicion, but she wasn't totally sold, especially after Rosie said something about you bailing on her."

I groan. "Stevie knows?"

He shrugs. "Not formally."

"Good. She better not find out."

"Oooh. Are we sharing secrets?" Rosie falls onto the bench across from us. "Who are they about? Tell me everything."

My heart begins to hammer wildly in my chest. Where the hell did she come from? And did she hear any of that? Based on the way she's staring at us both with wide, curious eyes, I'm going with no.

"Hey, Ro," I say to her.

She narrows her eyes. "Ro?"

Oh fuck.

"Sorry, I meant Rosie. I don't know why I said that." I swear my face is on fire as her green eyes bore into me.

Greer presses his hand to my shoulder. "I'm going to go check on Stevie now that the line has died down." He winks at Rosie. "*Ro.*" He walks behind her, pointing at her, then to me, then he makes a circle with his right hand and pokes his left index finger in and out of it, all while grinning like an idiot.

I want so badly to flip him off, but I know that's going to make everything entirely too fucking obvious, so I don't.

She shrugs. "It's fine. I've never had a nickname before. I like it."

"Nobody has ever called you Ro before?"

"Well, they sort of have." She doesn't elaborate on that, but she doesn't know she doesn't have to. "I've just always been Rosie. Even my…" She pauses, then swallows thickly. "Just Rosie."

I nod. "Well, Ro it is, then."

She grins, and I realize at this moment I missed that grin over the last few days more than I missed my strawberry smoothie and donut fix, and that's saying something.

"So, Fitz…" She links her hands together, then rests her arms atop the table, leaning closer to me.

"So, Ro…" I mirror her movements, loving how much sweeter she smells the closer I get.

The corners of her mouth tug up, but it doesn't last. "Why'd you ditch me at Slapshots?"

I sputter, completely caught off guard by her blunt question. She just went right for the jugular. Rip the Band-Aid off and whatnot.

"Um…" I reach up with my hand, lifting the hat I'm wearing and running my hand through my hair, then tugging the cap back down, this time backward. "I had to get home to someone."

"Yeah, you said that. I'm assuming they're okay. I mean, you were off playing hockey and stuff. If it was serious, you wouldn't have been."

"Yeah, everything is okay."

"Oh. Good. I'm glad."

She somehow looks upset by my answer, and I hate that. I hate that she doesn't like it. I hate that there are probably a million questions and scenarios running through her head.

I clear my throat, which suddenly feels so fucking dry, then sit forward once more. Rosie looks up at me with unsure eyes.

"Do you want to know what I was doing?" I ask.

She twists her lips, flicking her eyes away before looking back at me. She nods once. "Please."

"My cat."

Her brows slide together, a deep wrinkle forming between her eyes. "Huh?"

"Carl, my cat. For some reason, she loves sneaking into my pantry and sitting on the bread loaf in there. Don't ask me why because I don't know. She's weird. Anyway, I have this app on my phone that shows me a live feed of my place while I'm away, and I got a notification that she was in the camera's view. I saw her go into the pantry. It wouldn't be a big deal if the latch didn't stick so badly, which is why I never close the door fully. So, when it shut behind her…"

"You had to go rescue her."

I nod. "Exactly. I'm sure I could have explained that the other night, but I was worried because she's scared of the dark, so I just…"

"Left."

Another nod. "Yeah. I'm, uh, sorry about that. I'm

kind of clueless sometimes in social settings. I guess it's the loner in me."

Rosie doesn't say anything. She just stares at me. It's not a blank stare or an angry stare. It's just...a stare, and it has me twitching in my seat because I don't have a damn clue what it means.

"Um, Rosie?"

"I have so many questions," she blurts out. "I'm trying to figure out where to start."

"I'll answer them all."

"Okay..." She leans forward, counting off the first question on her finger. "One: your *female* cat's name is Carl?"

I chuckle because I knew this question would be first. It's always everybody's first one.

"Yes. *Her* name is Carl. I found her one night when I was out for a walk." Before finding Rosie's stream, I used to take them at night all the time when I couldn't figure out how to calm my brain down. For obvious reasons, I don't tell her that. "I saw this cat down in the alley, just a little thing, maybe six months old and skinny as hell. It had part of a Styrofoam cup from Carl's Burgers around its neck. The cat was trying to get it off and couldn't. It was so scared it scratched me all over the damn place when I tried to pick it up. When I got hold of the thing, I got the trash off, but I just couldn't leave it on the street alone. I took it home and let it stay the night, then took it to the vet the next day. That's when I learned it was female. I tried to change her name to something else, but she refused to respond to anything other than Carl, so it just stuck."

Rosie's grinning by the time my story is over, and… "Are you crying?"

"What? No!" She swipes at her obviously wet eyes. "Shut up. You're crying."

I laugh. "I'm not right now, but I totally did then."

"Did you really?"

That same blush from before creeps back in. "Yeah. Now shut up."

Rosie wipes at her eyes again with a sniffle. "Okay. That story is really sweet and also strange, but I have more questions. So, number two: Carl is afraid of the dark?"

"Oh yeah, big-time. She hates it. I keep a night-light on in every room so if she's up roaming the apartment, she doesn't get scared."

Her mouth drops open.

"What?" I ask.

"That is…"

"Weird? Yeah, I know."

"Sweet, Fitz. It's incredibly sweet."

I shift around, trying really fucking hard not to let that godforsaken redness creep back into my face.

"Question three: You have a camera for your cat?"

"Sure do." I take my phone out and pull up the feed, then slide the device across the table. I point to the screen where Carl is sitting on her tower, lazing around in the morning sun. "See."

"Aww, she's so cute."

I smile like a proud dad. "She's a handful." *And a total cockblock.*

"Clearly." She gives my phone back. "That's…*cute.*" She winks. "All right. I forgive you, then."

"Wait—no questions about why she likes to lie on the bread?"

She shrugs. "Bread is soft. Totally makes sense."

I laugh. "Right. Of course."

Quiet falls over us. It's almost awkward, but not quite there.

"So…" I start, trying to preserve the moment as long as I can. "Are we good?"

Rosie nods. "We're good. Just maybe next time give a girl a short description of why you're leaving so she doesn't think you're running off to a girlfriend or secret wife or booty call."

A look crosses her features, one I know…one I've seen from several of the guys on the team before, especially when someone flirts with their girl.

It's jealousy.

And a little worry.

"I don't."

"Huh?"

"I don't have one, a girlfriend or secret wife or booty call."

"Oh. Okay."

"Okay?"

She bobs her head up and down slowly. "Okay. Good."

Good.

I don't know what it means. I don't know what I *want* it to mean, but I do know it can't mean anything.

"Are you going to the Halloween party tomorrow?" she asks.

I suppress a groan. I *hate* going to parties, and I really hate going to costume parties. But I find myself nodding anyway. "Yes. I have to. I'm pretty sure if I don't, Lowell might rip my balls off, and since I'm kind of a big fan of those, I'd rather that not happen."

"Nah. He's getting soft in his old age, especially with that adorable baby of his and now that Hollis just had their second baby."

She's not lying there. I used to hear rumors of Lowell and his one-timer ways, but now he's fully committed and settled down, officially a dad of two.

"Dammit, Greer, did you put her up to it?"

We both look to the donut truck, where Stevie is looking at Greer like she's about ten seconds away from murdering him. He has his palms up in the air, doing his best to look innocent, though there is no doubt in my mind he's not.

"Me? Never?" He bats his lashes, but she doesn't buy it, and I don't blame her.

Rosie hitches her thumb over her shoulder. "I should get back before I have to help Stevie bury a body."

"You'd do that?"

"In a damn heartbeat." Rosie rises from the table but doesn't make a move to walk away. "Thanks for explaining things to me. I look forward to hearing more stories about what a troublemaker Carl is."

"Wait until I tell you about the time she snuck out and my neighbor, Miss Drake, brought her back wearing nothing but a G-string bikini. She's eighty." I shudder just thinking about it.

Rosie laughs. "It's a date, then."

She gives me a small wave before sauntering back to the donut truck, and I'm ashamed to admit I watch her ass the entire time. I mean, can I really be blamed? Especially when the material hugs all of her curves like it was made specifically for her?

When she's about to step back inside, I realize something.

"Hey, Ro!" She spins around, her brows raised in a silent question. "Are you going?" She tips her head to the side. "The Halloween party."

Please say yes.

"I'm not sure." She tucks a strand of hair behind her ear with a grin, and it takes everything I have not to march over to her and pull it loose again so I can feel it between my fingertips. "Maybe."

"Well, then maybe I'll see you there."

That small smile? It turns into a full-on beam.

Maybe this party won't be so bad after all.

CHAPTER 8

ROSIE

RoPlaying: So, I finally talked to The Guy.

ShootsAndScores: Yeah? How did that go?

RoPlaying: Good. Really good, actually. He gave me a totally legit reason for leaving like he did.

ShootsAndScores: And you believe him?

RoPlaying: I might be crazy for it, but I do. If you knew him, you'd understand. He's just this…well, really sweet guy, so I can see it.

·　·　·

ShootsAndScores: Well, good. I'm glad you got it sorted out and you're back on good terms.

RoPlaying: Me too.

RoPlaying: I think I may have you to thank for it.

ShootsAndScores: Me? Why?

RoPlaying: You convinced me to give him a shot at explaining himself. So, yeah, thanks for that.

ShootsAndScores: Well, then you're welcome.

RoPlaying: You're a good friend.

When he doesn't respond after two full minutes, I click my screen off and slip my phone back into my pocket. I might be a lovesick fool or the most gullible person on the planet, but Fitz's reasoning for ditching me at Slapshots was the sweetest thing ever.

It was so…*Fitz*.

He left to rescue his cat who is afraid of the dark because he didn't want her to freak out? He may as well have been holding a lighter under my dress because I swear my panties melted right off.

"Oooh. You look like you're thinking of something panty-melting. Tell me."

Stevie rests her arms on the countertop beside me. The morning rush is gone, and we're all out of things to do until it picks back up at eleven when people come in for their midday sugar coma.

"Fitz rescued his female cat who is afraid of the dark and likes to sit on bread and is named Carl, and I'm pretty sure it makes him the most beautiful man alive."

When Stevie doesn't say anything, I peek over at her.

"Did you hear what I just said? Fitz rescu—"

"I heard what you said. I also heard what you said yesterday when you told me this same story."

"So why aren't you swooning?"

"Oh, I am, because that is sweet as hell, but I also don't want to be creeping on your man."

"My man?" I scoff. "He's not *my* man."

"But he could be." She bounces her brows up and down a few times. "Maybe even tonight at the party."

"Ugh, the party. I still don't know if I'm going."

"What!" she explodes. "Of course you're going. You *have* to."

I don't *have* to, but I'd be lying if I said a little part of me didn't *want* to go. Fitz seemed excited by the idea of me going, and that made *me* excited about the idea of going. And who knows? Maybe this could be our shot. A loud party with flowing drinks, something to help ease the tension.

"I don't have a costume," I complain.

"Just wear your streaming getup. It's not like anyone is going to know it's you. Nobody knows you stream, right?"

I shake my head. "I haven't told anyone."

Not because I'm ashamed of what I do, because I'm not. It just hasn't naturally come up in any conversation. And besides, when people ask me *why* I do it, I'm not sure I'm ready to explain the whole paying-for-school aspect of it because then I'd need to explain *why* I'm going back. I'm not ready to divulge that information to Scout yet.

"Then wear that. It's sexy and it's fun. *And* it shows off the incredible curves you have." She bumps her shoulder against mine.

I used to be ashamed of my curves. I hated that my boobs were big and my ass spilled over the seats at restaurants. I especially hated the folds on my belly every time I bent over and the stretchmarks that lined my skin. I remember a time when I wore baggy clothes and gym shorts, doing anything and everything I could to not have something clinging to me.

Then, after everything that happened with Levi and I vowed to never be that meek little girl again, I did something daring—I wore a shirt that was actually my size. Sure, I still had my saggy basketball shorts on, but it was a huge feat for me. It took time, but eventually, I got to a point where it felt wrong to wear something that *didn't* show off my body. Now, I'm proud of what I'm rocking, rolls and all.

"Whatever you wear, it's going to have Fitz drooling, I know that."

"And what if I show up to this party and he doesn't recognize me and then we spend the entire night not talking or being awkward around one another?"

"Well, there is no doubt in my mind Fitz is going to be awkward because that's just how that adorable shy boy is, but I know you're not going to be. It'll be a total movie moment: you walking in looking all hot, the music coming to a dramatic pause, and then he'll see you and you'll fall into each other's arms and ask Lowell to use one of his rooms."

"Not one of his rooms," I remind her. "It's a rental."

"Even hotter because you don't have to worry about leaving the room all messy. Actually, maybe I can sneak off with Greer…" The wheels start turning in her head, and I have no doubt she's already plotting ways to get him up to a room—not that she'll have to work hard. Greer is obsessed with her, and he's not afraid to show it no matter who is watching.

She gives herself a shake. "Anyway, that's what's going to happen. Mark my words."

"Oh, yes, I'll just start holding my breath now." I roll my eyes. "Don't we have work to be doing?"

She groans. "Yes, but I don't want to do it. I hate working here."

"So why do you?"

She twists her lips back and forth a few times before saying, "Because it's easy, and sometimes easy is nice. But what I really want is to do something else, maybe even teach."

"You want to be a teacher?"

"I think so." She bites on her bottom lip. "Do you think that's crazy?"

"What? No! I think it's a great idea! I mean, they're tragically underpaid, so that part sucks, but I think it would be a good fit for you."

"Really? Because I do too. I don't think I've done a bad job with Macie, so working with other kids could be fun."

"I think it's the perfect job for you."

This is it, Rosie. This is your chance to tell Stevie about wanting to open your own bakery.

"And this is the perfect job for *you*, you know. I don't think Scout or I tell you enough, but we really appreciate what you've done here, stepping up to give her room to fulfill her writing dreams. It means a lot, and *you* mean a lot to us."

Guilt eats at me more and more with every word that leaves her mouth. I love this place. I love Scout and I love Stevie too, but making donuts isn't my dream. I want to do more. I want to make more. Hell, I might even want to cater some events.

I can't tell Stevie that now though, not when she's just said all these incredible things about me. It'll only make her sad.

"Thanks," I say instead. "You two mean a lot to me too."

She smiles, then bumps my shoulder again. "All right. Enough sappy shit. Let's get this place ready before all the fancy business boys come for their midday hit of caffeine so we can get out early and get ready for the party tonight."

For the first time since she asked me to go, I'm actually looking forward to the party because I have a feeling Fitz will be there, and tonight, I plan to tell him just how I feel.

"Great. Now I'm the weirdo who showed up to the party in an Uber instead of driving because she got nervous and did three shots before she left her apartment."

"Um, ma'am, this is an Uber, not a confessional, and I have other rides to pick up."

I wince. "Right. Sorry," I tell my driver. "Thank you for the ride. Five stars."

"Fucking better be," the guy mutters as I push the door open and climb out of the old Honda Civic.

I shut the door, he peels off, and I think for a second about removing one star just because, but I know he doesn't *really* deserve it. I mean, I did just sit in

132

the back of his car muttering to myself for a full ten minutes.

I give him five stars and a hefty tip, then slip my phone back into my purse before I do something dumb like read over my messages with ShootsAndScores again. He still hasn't responded from earlier, and for some reason, it's not sitting right with me.

I do my best to brush it aside and focus on the here and now—this damn Halloween party. I've never been a big party person, and this one has butterflies swirling in my belly because I'm not sure what to expect. Fitz seemed excited about the idea of me coming, but I wish I knew why. As a friend? As potentially more? I don't know, and not knowing is killing me.

"Well, there is only one way to find out," I say.

I stare up at the sprawling mansion Lowell rented for the party. I can hear the music from out here, and I just know it's going to be a madhouse when I get inside. I mean, it's a bunch of professional hockey players; they aren't exactly known for keeping things tame.

I blow out a breath, pull my skirt up, and make my way up the stairs. I don't bother knocking—it's not like anyone could hear me anyway—and push the door open. I'm immediately assaulted by the thumping bass of whatever rap song is blaring through the speakers. It's so loud I can *feel* it in my chest, and I already regret coming.

"This is so not my scene," I murmur as I wade through the groups of partygoers.

There are so many people, many more than there are

on the team, that's for sure. They're all dancing or talking, and some are even kissing. It's exactly what I imagined a party with a bunch of hot hockey players would look like—pure chaos.

"Hey! You made it!"

I spin to find Stevie walking toward me, a black and orange cup in each hand. She's decked out head to toe as Elsa from *Frozen*. She wraps me in a hug, and it's apparent I'm not the only one who has already had something to drink tonight. I can smell the booze wafting off her.

"You look great!" she shouts in my ear, giving me a big smile. "Fitz is going to love it." She points to the room behind her. "He's in there somewhere. Last I saw he was on the couch being a party pooper." She juts her bottom lip out, and I laugh.

"You look amazing, too. I love the wig." I finger the braid that's hanging over her shoulder.

"Isn't it great? Greer said he already has plans for later, something about acting out a dirty Disney version, one where I'm on my knees and he's the evil guy who is going to spank me instead of trying to take over my kingdom, and I cannot wait." Her eyes widen. "Oh my god, pretend I didn't say that. I'm drunk."

"You don't say," I tease. "Where's everyone else?"

She nods toward another side of the house. "Lots of them are over there. Some are in the kitchen, a few in the basement. I think they're playing strip poker? I don't know. Oh!" She smacks her forehead with her wrist, and whatever alcoholic beverage she has in her cup sloshes over the side. If any gets on her, she doesn't seem to care. "I almost forgot. We need your phone."

"My phone?"

"Yep. Them's the rules, straight from Lowell's mouth. No phones because it means evidence, and if things go awry, as captain, he's the one in trouble."

"Okay…" I dig into the small clutch I brought, then hand it over.

She tosses it into a bucket near the door that's already overflowing with other devices, then leans in close to me. "Don't tell Lowell, but I totally have my phone on me. I have a kid, dammit! I have to know if she's okay."

I mimic zipping my lips. "I won't say a word."

She winks and bumps me with her hip. "Come on. Let's go show everyone how hot you look."

I shake my head at her, letting her lead the way.

"Hey, guys, Rosie's here!" she announces to the room.

I stop dead in my tracks when I see what's before me.

"Is that… Is that Collin's ass?"

Stevie barks out a loud laugh, pulling just about everyone's attention since the music is a little quieter back here.

"It's beautiful, isn't it?" says Harper, who, based on the mask that's pushed up on the top of her head, is dressed as Michael Myers. She smacks her husband's exposed cheeks.

"Hey!" Collin whirls around, glaring at her. "What'd I tell you about that, woman?"

"That I'm your wife and I'm legally allowed to smack your ass?" she challenges.

He shakes his head, pretending to be mad, but it's obvious he's enjoying her ogling him.

"Wait. If you're Michael, then he's..."

"Laurie Strode circa *Halloween II*. The first time we came to one of these, he dressed as Michael, and I was Laurie. Figured we'd switch it up this year." She shrugs. "Why he insisted on not wearing any damn underwear under his hospital gown is beyond me."

"Because it's *funny*." Collin rolls his eyes at his wife.

She holds her fake knife up to him. "Keep it up, babysitter. I'll cut you."

"And I'll escape. It's what I do."

"I swear this is foreplay for them and we're all being forced to witness it," Rhodes grumbles from the other side of the counter.

I'm shocked to see him in costume, but when I notice who he and Ryan are dressed up as, it makes total sense.

"Beauty and the Beast, huh?"

Ryan grins over the rim of her cup. "Fits us perfectly, doesn't it?"

"I love it," I tell her, and I do. He's the big scarred grumpy man and she's the beauty queen of YouTube who is currently in talks with a major makeup company to launch her own line. It's totally fitting for them.

I check out the rest of the group's costumes. Smith and Emilia are dressed as The Big Bad Wolf and Little Red Riding Hood, which seems appropriate for them.

Though I'm surprised to see them here with the new baby at home, I love that Hollis and Lowell are dressed as two different versions of Freddie Mercury, looking seconds away from bursting out into "We Are the Champions." The new guy, Ford, is dressed as Han Solo (I guess a play on his name), and his girlfriend is Princess Leia. I don't know either of them very well yet, but I'm excited to have new faces showing up at the truck.

After seeing Stevie's costume, I'm not surprised to find Scout dressed up as Anna, nor am I shocked to find Miller as Kristoff. But the one that really gets me is the nose that's on a very, very grumpy-looking Greer.

"What?" he growls at me.

I tuck my lips together, refusing to laugh, mostly because I'm a little scared of him.

"Nothing. I like your cos—" The word ends with a laugh because I cannot hold it in any longer. "Really? That's the best you could muster up?"

He glowers at me. "Shut up. I make a damn fine Olaf, thank you very much."

He's wearing a full-on snowman costume complete with a fucking carrot for a nose. He looks ridiculous, and I love it.

"You look great," I tell him, speaking honestly. I really love seeing the big grump be miserable.

"Doesn't he? We're playing find the carrot later."

"Jesus," Greer mutters, pinching the bridge of his nose, then setting down his drink. He wraps his arms around Stevie's waist. "That's it—you're cut off."

"Oooh, are we starting now?" She grabs him through his jeans. "I found something long and hard!"

Everybody laughs as he carries her from the kitchen.

"Please nobody hold this against her. She doesn't drink often," Scout says in defense of her sister.

I hold my hand up. "No judgment from me. I don't hold my liquor very well either."

This is exactly why I stopped at three shots before I left, and I'm refusing to let another drop of alcohol touch my lips tonight. I'd rather not be completely obliterated just in case I do happen to run into Fitz.

"So, what's your costume?" Scout asks.

"Oh." I glance down at my outfit. It's not far off from what I'd wear for my live streams. I paired my usual lingerie with a long, silky black skirt with a slit that sits dangerously high on my thigh. "I'm not sure. I just threw something together."

"It looks familiar," says Hayes, who is just wearing his jersey, eyes narrowed as he takes me in.

I shrug, hoping he doesn't know what I spend my evenings doing.

"Well, it's cute. I love the top. I wish I were brave enough to wear something like that."

"Um, you do all the time for me, babe." Miller presses a kiss to her head. "Not that it's on long before it's on my bedroom floor."

"Miller!" she hisses.

He doesn't look the least bit sorry.

I slide my eyes around the room, hoping maybe he

abandoned his spot on the couch and decided to join us, but with everyone wearing costumes, it's hard to figure out who he is. I glance through the dining room and into the second living room, and I stumble back when I find someone standing in a corner, staring at me intently.

He's not dressed as anything I recognize, wearing a simple black suit and a mask that's similar to mine, just inverse in coloring. His eyes are burning a hole right through me, like he couldn't look away if he tried, and frankly, I don't want him to.

Something about him seems familiar…like I should know him…

Someone passes by, and by the time they clear the area, the stranger is gone.

Huh. Weird.

"Hey, I think I just saw Fitz head into that room," Collin says, pointing in the direction I was just looking. "Someone go get his antisocial ass and bring him in here."

"I'll do it," I find myself saying before I realize what I'm doing.

Oh my god, can I be any more obvious?

If anyone is shocked by my volunteering, they don't show it.

I weave my way through the crowd, trying to avoid the drunken bodies that are moving all over the room. When I finally make my way to where Collin pointed, I know Fitz the second I spot him.

He's leaning one arm against a floor-to-ceiling

window, looking out over the dark yard. One hand is in his pocket, and even from here, I can tell he's lost in thought. I don't expect him to spot me when I move closer, but the shift in his posture is clear—he knows I'm here.

He turns toward me, a grin spreading across his face, showing off that toothless smile that makes my stomach do all kinds of flips. The gold and black mask he's wearing shifts with the movement, and he takes a step closer. The scent I love so much, fresh linen with a hint of lavender, hits me all at once, making me feel safe and comfortable.

He takes another step. Then another.

And suddenly, he's only inches away. So damn close that if I moved *just a little*, we'd be touching, and I really want to be touched.

He leans toward me, his breath tickling my ear. "Evening, Ro."

Two words…that's all he says. It's all he *has* to say.

And I know without a doubt there is no way I'm leaving this party without making him mine.

CHAPTER 9

RoPlaying: You're a good friend.

I've read her message no less than fifty times since she sent it earlier.

I'm not a good friend. In fact, I'm the worst fucking friend ever. I'm lying to her. Hell, I've *been* lying to her for months, in more ways than one.

A good friend wouldn't do that. A good friend would be honest. They would walk up to her and say, *Hey, I like watching your streams. I'm proud of you.* A good friend would definitely not reach for his cock in the shower, thinking about the lacy top his friend was wearing during her last stream.

But that's exactly what I fucking did not even an hour ago as I was getting ready for this stupid party. I felt awful afterward and promised myself I'd never do it again, but seeing Rosie stand just a hundred feet away from me completely decked out in her RoPlaying ensemble, I know that's a promise I'm not going to be able to keep.

She looks incredible. Her tits are pushed up high, threatening to spill over the top of her lacy bustier with every move she makes. And that fucking slit in her skirt? The one practically painted onto her body? I want to rip it off and do very, very naughty things to her.

It's taking everything I have not to cross the room, grab her hand, and haul her away.

She's laughing at something Greer says, then I watch as he grabs his girlfriend by the waist and pulls her away from the rest of the group.

"Fitz!" she calls out to me. "Rosie's here. She wants to bang you."

"Holy fucking shit. Shut up, Stevie."

"What?" She shrugs. "He totally wants to bang her too. They just need to do it already."

"Fucking Christ," Greer mutters. He looks over at me and shakes his head. "Ignore her. She's——"

"Plastered? I can tell."

He grins, then drops his head closer. "But really, she isn't lying. Rosie is totally into you, and I don't think it would be such a bad thing to see where that goes."

I pull back, surprised this is coming from a guy who just earlier this year swore up and down he'd never, ever fall in love.

He shrugs. "I'm a changed man," he says like he can read my mind. "Besides, being in love is fun."

"Your girlfriend is drunk off her ass, and it's barely nine."

"Yeah, but she's cute when she's like this. Besides, between you and me, you could really loosen up out there on the ice. You're tight."

"I already have five goals this season."

"Right, but you could have ten."

I shake my head. "I'm not doing that. I'm not going to try to get into Rosie's pants because I think it will help me play better hockey."

"Then don't, but at least try to get into her pants because you really fucking want to and this damn dance you two idiots have been doing is getting tiresome to watch. She's clearly into you."

I peek over at where she's still standing, talking to everyone else. She's wearing her pink wig and mask, and I want to march over and pull them both off so I can see the real her.

I like Rosie. I've liked her for a while now, long before I even knew about her streaming. Never thought I had a chance in hell, but now...

"You think?"

"Dude, I *know*. Just trust me on this."

Stevie drops her head to Greer's shoulder. "Jacob..." She moans his name, and I have a feeling the rest of Greer's night is going to be spent sitting up with her in the bathroom.

He sighs, but it's one of those sighs that comes out sounding sweet.

"I need to get her upstairs. Just…" He looks over his shoulder at the baker, then back at me. "Don't fuck it up, man. I really fucking love those donuts."

"Hey! I'll make your donuts. You don't have to pimp Fitz out for donuts. I can make them just as good as—oh, who am I kidding? I hate making donuts. I'm awful at my job."

I chuckle at Stevie's drunken rambling. "Go take care of her."

Greer hauls his girlfriend into his arms, then carries her up the stairs. I'm about to move from my spot when something catches my eye.

Rosie.

She's looking over. No—scratch that. She's looking *at me.*

Her green gaze is locked on to me, and I couldn't walk away if I tried, not when she's practically staring into my soul like she's searching for all of my deepest, darkest secrets.

Does she know what I did an hour ago? Does she know I had my hand wrapped around my cock as I thought of her? Does she know at all what she does to me? The power she holds? The power I *want* her to hold?

I don't think she does because if she did, we wouldn't be having this staring contest we're participating in. We'd be upstairs in one of the unoccupied rooms, and I'd be showing her the effect she has on me, showing her how badly my cock is aching inside these tight slacks.

I need to move before I do something crazy like

march over and pull her into my arms. When someone passes by, I use it as my opportunity to slip into the party, then I make my way to the great room.

In an effort to cool down, I lean my forehead against the glass of the giant window that overlooks the sprawling backyard. I have no clue how Lowell finds these places, but it's the perfect mixture of seclusion so we can all have fun while still being elegant.

I take a few deep breaths, trying to talk my dick back down and regain a sense of control. It's a futile attempt, especially when I *feel* the moment she walks into the room.

I focus my eyes on the reflection in the window and watch—always fucking watching—as she scans the crowded space. I already know it's me she's looking for, so when her eyes land on me, I'm not surprised by the small smile that plays at the corners of her lips.

She saunters into the room. That slit that's already too fucking high moves with her, inching up and up until it's touching dangerous territory…territory I don't want anyone else to see.

I spin around and stuff both hands into my pockets, telling myself it's for her own good, and let a slow smile spread across my face. Unable to stop myself, I take a step toward her, and my favorite scent in the entire world hits my senses.

Strawberries.

Another step.

She doesn't move. Doesn't try to stop me. It's like

we're the only two in the room, and fuck how I wish that were true.

When there's barely any space left between us, just enough so we're not touching because I know I'm a fucking goner if I touch her, I lean down so she can hear me and say, "Evening, Ro."

The hitch in her breath is clear, and I love how it sounds.

"Fitz," she whispers.

I step back, letting my eyes roam as if I haven't already memorized every single thing about her. "You look incredible."

Color creeps into her cheeks, her jade eyes sparking with delight at my words. "Thank you. You don't look too bad yourself. Who are you supposed to be?"

"A guy who put his costume together at the last minute."

She laughs. "I like your mask."

Thanks. I picked it because it reminded me of yours. But I don't say that.

"It's Venetian."

No shit, you idiot.

She smirks. "You don't say."

Feeling the heat spreading across my cheeks, I blurt out the first thing that comes to mind: "Did you see Wright's ass?"

She blinks twice, then a loud laugh tumbles out of her. "Unfortunately, I did. Actually, who am I kidding? It's a great ass. Nothing unfortunate about it."

The overwhelming urge to find Wright and tell him to cover his shit up hits me, and I have to physically pinch myself to keep from doing just that.

"I think Greer as Olaf might be a favorite, though," she says with a smirk.

"I offered to give him a warm hug and he punched me."

"That sounds exactly like Greer. Between everyone teasing him about it and Stevie being hammered, he's in for a long, long night."

"Good. Serves the asshole right."

"Poor Stevie."

"*Brave* Stevie."

Rosie laughs. "You got that right. I'm not sure how she puts up with his gruffness, but she's totally into it. In fact, she told me they're off to play a game of find the carrot."

I shake my head. "She's had a bit too much to drink. Speaking of…can I get you something? A vodka soda?"

"You know, I said I was done drinking, but I think I could use one right about now."

You're telling me.

I place my hand on the small of her back, steering her toward the bartender in the corner. Lowell always goes all out with these things, and there are about six different bars set up around the house.

I order myself a beer and a vodka soda for Rosie.

"You remembered," she remarks.

Of course I did. I remember everything about you.

The bartender slides our drinks over to us, and we step to the side.

"So, how's Carl doing?" she asks before I can say anything stupid like what I just thought. "Has she trapped herself in the pantry lately?"

"Worse—she snuck out again when I was bringing in the groceries, darted right down the hall to my neighbor, Miss Drake's, apartment."

"Aw. Does your neighbor not like Carl?"

"Oh, she *loves* Carl. The problem is my neighbor also loves walking around her apartment in the nude. So, when I went to retrieve my shithead cat…"

"You got to see granny in the buff?" She winces.

"Unfortunately. And unlike with Wright, I very much mean *unfortunately*."

Rosie laughs, then taps my cheek a few times with her palm. "You poor thing, you. Are you traumatized? Do I need to kiss you to make you forget all about Miss Drake and her hot bod?" Her eyes widen when she realizes what she's just said, and she slaps her hand over her mouth. "Oh my god. Pretend I didn't just say that," she mutters through her fingers.

I don't want to pretend she didn't say that, and I really don't want to pretend I don't want her to follow through. Before I think too much about it, I step into her, not missing when she swallows roughly.

"And what if I want you to kiss me?"

Several seconds pass. Too fucking many seconds, in fact.

We stand there so damn long just staring at one another that I'm pretty sure I just completely overstepped and messed everything up.

But then, Rosie runs her tongue over her lips and says, "Hey, Fitz?"

I swallow the lump that's stuck in my throat. "Yeah?"

"Do you want to get out of here?"

I don't think. I act.

I grab her by the waist and pull her to my side, marching us both through the party and up the stairs. I open the first door I find.

A bathroom. It will have to do, because there is no way I can wait another second to feel her mouth on mine. I tug her inside, then close the door behind her, pressing her back against the wood.

She gasps when I press myself flush with her body, and I have no doubt it's because she can feel how fucking hard I am. I want this. I want *her*. In fact, I can't remember a time when I wanted anything more, when I've craved something so damn badly. Maybe when I was in a Game Seven final? I don't know, but it felt different than this. This feels…like more.

I peer into her eyes, the beautiful green ones that are wide and full of so many questions, yet also so much lust. I run my thumb over her cheek, savoring this moment… this heated look in her eyes. She's gorgeous, her cheeks tinged with a bit of pink, lips parted as her chest heaves heavily against me.

She wants this as much as I do.

I have no clue who moves toward who first. All I know is the moment her lips touch mine, I'm absolutely fucking done for. Her mouth is soft and sweet like she might have snuck a piece of candy or two before coming to find me.

She moans when I brush my tongue along the seam of her lips, and they open effortlessly. Her hands twist into my hair, finding the tie on my mask and tugging it free. We break just long enough for me to take it off and set it aside.

"God, I've been dying to touch you," I whisper against her lips, running my palms over her hips, feeling every fucking delicious inch of her. It's heaven and sin all at once, and at this moment, I'm totally okay with going to hell for this.

"I've been dying for you to touch me," she says back as her lips ghost over my chin. She nips along my jawline until she hits my ear, then she sucks the lobe between her teeth and bites me just hard enough for it to sting, and I fucking welcome it.

My grasp on her tightens, tugging her close, begging her to keep going, and she does. She bites at me gently, then runs her tongue over each and every place she's just sunk her teeth into. I groan when she hits that spot just below my ear, and she doesn't miss it.

"Ro…you smell like strawberries." I nuzzle my nose against her neck. "I fucking love strawberries."

"I know." She kisses me again. "They're your favorite."

"*You're* my favorite."

She grins against me as I capture her mouth in another kiss, plunging my tongue inside. She kisses me back with fervor, pulling on my suit jacket and yanking me closer. I reach down and bunch her skirt in my fists, lifting it high enough for me to press a knee between her legs, thankful as hell for the high slit that gives me more room to work with.

She groans the second she makes contact with my thigh and begins rocking against me, trying to find the angle that works best for her. I drag my hands back up her body, loving how soft she is beneath my palms, and I don't stop until my fingers are at the top of the lacy dark purple bustier she's wearing. Only then do I break the kiss.

I search her eyes in a silent question. *Can I?*

She nods, then watches as my fingers work to unhook the lacy material. My mouth fucking waters like a teen seeing boobs for the first time the minute she spills out of her top. Her tits are big, definitely more than a handful, and her nipples are the exact shade of her rosy lips. I want to kiss them just as badly as I want to kiss her.

"Fitz…" she pleads, likely tired of me just standing here looking at her like the angel she is and wanting me to touch her. "Please."

I can't deny her what she wants, not when her voice comes out as nothing but a strain.

I capture a nipple between my lips, sucking the sweet bud into my mouth. She groans and shifts her hips against me harder...faster. I take my time tasting her, learning what she likes and what she doesn't. Based on the way she slips her hands into my hair and holds me to her when I use my teeth to tease her, she really likes that.

"I need..." I hear her say, and I pull away, understanding exactly what it is she needs.

I drag her by the waist, setting her in front of the mirror as I take my place behind her.

"I want to watch you finger your cunt, Rosie," I say against her ear. "Can you do that for me?"

She gulps loudly and nods. "Yes."

"Good. Very good. Take your panties off and put them in my pocket."

She bends, making sure to press her ass against me, and grabs them. When she straightens, she slides them into the pocket of my pants, knowing exactly what she's doing when she brushes her knuckles against my cock, which is rock hard inside my slacks. I hiss at the contact, and she smirks.

"Evil," I mutter, and she laughs.

She rests her back against me and spreads her legs as I bunch her long skirt up in my hands, pulling it up until her pussy is exposed. Her thighs are thick just like the rest of her and rub together.

I bet they'd feel incredible wrapped around my head.

I intend to find out, but not tonight. Tonight, I want to watch.

I hold the material and watch as she slides her hands down her body, something I've seen her do countless times on her streams. She's taunting me, and I love every single minute of it. My mouth is literally watering with anticipation as she takes her time getting to where I want her. It's like she *knows* I need this buildup.

She runs her fingertips over every curve and dip until she gets to her mound, which is neatly trimmed. Only then does she slip two fingers between her legs, parting her pussy and giving me my first glimpse of her.

Fucking shit.

She's wet and pink and absolutely fucking everything I thought she should be.

"You're beautiful," I tell her, not caring when my voice comes out all scratchy. "Fucking perfect."

A sickly-sweet grin curves her lips, then she slides her fingers over her clit, not taking her eyes off me as she plunges two fingers inside.

"Oh god," she mutters as she begins to fuck herself, grinding down on her hand and using her palm to stimulate her clit.

It's perfect. *She's* perfect.

I tell her just that, and she sighs at my words.

I lift my eyes from what she's doing between her legs to look at her face, and I'm surprised when I find her staring right at me in the mirror. She's not watching herself. She's watching me watch her, and I swear it spurs her on even more.

My knuckles are pure white at this point and there's no way it won't be obvious her skirt was in my hands with how wrinkly it will be, but I don't care. Not when I have this fucking goddess in front of me. Not when her panting picks up and her chest begins to move rapidly. She's close, and I want nothing more than to watch her fall apart.

"Get yourself there, Ro. I want to see what it looks like when your cunt is squeezing your fingers."

My words motivate her, and with just a few strokes, she's detonating before my eyes, her body going rigid, her lips parting, but that's not what gets me. That's not what sends me completely over the edge.

No.

It's my name tumbling from her lips as she rides out her orgasm.

"*Ivan.*"

I'm ashamed of what happens next. It's something I can't control, something that's never happened before.

I come in my fucking pants.

Like some teen who can't control themselves, I fall apart right along with her, pressing myself against her as waves of pleasure crash over me.

The second I've regained my breath, I spin her in my arms and crash my mouth to hers, desperate to taste her again. She groans against me, tugging me closer until I'm not sure where I end and she begins. I kiss her lips, up her jaw to her ear, going as far as I can until her mask gets in the way. I slip my hands into her hair, searching for the tie, never taking my lips from her body.

"I always wondered what it would feel like to peel this

off you," I mutter against her when my fingers finally find the end of the string.

She goes limp in my arms, and I feel it instantly. I pull back to search her eyes, worried I've done something to hurt her.

"Is every——"

"What did you just say?" she asks sharply, those green eyes I love so much darting back and forth between my own hazel ones.

"I said, I always…"

The rest of the words die on my lips because I know. I fucking *know*.

I messed up. No, I more than messed up. I wrecked this. Completely fucking ruined it. Obliterated any chance we had.

She shoves at me, and I stumble backward, letting her push me out of the way; I deserve it. She crashes her hands through her hair, ripping her mask off, letting me see all of her for the first time tonight.

"Do you…" She sucks in a deep breath. "Fitz, do you *watch* me?"

I could lie. I could make something up, could find a way out of this.

But I have no fight in me. So, I tell her the truth.

"Yes."

Her jaw drops, but no words come out of her mouth. She shakes her head a few times. She appears disgusted with me, like she can't believe the person she's looking at.

I take a step toward her. "Listen, I——"

"How long?" she interrupts, holding her hands up to stop me.

"Excuse me?"

"How long? How long have you been *watching* me?" I hate the emphasis she puts on the word, like she's completely revolted by the idea even though *she's* the one who gets paid to be watched. "How long have you known?"

I gulp. "A few months."

"Months? *Months*, Fitz?!" I hate the way my last name drops off her tongue, especially now that I know what it's like to hear her speak my first name.

She gasps, her hand going to her chest, and I know what she's going to say next.

"You're ShootsAndScores."

I say nothing. I don't confirm it, but I don't deny it either, and that's enough for her.

She scoffs, shoving her skirt back down into place and pulling her top back up, covering those very tits I just had in my mouth, the ones I know taste so damn sweet.

She grabs the door handle, shooting me a glare. "You're nothing like I thought you were, Fitz."

Then she's gone, disappearing right out the door before I can stop her.

Everything I ever wanted flashes before my eyes, then shatters like someone just shot a hundred-mile-per-hour puck right at it, everything inside me breaking right along with it.

I need to fix this. I *have* to fix this. She can't leave.

I yank the door open, praying and hoping she's not gone. I spot her at the end of the hallway, one foot already on the top stair, ready to flee.

"Ro!"

She pauses, then looks back at me. "Don't ever call me that again." She spins on her heel and leaves...taking every bit of my heart along with her.

I am so completely fucked.

CHAPTER 10

Fitz watches me.

Fitz subscribes to my channel.

Fitz is ShootsAndScores.

Fitz *pays* me.

That's all that's been playing in my mind for the last three days as I've lain in bed. I've skipped work, leaving Stevie to pick up my slack. I've even skipped classes. I sure as hell haven't done any streaming, leaving my subscribers to resort to DMing me trying to figure out where I've gone to. I have no doubt I've lost a few of them by now, but I can't be bothered to worry about losing that income. I'll figure something else out, possibly something that has nothing to do with being on camera · because right now, just looking at my computer has my stomach rolling.

Fitz watches me.

I can't believe it. I can't believe the sweet guy behind the keyboard, the guy I thought was just being friendly… it was the guy I've been crushing on the entire time.

Every conversation, every gentle push to give Fitz another chance…it was all him.

I'm hurt.

I'm mad.

I'm…still craving his touch.

God, how messed up does that make me? Probably pretty damn fucked in the head, but I can't help it. Having his hands on me…his lips…having him watch me as I fingered myself to release…it was everything I didn't know I needed. I loved every minute we shared in that bathroom—until he uttered words that changed everything.

I steer my car into the gravel lot and pull into my familiar parking spot. I shift into park and finally drag my eyes to the place I've been avoiding for days now. It still looks the same, the bright baby blue truck with the cute little awning and the books stacked on a shelf that sits off to one side. The picnic tables each have a basket of napkins and a small vase filled with fresh flowers from the market down the street. Everything looks the same, but it all feels so different. This is the place I first met Fitz, and now it feels tainted too.

Stevie is moving around inside the truck, bustling from one side to the other as she preps the donuts for the day.

I owe her so much for covering for me. I know there's no way she wasn't completely hungover after the party, and I know Sunday must have been nuts because it's always packed. Monday tends to bring a crowd too. I'm awful for letting her manage this all on her own, but I couldn't bring myself to show back up here. Not after everything.

I check the clock on the dash of my Toyota: we're set to open in half an hour. I should really get in there and help her.

"You can do this, Rosie," I mutter. "You're a badass who has handled heartbreak before. You got this too."

I let out a heavy sigh, shut my car off, and push my door open. I grab my purse from the passenger seat, then step out. Slowly, I make my way toward the truck I'm dreading walking into.

When I'm halfway there, Stevie spots me, and the smile that fills her face makes the guilt that's sitting in my chest feel ten pounds heavier.

"You're here!" She claps her hands together, looking like her usual sunshiny self as she bounces on the balls of her feet. "I missed you!"

I smile for the first time in days. "I missed you too."

And it's true. I did miss her. It was never her I was upset with or avoiding.

It's *him*.

I cross the rest of the way to the truck, and the minute I'm inside, Stevie's throwing her arms around me, pulling me into a hug.

"Oh my gosh," she practically squeals, hugging me tightly. "I was starting to worry I'd never see you again." She pulls back, her eyes scanning over me in that typical mom look they all give a child they're worried about. "How are you feeling?"

There's so much sincerity in her words and in the stare she's giving me, and before I know it, my chin is wobbling and I can *feel* the stupid tears forming in my eyes.

Stevie's face falls. "Oh no, what's wrong? What happened?"

And then the tears fall free.

She steers me over to the chair we have in the back, the one that hardly ever gets used inside the truck, everyone always opting to take it out back and into the sunshine. She pushes me into it gently, then kneels on the floor in front of me. She sits there for several minutes, not once rushing me or asking me to talk to her. She just rubs my arm, letting me work through whatever this is.

I can't remember the last time I cried like this. Maybe when Levi told me he was leaving? But this…this feels different.

When I've finally calmed down enough, I wipe my tears from my face and blow out a breath.

"I'm sorry," I say to her.

She shakes her head. "Don't you dare apologize to me. I'm just… Are you all right?"

Now it's my turn to shake my head. "No."

"Do you want to talk about it?"

"Not really, but I probably should."

She smiles sadly. "I know how that is."

I sigh shakily, then roll my tongue over my lips,

tasting the salt from my tears. "It's…" The words get stuck in my throat.

It's hard because it hurts but also because it's so damn embarrassing. How stupid am I? How could I not have known something like this would happen?

"Is it Fitz?"

My eyes snap to Stevie's. "How…"

She shrugs. "He's been coming by every day since the party asking for you, and every day, he looks worse and worse. You weren't coming in and he looked like crap and I might have heard from my sister and Miller that they saw you run away from the party, so I just kind of assumed…"

"Oh." I nod, squeezing my eyes shut, holding back the tears that threaten again. "It's Fitz."

"What happened? I thought maybe the party was finally your chance. I mean, I was pretty drunk"—she grins sheepishly—"but I *saw* how he was looking at you. He was totally into you, and I know you're into him. What'd I miss?"

"It's kind of a long story, and we don't have long before we open…"

"If you think opening this truck is more important than whatever's going on, you're wrong." She squeezes my arm. "Talk to me."

I sigh, then launch into the long story of everything that's happened with Fitz over the last few weeks, including what happened at the Halloween party over the weekend. She listens to every word, not interrupting, letting me get it all out.

When I'm finally done, she gives me a soft smile. "He's a fucking moron."

A laugh bubbles out of me, and it feels so damn good. I needed it more than I realized.

"He really is," I agree, and I mean it.

"But…" Stevie sighs. "Please don't get mad at me for saying this, but I don't think he meant any harm."

I nibble on my bottom lip, because as much as I hate to admit it, Stevie's right. That's just not who Fitz is.

"He's too nice for his intentions to be malicious. I mean, hell, you've seen the guy—he's always blushing, almost never talks, and he's just… Well, he's Fitz. He's quiet and polite and just so…*nice*."

"I know," I say, nodding a few times. "He is all those things. But he also lied to me."

"He did, and that was wrong, and you have every right to be mad at him, but…"

"But I don't think he did it on purpose," I finish for her. "I don't think he set out to be deceitful."

"Yeah, me either."

That's the hardest part of this. I *know* Fitz. Doing this…it's not him. A part of me wishes I could say it is, could say he's nothing but a jerk and doesn't deserve my time…but I can't say any of that because I don't feel like it's true.

"He's been here every day," she says. "Like *every day*.

He comes in the mornings before practice. He just sits on one of the benches out there and waits for you. I tell him you're not coming, but he doesn't believe me. He just… waits. Then he comes back after practice and does the same thing. It's been like that every day, and I'm sure the only reason he's not here now is because they play in New York tonight, but tomorrow, he'll be back. I guarantee it."

I hate that my heart skips a beat with every word she utters. I hate that I love it that he's shown up here, but I do. I do love it—so damn much.

"I should talk to him."

"You should," Stevie agrees. "Because I think if you two work this out, you could be something great together. I mean, you like being watched and he likes watching, so it works." She waggles her brows and grins.

I smile back, but it's gone as quickly as it came, unease settling into my belly.

"What's wrong?"

I bite my bottom lip. "Am I… Is it weird that I like it? Being watched? That I liked it when he…when he just watched and got off on it?"

She's shaking her head before I even get the entire question out. "No, not at all, but I understand how you feel, why you'd feel that way. I thought something was wrong with me and my…tastes too."

My brows crush together. "Do you like being watched too?"

"No. I mean, I don't hate it if it's Greer, but it's… other stuff. Greer is… He's rough, you know? He's commanding and he likes it that way. And *I* like it that way. I didn't think I would after..." She trails off, her eyes dropping to the floor of the truck, but I know what —and who—she's referring to. It's her ex. "I didn't think after the abuse I went through that it would be something I'd like, didn't think I'd crave the roughness and him bossing me around, but I like it. I *want* to please him. I want him to tell me when I'm doing good for him, you know? It makes me feel good, powerful, like I'm taking back everything that was taken from me. I think it's because even though I know Greer's the one doing the bossing, I'm really the one in charge, and if I ever want it to stop, I only need to utter a single word and he'll back off. I feel safe with him, comfortable." She finally looks up at me. "Is that how Fitz makes you feel?"

Yes.

Not once during our time in the bathroom did I feel unsafe. It's not that I ever feel unsafe on my streams or anything, but with Fitz it just felt...different. It felt right, like that's how it's supposed to be. Never mind that orgasm I had. It was easily the most intense of my life. I can't remember ever getting so damn aroused by fingering myself, and I masturbate regularly.

"It is," I tell her.

"Then don't let it pass you by. Give him a chance to explain."

I nod. "I will."

"And if it makes you feel any better, my first sexual

experience with Greer sucked too. Well, I mean technically *I* sucked, but still."

"Stevie!" I admonish, and she laughs. "But seriously…what happened?"

She tells me about going down on him the first time and then him leaving immediately afterward.

"Wow. These hockey boys are idiots, huh?"

She nods. "You have no idea. But after he explained things, I understood. I mean, he'd never been with someone he actually cared about before. He had no clue how to act. And plus, he was worried about how I'd react to his roughness. He didn't realize I was totally into it and would have been more than fine with the night continuing."

"And now you two horndogs can't keep your hands off each other, Miss Plays Find the Carrot in Front of the Entire Halloween Party."

She buries her face in her hands. "Oh my god. I still can't believe I did that. Drunk Stevie is a whole other version of me."

I laugh because she's not wrong. "It was fun. I'm sure everyone's forgotten by now."

She gives me a look that says I'm full of shit, and I don't blame her. There is no way anybody is letting her live that down.

"All right," she says, shoving up from the floor, then holding her hands out to me. "Come on. Up." I let her tug me out of the chair. "Today, let's focus on donuts. Tomorrow, we'll fix your broken heart, deal?"

I nod. "Deal."

So that's what I do. I throw myself into work. I knead dough, I shape donuts and ice them, and I refill coffee, rinse and repeat for hours and hours.

And the entire time, I think about one thing: Fitz.

CHAPTER 11

FITZ

"Yo, Fitzy Baby! Come here!"

I suppress the groan crawling its way from my throat. The last thing I want to do is go talk to Greer. In fact, I don't want to talk to fucking anybody. It's been days since I've seen Rosie, and all I want to do is get out on the ice and beat New York so I can get back on the plane and home to her because I *need* to fix things.

I've gone to the donut truck every day since the party. I've been attached to my phone and computer, waiting for her to get on her stream. I've even tried messaging her on MyFans, but nothing. Not a damn thing from her. It's killing me, tearing me completely apart. I haven't even had a strawberry since Saturday morning because I can't stand the fucking sight or smell of them. All it does is remind me of Rosie.

I shove my phone into my pocket and spin on my heel, backtracking across the parking garage toward Greer, who is standing beside the bus we just got off.

"What's up?" I ask him.

"Over here. Got something I want to show you," he says, motioning for me to follow him around the other side of the bus.

I have no clue what's going on and don't really have the patience for this, but I follow him anyway. I regret it the second I round the vehicle because all of a sudden I'm being slammed against the big rig and there's a forearm pressed heavily against my throat.

"W-What the…" I manage to sputter out. "Get the fuck off me."

"Not a damn chance." He shoves me harder, sneering. "What the fuck, man? What'd I tell you?"

"What?" I cough, slowly losing my ability to breathe. "What are you talking about?"

"Rosie, you fucking asshole. That's what I'm talking about. I just got off the phone with Stevie, and I swear to god, if you don't tell me what the hell crawled up your ass, you'll be walking back out there with a black eye, which I'm sure you'll have great fun explaining to the press and Coach."

"Fuck," I mutter, dropping my head back against the bus. It hurts, but I welcome the sting.

"Yeah, *fuck* is right. What the hell, man? What'd you do?"

"Can you let me go?"

He laughs, and it's downright fucking scary. "Not a chance."

I sigh. Since he's not going to let me go until I explain things, I tell him. Everything.

Only when I'm finished does he finally let me go, and I drop back to the flats of my feet and reach for my throat, massaging it. It's aching and I'm definitely going to be hoarse, but honestly, I deserve it. Hell, I deserve worse.

"What the hell, man?" he asks again. "Why?"

I shrug. "I don't know." But that's not true. I do know. "I just...couldn't stop myself. I couldn't help it. I wanted to be close to her. No...I *needed* to be close to her, and this felt like the only way."

"You couldn't have, I don't fucking know, just asked her out?"

"I..." I drag a hand through my hair. "I didn't think she'd be into me, you know? I'm not exactly smooth with the ladies." I show off my missing tooth. "And then there's this ugly fucking thing."

"Your missing tooth?" He rolls his eyes. "You're kidding, right? That's basically real-life porn to women, *especially* the ones who love hockey. Rosie loves your damn missing tooth. Hell, *I've* seen her swoon over it before. I don't know how your stupid ass has missed it, but she's totally into you."

"Well, I know that now."

He laughs, but there's no humor in it. "You're an idiot."

"I know."

"Like Miller-level idiot."

I half expect the man in question to come out of nowhere and yell at us in protest, but he doesn't.

"Yeah, I know," I tell Greer. "But I'm going to fix it."

"Good. You fucking better."

I glare at him. "I will."

He eyes me hard, possibly harder than he ever has before. "You really like her, huh?"

I nod. "So much. I have for a while, before I even found her stream, but I've been so focused on hockey I didn't let myself really think much of it, you know? I know this season means a lot to Coach, and I want to focus on it for him and for the team. Then I found her stream and I thought, this is it. It was my way to be close to her without worrying about screwing with my game. It felt like it was meant to be…but I couldn't stay away."

With how things played out, a huge part of me wishes I could have kept my distance, but now that I know how good she tastes, how good she feels…I was doomed from the start.

And dammit if I'm not okay with being doomed.

"I get it, man. I do. I didn't want to get involved with Stevie, but…" He shrugs. "Here I am, completely fucked for that woman."

I grin, because it's still so weird to hear him say that. "You're totally whipped, man."

He lifts a brow. "Like you're not screwed when it comes to Rosie?"

I wince, because I am. I'm completely screwed, and

171

now I have to fix it before she realizes how much better than me she can do.

"That's what I thought." He shakes his head. "Damn, man. We have some dumb people on this team who have done some really dumb things, but this…" He whistles. "You've been lying to her for months, pretending to be someone else."

"I know," I say, shoving off the bus. "I fucking know. I'm going to fix it."

He gives me another hard stare, then nods once. "All right. I'm giving you a chance, but if you don't—"

"You'll beat me to a pulp—yeah, I got it."

What he doesn't know is I'd let him. I'd certainly have it coming. I just hope it doesn't come to that. I hope I can fix things with Rosie.

I *have* to.

"I'll fix it," I promise, but I'm not sure if I'm talking to Greer or myself.

Either way, I hope it's a promise I can keep.

We beat New York, no fucking thanks to me and all the asinine penalties I took. Stupid stuff, stuff I know I shouldn't be doing but did anyway. Too many crosschecks right in front of the linesman. Straight-up tripping someone and not even trying to hide it. Slashing.

And that was all in the first period.

I played so awful Coach benched me for the last ten

minutes of the game, and I don't blame him. He refused to talk to me afterward, so I'm dreading going to practice this morning because I know I'm going to get my ass reamed for my behavior. My list of people I need to fix things with just keeps growing, and it's really starting to feel like a bad omen.

I lift my head, watching the robin's-egg blue truck get closer and closer as my feet pound heavily against the pavement.

Please let her be here. Please let her be here. Please let her be here.

I repeat it with every step I take until I skid to a stop in the parking lot. The closed sign is still up on the counter, but the window is open, and I hold my breath, welcoming the ache in my lungs as I wait to get my first glimpse of her in days.

I don't have to wait long because not even fifteen seconds later, she's there. There's a giant box in her hands. I can't make out from here what's in it, but it looks heavy, and I want so fucking badly to waltz into the truck and take it from her like some knight in shining armor so I can prove to her I'm more than just some asshole.

Even from here, she looks beautiful. Maybe a little tired, but still gorgeous. Always fucking gorgeous. Her hair is tossed up in her usual bun and her trusty apron is tied around her waist, covering all those curves I know she has, those same curves I committed to memory the other night at the party and really fucking want to touch again.

As if she can feel my eyes on her, she lifts her head and looks directly at me.

And I…wave.

I lift my damn hand and *wave*.

God, what a moron.

Both of her brows rise and I swear I see her lips mutter *idiot*, but that's all that happens. She doesn't run away. She doesn't try to hide from me.

No. She does something worse.

She pretends I'm not even here.

Rosie returns her attention to the task at hand, and it hurts more than if she were to march out of the truck and tell me off. I press my palm to my chest, an ache forming that I wish I could never feel again because I hate it so much. Is this how Greer felt when he screwed everything up with Stevie? This blows, and I need to make it go away. *Now.*

I pull my headphones from my ears and tuck them into my pockets, then cross the lot to the truck. Rosie lifts her head when she hears the gravel crunching beneath my feet, but she doesn't tell me to fuck off. I take that as a good sign and keep moving forward.

In fact, I don't stop until I'm at the end of the truck. The doors are open wide, and I peer inside. She's standing there, just staring at me. Watching. *Waiting.*

I take a step in.

When she doesn't protest, I take another. Then another.

I reach over to grab the bar that's holding the

window open and give it a tug. It folds in on itself easily, trapping us inside under the low interior lights. Rosie still doesn't say anything, and part of me wishes she would. I wish she would yell or call me names or tell me to get lost. Something. *Anything.* God knows I deserve it.

But she doesn't. She just stands there, her arms folded over her chest, her brows lifted high as she takes me in, sweaty state and all.

I grab a plastic cup from the stack, retrieve the pitcher of water I know they keep in the fridge, and I pour myself a glass. I chug it in five seconds flat, then refill it just to do it all over again.

I drag my hand over my mouth and meet Rosie's hard stare. "I—"

"Oh, no. You don't get to talk first, Fitz."

Fitz.

She's called me that before. Hell, except for the one time, it's all she's ever called me. Nobody ever calls me by my first name; they haven't since middle school. It's always been Fitz or Fitzgerald, never Ivan…until her.

I want to be Ivan again.

"You're a dick."

I swallow the lump that seems to be superglued inside my throat. "I know."

"Like a major, massive dick that's covered in warts and moles and all kinds of other awful things I can't think of right this moment because I'm so damn mad at you."

"I know."

If it's even possible, her stare hardens further. "You hurt me."

"I—"

"You led me on. You pretended to be someone else. You *manipulated* me into letting you apologize for ditching me at Slapshots. You *lied* to me, Fitz, and it fucking hurt."

I just nod, not because I don't have things to say, but because I know she doesn't want to hear them.

"I thought you were different. I thought you were better than that. I thought..." She looks away a moment, then rolls her tongue over her lips. "I thought I knew you."

I take a step toward her, unable to help myself. To my surprise, she doesn't move back.

"You do know me, Rosie. You do. I'm still the same guy. I just..." I drag my hand through my hair. "I just fucked up. You're so..." I gesture toward her. "Well, *you.* You're comfortable with who you are, in your body. It's kind of intimidating sometimes. I didn't think... I never thought someone like you could be into someone like me."

"What's so wrong with you that you thought that?"

I shrug. "I don't know. I mean..." I flash her my smile. "This, for starters."

"That? Are you kidding? I wanted to throw my panties at you the first time you smiled at me, and about ninety percent of that was because of your missing tooth. It's cute, Fitz."

"It bothers me."

"So get it fixed."

I give an *Are you serious?* look.

"Oh. Right. Hockey."

I nod. "Hockey. Sure, I could do flippers or something, but why bother while I'm still playing? At first, I was cool with it, you know? It felt like a badge of honor or something. But then some comments...the stares I'd get...I don't know. It just all added up to me feeling incredibly self-conscious about it."

"I like it."

"I know. I mean, *now*—I know that now. But still."

She gives me a sad smile. "What else? Why do you think you're not good enough to just ask me out?"

"Well, there's the watching thing. The...voyeurism." It's the first time I've said the word out loud. Sure, I've googled it countless times, but I've never acknowledged that I might have a kink like that.

"What about it?"

"It doesn't...bother you?"

"Um, hello." She waves both hands. "I'm basically a cam girl over here. I think you *know* I like being watched."

Images of what it was like the last time I watched her flash through my mind. Heat creeps up my neck and into my cheeks just thinking about how beautiful she looked as she fell apart in front of me.

"Did someone tell you it's not okay?"

That fucking lump returns, and I try to swallow around it.

"Please tell me you told them they're completely in the wrong."

"She wasn't really wrong. It is weird, right? I get off on watching someone have sex more than I like having sex. That's fucked up, no?"

"It's not fucked up, Fitz. It's just who you are, and that's okay. Would you tell me I'm fucked up for liking being watched?"

"No! No. Never."

"Okay." She shrugs. "Then you're not fucked up either."

When she says it all out loud like this, it sounds… reasonable. It sounds okay. It sounds like something that could work…like *we* could work.

"Rosie, I…" I swipe my tongue over my lips, then take another step toward her because I *need* to be close to her. "I'm sorry. I'm sorry I lied to you. I'm sorry I tricked you. I'm sorry I didn't come clean from the beginning. Hell, I'm sorry I kept watching your videos even when I knew it was you. I just…I really like you. Like, a lot. And I'd really, really like it if you gave me another chance. I'd like a chance to be real and honest with you."

Her green eyes bore into me, her teeth clamping tightly on her bottom lip as she considers my words—my *plea*.

That's what this is. I'm a desperate man in a desperate moment. I need her to believe me, to give me another chance. Because there is no chance in hell I'm going to be able to stay away from her. Not now. Not after everything.

"How?" she says softly.

"Sorry?"

"How did you know it was me?"

"Oh." I take another step forward, lifting my hand. I pause just a moment before I touch her, making sure it's okay. She doesn't move or tell me no, so I reach out, cupping the side of her face and running my thumb over her cheek. "Your eyes. I knew because of your eyes."

Her brows pinch together. "Lots of people have green eyes. I—"

"No." I shake my head, lifting my other hand to her face, using my thumb to trace the freckle that sits just below her eye. "Not like yours. They don't have green eyes like yours, Ro. I'd know them anywhere."

She swallows harshly. "Oh."

"Yeah. Oh."

She's back to nibbling on her lips, and all I can do is watch as she works through everything in her mind.

Please give me a chance. Please, please, please.

After what feels like hours of us standing here, of her just chewing on her lip, she drags her eyes back to mine. Her jaw drops, and I worry for a moment she can hear my heart beating in my chest because I swear it's moving harder and faster than it ever has before.

"I—"

"What the hell?" A muffled voice breaks the moment,

and I turn around just in time to see the back door being ripped open.

"What in the actual fu—oh."

Scout, the owner of the truck, is standing at the back door. She has one foot inside, her eyes wide and her face full of shock.

"Scout, hi," Rosie says, stepping out from behind me.

"Um, hi," Scout says tentatively, her gaze flitting from me to Rosie and back again. Her brows slide together. "Is everything okay?"

"Yeah, everything is—"

"I wasn't asking you," Scout says tersely, cutting me off. She looks at her head baker, checking in with her directly. I love it. I love how protective she is. "Rosie, is everything okay?"

I peek back at Rosie, who sends Scout a soft smile.

"Yeah, everything is okay," she tells her. "I'm sorry. We were talking and I—"

Scout holds her hand up. "Is everything ready to go?"

"Yes. All the donuts are prepped, coffee is made, and the drawer's been counted in. We're good."

"All right. We open in ten minutes, so whatever this" —she waves her hand between the two of us—"is, just wrap it up."

Rosie nods. "We will. Thank you."

"Of course." Scout looks at me, her eyes still hard. "I have a feeling you're being dumb, aren't you?"

I grimace and nod.

Scout rolls her eyes and mutters, "Fucking hockey

players." She walks out of the truck, shaking her head and pulling the door shut behind her, bathing us in the low light once more.

The moment she's gone, I turn back to Rosie.

"You know, I'm really starting to think that whole *people believing hockey players are stupid* thing is true."

Rosie arches one brow. "Sometimes it is."

I nod. "I deserved that."

"You did."

Silence falls between us again, and I hold my breath once more, waiting for her answer, hoping and praying she'll tell me what I want to hear.

"You're kind of killing me here, Ro," I say after several minutes. "And we are on a time crunch."

She glowers, and I can't help the smirk that curls up one side of my mouth. She's being sassy with me; I like it when she's sassy with me.

Then finally, after another minute of silence, she utters a single word.

"Okay."

My heart stutters in my chest. *Did she just say what I think she did?*

"Okay?" I ask.

She nods. "I'll give you another chance. But, Fitz? I need you to be honest with me. Completely."

"It's not Carl who is afraid of the dark. It's me."

"What?"

I lift a shoulder. "You said you wanted honesty. The reason I keep night-lights in every room is because *I'm* scared of the dark. I mean, Carl isn't the biggest fan, but she's got that cool crazy cat vision. I don't and am totally afraid a monster is going to reach out and grab my leg and drag me away to hell. When I go on the road, I take a night-light with me and plug it in. I tell everyone Miller does it to make myself feel better, but he doesn't. It's all me."

A laugh bubbles out of her, and not until this moment did I realize how much I missed hearing that sound over the last few days. This is the longest I've gone without seeing her for months, and I needed it more than I knew.

"That's a good start. I was thinking more like you could not pretend to be someone else, but that works too."

"That's a fair request."

"Speaking of requests…" She clears her throat. "I'd like it if you… Will you unsubscribe?"

A heaviness hits my gut. I hate the idea of not being able to see her.

But…I get it. It's probably weird. I mean, she's working; why would she want me to watch her?

"It's just…I'd feel weird if we're dating and I'm accepting money from you like that."

Oh. Well, that makes sense too.

"Okay," I tell her. "I'll unsubscribe as soon as I get home."

Then her words hit me.

"Wait… Are we?"

"Are we what?" she asks.

"Dating. Are we dating?"

"Yes."

My chest fills with something I haven't felt in a long damn time, and I love it.

I take another step toward her, closing that distance we created when Scout interrupted us. I cup her face once more, loving how soft her skin is under my touch.

"I know I'm not in any position to request something of you, but…can I kiss you?"

A slow smile spreads over those lips I know taste so damn incredible.

"I thought you'd never ask."

I don't hesitate, don't waste another second. I capture her mouth with mine, and a groan leaves me the second our lips collide because kissing her feels so good, so right. Like coming home after a long road trip, it just feels *right*.

I gather her in my arms, hauling her to me, reveling in the way she feels pressed against me. I know I've only had it once before, but I missed this. I missed *her*.

And this kiss? It feels so different than our last one. That one was great, amazing even, but this? This feels like more than that. It feels like how our first kiss should have been—*us*.

I run my tongue along the seam of her lips, loving how she easily opens for me, giving me a taste of her.

Strawberries.

I love it, and it eggs me on. I slide my hands under

her shirt, and she sighs when my palms coast over her body.

"Ivan…" She groans my name, and if I wasn't holding on to her, I think my knees might buckle under me at the sound of it falling from her lips.

I kiss her harder, grinding my hips against her so she can feel what she's doing to me under my running shorts. I have no idea how long we kiss, but it's long enough for Scout to bang on the back of the truck.

"Wrap it up, you two!" she shouts.

"Yeah! I want donuts, dammit."

I pull my mouth from Rosie's.

"Is that…"

"Miller?" Rosie finishes for me.

I groan, resting my head against hers. My cock is hard as hell, and there is no way I'm going to be able to hide it.

"Think of something terrible, Ivan," I mumble to myself.

Rosie laughs, and it does nothing to help.

"Stop that," I tell her, pulling away, putting distance between us, hoping it will help with the situation in my pants. "You're making it worse."

"By laughing? That's turning you on?"

"Rosie, everything you do turns me on."

She grins up at me, clearly proud of herself.

"Stop smiling."

"Why?" she asks, taking a step forward.

I retreat, glaring at her. "You know why."

She doesn't stop moving toward me, and fucking hell, I'm running out of space behind me. Truthfully, I'm okay with that. I *hope* I run out, because that means I get to touch her again, and I really want to touch her.

"I don't. Can you enlighten me?"

"Rosie…"

"Ivan…" she teases, my name rolling off her lips like it was always meant to be there.

"You're playing a dangerous game."

She's close, so damn close if I really wanted to, I could bend down just slightly, and my lips would be on hers.

She presses up on her tiptoes, narrowing the space between us even more. "A game I intend to win."

"Oh, fuck it," I mutter, then I crush my mouth to hers.

She sighs against me like I haven't kissed her in years, never mind that we were just locked together.

Another loud knock sounds on the door, and it's enough to break the kiss.

"Come on, man! I'm fucking starving. My woman didn't make breakfast this morning."

"Um, probably because you have two hands that are perfectly capable of making their own breakfast, you butthole."

"Did Scout just call Miller a butthole?" I whisper.

"Did you just call me a butthole?" Miller echoes my words unknowingly.

"You're damn right I did. Keep it up, and I swear, I'm going to pinch you, Miller."

"Aw, come on. You know you love me."

"Not today I don't."

I can just picture Scout stomping away and Miller chasing after her like the lovesick man he is.

"Those two are something else," I remark.

"Yeah, but they're cute together. They work."

We work.

But I don't say that.

"I should go," I say instead.

She nods. "I think that's probably best."

I press one last soft kiss to her lips, then move as far away as possible before I do something crazy like kiss her again. "Can I make you dinner tomorrow?"

"Will Carl be there?"

"Yeah, it's kind of her apartment too."

Her smile is so bright. "Then, yes. I'd love that."

"Good." I step toward her but catch myself before I can go any further, and then I open the back door.

Something hits me before I leave, and I turn back to find her still watching me.

"Hey, Ro?"

"Yes?"

"Your live streams…do you ever accept private video requests?"

She shakes her head. "No. Never."

"Good. Keep it that way."

Then I disappear out of the truck.

Somehow, I don't run into Miller as I leave, and I've never been more thankful in my life. It's already awful enough I have to run home with my cock rock hard. I don't need to deal with Miller's crap too, though I'm not sure it could ruin my mood.

Because kissing Rosie? It's my new favorite thing, and I can't wait to do it again.

CHAPTER 12

I'm not sure what it says about me, but I spend more time selecting my outfit for my date at Fitz's place than I do for my live streams where thousands of people watch me in lingerie.

Maybe it's because I'm far more nervous to spend time alone at his apartment than I am hitting that *Go Live* button. I don't know if that means anything either, but I push the thought away to deal with later. Right now, I'm just focused on hitting the right floor number.

I double-check our texts from earlier, then hit the button for the sixteenth floor and hold my breath as the car takes me up, up, up. I was surprised as hell last night when, after I got home from my classes, there was a message waiting for me on MyFans from Fitz.

ShootsAndScores: Look, I know I said I'd unsubscribe, and I promise I will, but I realized I don't have your number. I thought about asking Greer to get it from Stevie, but then I wasn't sure how you'd feel about everyone knowing we're dating. So, yeah, here's my number.

I laughed, then sent him a text, and we set up a time for dinner. He begged me several times to let him pick me up, but it felt silly and totally unnecessary since he's cooking me dinner at his place, so here I am, waiting on the elevator to hit his floor.

A few seconds later, it does, and I blow out the breath I was holding, trying to calm my racing heart. I have no idea why I'm so nervous for this. It's not as if it's the first time I've spent time with Fitz, but somehow, that's exactly what this feels like. Actually, I guess that's what this is—our first date.

My first date with Fitz.

I reach down and pinch myself because *Is this real?*

"Ow," I mutter, rubbing at the spot I just pinched. "Yep, totally real."

I'm still reeling after his confession in the truck yesterday. He's worried he's not good enough for me? Is he insane? He's good enough for me and then some. It was hard to see him so down on himself about his tooth and his…kink, but I also liked how real it made him seem. He's a professional hockey player who makes millions of dollars a year; it was nice to see him knocked down a few pegs and have real-people problems.

I find his apartment at the end of the hall, then lift

my hand to knock. But before I can make contact with the door, it's being pulled open, and suddenly he's there.

Holy shit, hold my panties he looks incredible.

He's wearing a pair of dress slacks—maybe even the same ones he made a mess in on Halloween—and a simple gray button-down shirt. The top few buttons are open, and the sleeves are rolled up, showing off his impressive forearms. I kind of want to reach out and grab them, confirm that they're as strong as they look.

He's not wearing any shoes, but he does have on socks, and it's just all so...*cute*. I love that he dressed up for an at-home date.

"Hey, you found it okay," he says, stepping to the side. "Come on in."

With one last steadying breath, I cross into his apartment.

No turning back now.

Not that I'd want to, but still.

He closes the door behind me, then grabs the peacoat I'm wearing, tugging the material down my arms. He takes my purse from my hands and sets it on the table just inside the entryway.

"You look beautiful." He presses a soft kiss to the exposed skin of my shoulders. "I love this color on you."

"Of course you do," I say, turning to face him. I look down at the silky dress I'm wearing, loving how it hugs all my curves. "It's orange."

"So?"

I lift my hands, which I recently refreshed the color

on. "You were the one who requested I paint my nails orange. I just kind of took a guess…"

He steps toward me, and that scent of his I'm so damn familiar with floods my senses. He reaches up, grabbing hold of a piece of hair that's fallen from the clip I put it up in. He rubs it between his fingers, looking into my eyes.

"You wore my favorite color?"

Heat floods my cheeks. Since when did I get all blushy? Until Fitz, I hadn't blushed in years, but around him, I can't seem to stop.

"Yes," I confess.

"Good," he says. "Very good."

His words transport me back to the Halloween party. He said that exact same thing to me just before he demanded I take my panties off and stuff them in his pocket. I have no idea what he did with them since I never got them back after I rushed out, but a part of me doesn't want to know, nor do I care. I like knowing he has something of mine hidden around his apartment.

"Come on," he says, grabbing my hand and tugging me deeper inside. "There's someone I want you to meet."

"Carl?" I ask, practically bouncing on my heels.

"Yep."

He leads me to the kitchen, where I inhale deeply.

"Ohmygod." The words come out a moan. "It smells amazing in here."

"Thanks. I'm not the best cook in the world, but I

can whip up a few things. I hope you're okay with lemon pepper chicken over penne noodles."

"Are you kidding? That's my favorite! My mom used to make it all the time."

"I'm sure this isn't going to be anywhere near as good as hers, but I'm glad to know it's something you'll like. I probably should have asked first."

Now *he's* the one blushing, and all feels right in the world.

He pulls me to a stop in front of the famous pantry, then looks back at me. "You ready?"

"Yes, but why is she in the pantry?"

"Because if I don't lock her up, she'll escape, and Miss Drake's body isn't the one I want to see tonight." He says it so casually, like getting me naked is a guarantee.

And…I like it. I like how sure he is that this is leading to something more because I want it to be something more. Like *really* want it.

"She might run," he warns, hand on the knob. "One…two…three!"

He pulls the door open, and my heart damn near leaps out of my chest at the sight before me. There on the third shelf sits a fluffy white and brown cat right on top of a fresh loaf of bread. She's looking up at us with a glare, but it doesn't feel mean. It feels full of affection.

"She's on her bread."

"*Her* bread is right. I have Carl bread, and I have people bread."

It's the silliest thing I've ever heard, and possibly the cutest.

Fitz reaches into the pantry and scoops her into his arms.

"You can come out now, you little shit," he says affectionately, pressing a kiss to her head. "I want you to meet someone, and you're going to be nice, and you will not scratch her. Do you understand?"

Meow.

I grin. It's like she can understand him and is answering him.

Fitz turns her until she's facing me, and I tentatively reach out. She doesn't hiss or arch her back, just lets me run a few fingers over her soft fur. It takes several strokes, but it's not long until she's purring from my ministrations.

"Aw, she likes me."

"She wants you to *think* she likes you. She's banking on you bringing her treats. After you do, she'll forget you exist until she's hungry again."

"From what I've heard about cats, that sounds right."

He sets her on the floor, and she takes off like a shot, darting to the other side of the apartment, jumping on her tower with ease.

"Do you have any pets?"

I shake my head. "No. I've thought about it, but I'm nervous. I've never had one before."

"Never?"

"Nope. I grew up in kind of a…strict household."

"Really? That's surprising considering…" He clamps

his lips together, like he doesn't want to finish that sentence.

"Considering the MyFans account I have?" He nods, his cheeks ruddy. "That's kind of part of the reason I have the account. I didn't really get a chance to explore much of anything when I was younger. I had one life plan and that was it, no deviating. Obviously, I did, but even after that, I was still so…" I tap my finger to my chin, trying to find the right words. "Let's just say I was a much tamer version of who I am now and spent too much time letting everyone else make decisions for me."

Fitz's brows shoot up as he moves around me to the stove, flipping off a burner, then picking up a spoon and stirring the sauce.

"I can't imagine you being tame. I mean, it's not that you're out of control or anything, but you're…" He pauses, tipping his head to the side before settling on: "Strong. You're strong. You know who you are. You're confident. I like that about you. I like how well you know yourself."

His words surprise me. I never in my life thought someone would say I'm strong or confident or that I know myself. I know I've come a long way from who I used to be, but I don't always feel those things he says I am. Some days, I still feel like the little girl who had someone telling her how to live her life.

It's strange to hear Fitz describe me. What's even more strange is how much I *want* to be those things…for him.

"God, I'm a terrible host," he says, setting the spoon to the side and making his way to the fridge. "Would you like something to drink? I have wine, beer, soda, water. Dinner is just about ready."

"Sure, but I can grab it. You finish up what you're doing."

He nods and goes back to the stove as I round the island and start opening cabinets to find a glass. It takes me two tries before I get the right one. I grab two glasses, then open the fridge and pluck out a bottle of strawberry wine.

I grin, because it's just so...him.

Fitz reaches into the drawer nearest him and pulls free a bottle opener, then hands it to me without saying a word. And that's how we work—side by side in complete silence as I pour us some drinks and get the plates set out on the counter while Fitz finishes up dinner.

It's comfortable, like we do this every day. We don't *need* to fill the silence. We're okay with it.

When dinner is ready, Fitz brings the pan to the counter and fills both our plates. Nothing is said until I take my first bite, and it's me who breaks the silence.

"Holy hell," I mutter. "This is incredible. I'd never tell my mom, but this is a million times better than hers."

"Come on now. You don't have to lie to me."

"I'm not! Scout's honor."

His smile melts my heart...and my panties.

The conversation flows easily, and it feels like this is our hundredth date, not our first. We talk about the first time we met, when I totally picked on him for his strawberry donut habit. We talk about Carl and his love for her. We talk about the boudoir shoot that got me interested in taking sexy photos. We talk about so much that two hours pass before we even think about cleaning up dinner.

It's all so easy it feels like I've known Fitz my whole life, and not once has he judged me for anything I've said or done. He just accepts it. It's a far cry from anything I've ever experienced before.

"Can I ask you something?" he says as he scoops our leftovers into a dish. Those damn forearms that are still on display and still look entirely too lickable stretch with each movement, and I think I could watch him do mundane things like this forever.

I smile to myself, because isn't that what he's been paying me for? Watching me do silly, simple things?

"Anything."

He finishes what he's doing, then sets the dirty pot in the sink. He looks up at me. "Why don't you do private videos?"

It's not what I was expecting him to ask at all.

I take a sip of my wine and shrug. "I'm not sure. It would definitely bring in more cash, but to me there's a difference between racy photos and streaming like I do and doing private videos. Those usually lead to more, and I don't want that with just anyone."

He stares at me a moment, and I'm sure it's because my answer is probably strange to him. Is there a part of me that wouldn't mind doing private chats? Yeah. I can get pretty hot during the live streams and sometimes the idea of going into a private room with someone sounds nice, but I'm always scared of how I'm going to feel afterward.

Will I feel dirty for what I've done? Will I even like it?

"Would you ever do it?"

"With the right person, probably."

He swallows roughly, then turns on the water, adds soap, and fills the sink. He stands there with his hands on the counter, his muscles bunched as he watches the sink fill. His jaw is tight, and it's obvious he's grinding his teeth. I bet I could hear it if I listened closely enough.

"Ivan?" I say softly, and his head whips up my way. "Are you jealous?"

His knuckles turn white around the spatula he's holding. "I'm not sure how you want me to answer that."

"Honestly. We are still doing that, right?"

"Yes," he says quickly. "To both questions. The answer is yes."

My shoulders slump, and he sees it.

He drops utensils into the sink, bubbles and water going everywhere. He rounds the counter, pulling my chair until I'm facing him and he's standing between my legs. He cups my face, stroking my cheeks just under my eyes like he loves to do.

"Stop that," he says roughly. "It's not in the way you're thinking. I'm jealous because...because *I* want to be the right person, and I'm terrified I'm not."

"I'd do it with you," I tell him honestly. "I'd be on camera for you."

"You've already been on camera for me."

"I know, but you know what I mean. I'd do more for you. *Only* you. And if you want me to stop streaming, I'd do that too."

He's shaking his head before all the words are even out. "No, don't do that. I...I like it."

"You like other people watching me?"

He moves his head up and down slowly...like he's afraid to admit it. "Yes. It's... Fuck," he mutters. "I don't know. I just know it doesn't bother me because it's my name that's going to be falling from your lips when you come."

My mouth is completely dry. He's okay with me continuing my streams? He likes it? I'm surprised, especially since I expected him to ask me to stop, but I realize I'm glad he doesn't. I think he understands how important this is for me.

"Oh god. Does that make me fucked up? That I'm okay with my girl being seen practically naked by thousands of people? That I'm okay with her being watched?"

"No," I say adamantly. "No. It might not be traditional, but it's not fucked up. *You're* not either. I don't know who told you that, but it's not true."

He presses his forehead to mine, taking in my words.

"I really want to kiss you right now," he whispers.

"I really want you to kiss me right now."

He doesn't waste another moment. His mouth finds mine, and it feels like coming home.

I just kissed him yesterday, but it somehow feels like it's been years. I'm so desperate for his mouth, and it's startling because I've never felt this way about anything before.

I thought before with Levi that I wanted him. Hell, I pined for him for years, and I thought I knew what that felt like, needing someone so damn badly you can't breathe.

But I was wrong. So damn wrong. It was nothing compared to what it feels like with Fitz. I can be kissing him, like now, and still miss him, still *need* him.

His hands move from my face to the back of my head, and before I realize what he's doing, he opens the clip that's holding my hair back and lets my hair fall free. His fingers tangle in my blonde strands, tugging at them in that delicious painful-pleasurable way. I should be ashamed of the moan that leaves me just from him playing with my hair, but I don't care, not when a low growl rises from his chest.

He hauls me into his arms, picking me up as if I weigh nothing, even though I have no doubt I'm the heaviest woman he's ever been with. He sets me on the counter, fitting himself between my legs. He never stops kissing me, never stops stroking my tongue with his own. His hands continue to play with my hair, and I think I could probably get off on the sounds he's making and the way he kisses me alone.

Suddenly, he wrenches his mouth from mine, his hazel eyes full of lust and need.

"What do you need?" I ask him.

"What we did at the party..." He swallows. "Can we do that again?"

"You want me to touch my pussy while you watch?"

He groans and fire dances across his gaze.

"Yes." The single word comes out strained, like it's painful for him to talk.

I shove at his chest lightly, then nod toward the living room.

"Over there," I instruct, resting back on my palms and crossing my legs. "Sit."

He does as I say, dropping into the leather chair, spreading his legs wide, never taking his eyes off me. His lips are slightly parted, and his cheeks are flushed. His cock is already straining against his pants, and I've not done anything yet.

Other than the night of the party, I haven't done this in person. I've recorded myself privately doing this, just for practice, but never for someone else. I keep thinking any moment now I'll feel awkward being on display like this, but I don't. If anything, it's the opposite. This feels perfectly right.

I'm burning up under his gaze, can already feel sweat beginning to form on the back of my neck. I'm hot, and it's all because of the way he's staring at me.

I think maybe I should cool down...

I reach behind me to a fresh stack of dish towels he's

set on the counter, and I grab one. I turn on the faucet and get the rag nice and wet. When I turn back to him, he's still watching, and when I lift the fabric over my body and wring it out, letting the cold liquid slide over the silky fabric of my dress, his chest begins to heave as his breaths intensify.

The material clings to my body, leaving nothing to the imagination. My nipples are poking through, standing hard and ready, aching to be touched. With the rag still in one hand, I drag it over my neck, squeezing just enough to let the water run down my throat and between my breasts, using it to cool me down. It's just what I needed, and based on the way Fitz is gripping the armrests of the chair, it's just what he needed too.

I slide my free hand up my body, making sure to go slow and touching myself like I know he would touch me. I don't stop until I reach my aching nipple. I rub my thumb over the sensitive bud, letting out a low hiss at the contact I so desperately needed.

"I'm imagining it's your hands on me, Ivan. Your palms are the perfect mixture of rough and soft, and they feel so good on my tits, baby."

A hum of approval leaves him, and it spurs me on. I uncross my legs, letting them fall apart, giving him a glimpse of the white thong I'm wearing. His tongue darts out when he gets his first eyeful, and I fucking love it. I drop the rag, then grab the bottom of my dress, shimmying it higher so I can spread my legs wider.

"Fuck," I hear him whisper, and I grin.

I glide my hands over my thighs, getting close to my pussy but not touching it just yet.

Every time I get close, Fitz inches closer. I do it until he's resting his elbows on his knees, looking like he can barely hold himself in the chair any longer. Only then do I slip a hand between my legs and pull my thong to the side, giving him a look at my center. I drag a single finger through my folds, shuddering at how fucking good it feels, not just to be touching myself, but to have him *watch* me touch myself.

I slip a finger inside my pussy and immediately need to add another because one just isn't enough, not with how worked up I am.

"Tell me," he commands gruffly. "Tell me how your hand feels on your cunt."

"So good. It's soft and warm and wet. God, Ivan, I'm so fucking wet. Having your eyes on me…I'm soaking the counter." I rock against my hand, squeezing my eyes shut and biting my lip to keep from crying out. "I wish this was you. I wish these were your fingers inside me, wish you could feel what I do. My pussy is craving your touch."

The unmistakable sound of a belt being undone fills the room, and I open my eyes just in time to see him unzip his pants and pull his cock free.

"Oh god," I moan, sliding my fingers in and out as he begins stroking himself.

I've never found dicks particularly nice to look at, but him? He's beautiful. Not so long it's going to be uncomfortable and just thick enough that I know I'll stretch perfectly around him.

His movements are lazy and steady, and he never once takes his gaze off me. He alternates between watching my fingers disappear inside of me and my face. Every time he looks in my eyes, I tumble closer and closer to the edge.

As if he knows I'm getting close, he strokes himself faster…harder, rolling his thumb over the head of his cock.

"That's it, Ro," he says. "Get yourself there. I want to watch you fall apart. Make me jealous of those fingers in your pretty cunt. I want to see what me watching does to you. Coat those fingers with your release."

His words are just what I need, and with a few more strokes, my orgasm rocks through me, sliding all the way up my spine and spreading through my body.

Then suddenly he's there, dropping to his knees between my legs.

He doesn't hesitate, doesn't say a single word. He just knocks my hand out of the way, pulls my thong down my legs, drags me to the edge of the counter, and covers my pussy with his mouth. He plunges his tongue into my hole, groaning when he tastes the evidence of my release. He fucks me with his tongue just like I was fucking myself with my fingers, then moves to my clit, sucking it into his mouth with a fervor I've never experienced before.

A second orgasm races through me before I even

realize what's happening. I grip his head, grinding against his face as I ride it out and even through the aftershocks. He doesn't pull away, and I honestly don't want him to. I'm pretty sure I can live the rest of my life with Fitz's face buried between my legs.

I have no idea how long he slowly eats at me, but it has me shuddering once more, this orgasm far less powerful than the others but just as delicious.

When my third orgasm of the night subsides, he finally releases me, kissing the insides of my thighs softly before falling back onto his haunches, sucking in breath after breath. His once artfully styled hair is a wreck, and his face glistens with my cum.

He's never looked hotter.

He grins at me, and I realize I was wrong—*now* he's never looked hotter, smiling up at me with that damn toothless grin of his I love so much.

And I realize something scary…

I could get seriously used to this.

CHAPTER 13

If I thought I was addicted to watching her before, it's nothing compared to how I feel now after watching her with her hands on her pussy. When she first spread her legs and I saw how drenched her cunt was just from rubbing her hands over her body, it took everything I had not to leap out of the chair. Then when she fell apart... fuck. It *killed* me.

I've always been content to just watch, but I wanted to be next to her in that moment. I wanted to touch her, taste her. I *had* to.

It was everything I wanted and more.

"I've been dying to know what your thighs feel like wrapped around my head," I tell her after I've finally caught my breath.

She quirks a brow. "And?"

"Fucking glorious." I shove up to my feet and drop my forehead to hers. "I think I'd like to move in."

She laughs, but the sound is cut off when I capture her mouth with mine. She moans when my tongue tangles with hers, and I wonder if it's from tasting herself. She tastes good enough, that's for damn sure.

I slide my hands under her ass and lift her from the counter, carrying her through my apartment straight to my bedroom. I drop her onto the bed, loving how beautiful she looks sitting there. I feed the buttons of my shirt through the holes, then tug it over my head, tossing it aside. I shove my pants down my legs along with my boxer briefs, kicking them out of the way.

Then I reach for her, grabbing the hem of her dress and tugging the silky material over her head, and step back to admire how she looks. The luminosity of the moonlight shining through my open window, the way her pale complexion contrasts with the darkness of my blankets, the soft, dewy glow of her skin…she looks like a fucking wet dream come to life.

One I intend to have my way with.

I settle back between her legs, loving how she feels underneath me.

"God, your body is incredible," I tell her, running my hands over every inch I can reach. "I love how you feel against me."

"I love how *you* feel against *me*."

"Your curves…" I place a kiss to her collarbone. "They're my favorite."

"I used to hate them," she says quietly. "I used to hide them."

I pull back. "What? Why?"

"Because I was told to." She shrugs like it's no big

deal, but it is. I want to know who made her feel like she had to hide any part of herself.

"Who? Why?"

"Society. My parents. My...ex-best friend." Pink creeps into her cheeks. "It's why I stream—to make myself feel beautiful—and it does. I feel confident on camera. Desired. Sexy. *Wanted*."

I swallow the emotion in my throat because it makes my heart ache that she's ever felt anything but those things.

"Fuck all those people. You're beautiful. I love every damn dip and curve you have. You should never, ever hide."

"I know. I know that now. But sometimes..."

I shake my head. "Ignore the voices. If you ever think you need to hide, if you ever think you're not good enough, remember what you do to me. Just *watching* you gets my cock so fucking hard I can't think straight." I roll my hips against her, letting her feel the evidence. "You're perfect the way you are, Ro, and I promise to remind you of that every goddamn day if I need to, no matter how long it takes."

She smiles shyly, and it's still so strange to see her like that. It's a different side of her she hides so well.

"Okay?" I ask.

She nods. "Okay."

"Good. Can I start now?"

A laugh bubbles out of her, and she nods. I drop my lips to hers once more, kissing her with everything I have, making sure she knows I'm not kidding. She *needs* to know she's beautiful just the way she is.

I grind my hips against her, letting my cock slide over her heat, loving how wet and ready she is. If I moved down just a little, I could slip inside of her with ease. She rocks against me, searching for that friction we both so desperately seek.

"Ivan…" she whispers. "Please. I need…"

I know what she needs because I need it too.

I pull away and laugh when she reaches for me.

"No," she protests. "Don't go."

"Condom," I explain, pushing off the bed.

"I'm…" She rises up on her elbows. "I'm on birth control."

I pause at her words. I'm sure it's reckless, probably one of the dumbest things ever, but just the thought of taking Rosie bare… *Fuck.*

"Are you sure?"

She nods. "Yes. I'm diligent with it, and I've never had sex without a condom before."

I believe her. I know she would never lie to me about something like this.

"I'm good too. We get tested regularly, and I've never gone without a condom either."

She swallows. "Okay."

"Okay." I place my knee back on the bed and nod toward the white lacy bra she's still wearing. "Off. I want to see your tits bounce as I fuck you."

The hitch in her breath is unmistakable, and she

reaches behind her, undoing the hook, then slips the material down her arms, tossing it to the side. She leans back on her elbows, letting her legs fall apart.

I lick my lips—fucking literally—at the sight of her glistening cunt. She's still so damn wet and ready for me, and I love it so much. I want to take my time with her, want to be gentle and go slow, but I don't think I can. I need her too damn badly.

I crawl up the bed, fitting myself between her legs, then without another word or hesitation, I slide inside her. The sound that leaves me is feral as I sink into the most heavenly place I've ever been before.

"Holyfuckingshitohmygod," she cries out in one breath. "You're so…*oh god.*"

"I know," I tell her, because I *do* know. Her pussy squeezes my cock with the perfect amount of pressure, and I honestly don't have a single clue how I'm going to last. It's not going to be possible. She feels too fucking good.

I bury my face in her neck, trying not to blow. "Stop squeezing me."

She laughs, which only makes her contract around me more.

"Stop it."

Her body shakes with the laughter I can *feel* her holding in, and I move my hips, just to shut her up.

"Fuck," she moans, and now *I'm* the one laughing.

I lift my head, grinning down at her. "Not so fun, is it?"

"Actually, this is my exact definition of fun."

"Mine, too."

I roll my hips into her again, earning me another moan.

"More," she begs. "*Please.*"

I pick up my pace, fucking her with everything I have. We're a mess of sweat and moans, our skin slapping together, creating the most beautiful sounds I've ever heard.

I never want this to end. I want to stay buried inside of her until the end of time.

"Ivan! I…" She doesn't finish her sentence, so lost in her lust.

I push to my knees, not giving up my pace, just changing the angle as I slide one of her legs onto my shoulder.

"Yes, yes, yes," she chants when I set my thumb against her clit. "*More.*"

"Fuck, Ro, I wish you could see this," I tell her, watching as I disappear inside of her. "Your cunt looks so pretty stretched around my cock. Like a painting you'd see in a museum. Just fucking perfect."

"So good," she mutters, her eyes falling shut.

"No." I stop my movements. "I want to see your eyes when you come."

She peels her eyes back open, and the look in them as she gazes at me…*fuck*, it's going to be burned in my memory for the rest of time.

"Very good," I mutter, then I slap her clit.

"Ohgodohgod."

"I've been called a lot of things before, but not God. I'll take it."

She laughs, but it's short-lived, turning into a full-blown moan when I press against her clit again and rut against her harder than I have before.

"I'm so close," she tells me. "So, so…"

"That's it, baby. Milk my cock. Give me all you can."

One more stroke and her entire body shakes around me as she finds her release.

"Ivan, Ivan, Ivan," she says over and over again, keeping her eyes on me as I continue drilling into her, fucking her through her orgasm.

It's enough to send me over the edge, and I pull out at the last second, coating her belly in my cum. Seeing her covered in me…god, it's almost enough to make me blow again, and there's no mistaking the low growl that leaves me.

"Mine," I say.

"Yours," she promises.

Then, to my absolute shock, she reaches down, runs her finger through it, and lifts it to her lips.

"Holy fuck," I mutter. I press my lips to hers, not caring about the taste of my cum on them. I can't not kiss her, not after that.

I couldn't say how long we lie there, but at one point, we're not even kissing, our mouths just pressed together as we try to catch our breaths. It takes all my willpower to convince myself to roll off her, and the second I do, I miss her. So, I grab her by the waist and haul her to me, needing to feel her.

"That was…" she starts, her fingers tugging at the smattering of hair on my chest. "*Everything.*"

Yes, it was.

Because Rosie? *She's* everything.

And I know for a fact there is no way I'll ever be able to walk away from her.

Leaving Rosie behind in my bed this morning was the hardest thing I've ever done, and that includes when I was playing in Vancouver and we made it to Game Seven and I had to sit on the bench as the other team celebrated winning the Cup.

She looked so peaceful sleeping. I hated slipping out like I did, but I had to go. I'm already on thin ice with Coach, and I don't want to get higher on his shit list.

We landed in Minnesota, then headed straight for the rink for a short skate to get our legs going. Now we're sitting in the locker room with twenty minutes to go until we're done for the night. I haven't talked to Rosie all day, and it's slowly killing me.

"Come on, boys! Get fucking pumped!" Miller slaps his hands together. "We got this!" He bounces up and down on his skates a few times, then shakes his hands out.

At least someone is jazzed to be playing hockey. Right

now, for the first time ever, I wish I were back at home and not at the rink, and I know it has everything to do with the blonde I left in my bed.

"Dude, shut up," Greer snaps.

Miller ignores him. "We're down two, but that ain't shit. We can fucking do this."

"Shut up, Miller," Rhodes grumbles, looking every bit as salty as Greer does.

They might be telling him to shut up, but I know they secretly like it when he tries to pump us up like this. It's worked enough times for them to believe in it.

The clock in the corner of the room counts down the minutes, and when we're down to just one, I rise from my temporary stall.

Miller bumps his shoulder against mine. "You ready, Fitzy Baby?"

I grunt at him in response, and he juts his lips out.

"Aw, come on. Don't you be grumpy too. We can get back in this game."

"I just want it to be over."

He tips his head at me, and I get it. I never wish for games to be over, not even when we're losing. I love being on the ice even when we're down a few goals. But right now…right now, I want to be somewhere else.

"You got it so bad."

"Huh?"

He shakes his head, a grin spreading across his lips. "Don't play dumb with me. You know what I'm talking about. Rosie." He waggles his brows. "Someone's totally getting some."

I don't care that he knows about Rosie and me—I assumed he did from the other day at Scout's—but it doesn't mean I want him talking about her or our sex life in any capacity.

I glower at him. "Shut up, Miller."

He laughs, but only because he knows he's right.

We hit the ice and do a few warmup laps before the period is underway.

"Let's go, boys. Keep your head in it," Coach says from behind us, clapping his hands a few times.

The puck is dropped, we win the faceoff—something we've struggled with all night—and Lowell zips it back to Rhodes, who zings it to Wright. Our entry to the zone is clean, then the puck is on my stick, and I'm looking around for a good shot. I got nothing, so I shoot toward Rhodes, who bounces it over to Wright, who sends it back to me. It's just enough movement to screw with the other team, and I see my lane. I drag my stick back and let it rip.

The goalie flips his pad out, stopping the puck, but I'm rewarded with a juicy rebound, and I shoot it just over his shoulder, sending it right to the back of the net.

"Fuck yes!" Rhodes shouts, skating over to me and wrapping me in a hug, a smile on his scarred face.

"Hell yeah!" Wright says, tapping my helmet a few times.

"See? What'd I say?" Miller bumps his glove against mine. "Now, let's get to work and get this game tied."

And that's what we do. Two shifts later, Lowell is the one who rips the puck past the goalie, and suddenly, we're in a tied game. With just over two minutes left, everyone on the bench is thinking we're heading to overtime. The arena is buzzing, and the fans are going wild.

I step onto the ice and get right into the play, shoving the opposing player into the boards. I'm not even out there for five seconds before the whistle blows.

"You!" the official yells, pointing at me.

"What? What the hell for?"

"Holding."

Fucking shit. I hang my head, frustrated as hell as he makes the call and the whole arena cheers. It's the worst feeling, hearing a crowd of thousands celebrating your demise.

It's a bad call, and based on the way my bench is screaming, they agree with me, but I don't argue it because I know it's pointless. I climb into the penalty box, pissed as fuck and wanting to do nothing but break my stick, but I try to keep my cool. Some guys go nuts over a penalty, but I try not to let it get to me.

Luckily, Lowell's faceoffs have been much better this period, and he wins the draw. Normally he'd shoot it down the ice, but Rhodes is there, and he's on his horse, galloping away toward the Minnesota net. He's not usually a charger like that, so nobody is expecting it...

especially the goalie. He drags his stick back and shoots. It pings off the crossbar and goes directly to Wright, who picks up the rebound and zips it past the goalie for one of the prettiest short-handed goals I've had the pleasure of witnessing.

"YES!" I shout, banging against the glass as the rest of my team goes nuts, having capitalized on my fuckup.

They manage to kill off the penalty, and with just three seconds left on the clock, we win the game in the best comeback we've had in years. We're nothing but smiles as we hit the locker room and get cleaned up, and I don't even complain when I have to hit the press room. I'm feeling too damn good.

My high follows me along to the hotel room, and the minute my door shuts behind me, I have my phone in my hand, ready to call Rosie. I swipe past the messages of congratulations from my mother, mentally reminding myself to text her back later, and go right for Rosie's name.

I hit call and wait, settling onto my bed, my back resting against the headboard of the hotel room that looks exactly like every other I've ever been in.

It takes two rings before her face fills the screen.

"Hey!" she says with a grin. "How was your night?"

"It was fine."

"Just fine? Nothing special happened?"

I shrug, unable to keep my smile at bay. "Guess something did."

Her grin grows wider. "That was a beautiful goal."

"From who?"

She lifts a brow in warning. "Ivan…"

I swear, just hearing my name causes my cock to stir to life.

"Which did you like better, my goal tonight or the orgasms I gave you last night?"

"Wow, way to put a girl on the spot," she jokes before winking at the camera. The image shakes a bit as she moves through her apartment, and I don't miss her walking out of her streaming room.

She was online tonight.

I wait for the jealousy to settle into my stomach, but it doesn't come. I meant what I told her—I don't mind if she still streams because I know I'm going to be the one she ends up with at the end of the night.

My eyes fall to the rest of her, and I sit forward.

"What are you wearing?"

A seductive grin spreads over her lips. "Oh, this? It's nothing."

"The fuck it is. Show me."

She jostles around and sets her phone down, giving me a view of her empty bed. Then she's there, just at the edge of the frame, and she crawls onto the mattress, right to the center. A logo I'm more than familiar with fills the center of her chest.

"Turn around," I tell her.

She heeds my instruction, spinning around, then looking at the camera over her shoulder.

"Do you like it?"

Do I like it? Is she nuts?

If she could see how hard my cock is at this moment, she wouldn't be asking me that.

She's wearing my jersey, and the number 91 and my name stretched across her back does something to me I wasn't expecting. I've seen plenty of people wear it before, but never her. It means so much more than she could ever imagine.

"I swear to fucking god, Ro, you've never been more beautiful."

She giggles, then goes to turn around.

"Stop!" I shout.

She pauses, a brow raised.

"I want to see more."

A sly smile pulls at her lips. "How much more?"

"All of it."

Her teeth sink into her bottom lip as she reaches down, grabbing the ends of my jersey, then inching it higher and higher. She does it slowly, so fucking slowly that if I were there, I'd reach over and yank it up myself, that's how impatient I am right now.

The bottom of her ass peeks out, and I have to physically bite my lip to suppress my groan. She lifts it higher and higher until her ass is completely exposed, and that's when it hits me.

She's not wearing any underwear.

"Did you wear that on your stream?"

She shakes her head. "Nope."

"Good." I'm okay with her streaming, but I want this part of her to myself. "Show me more."

"More?"

I nod. "Bend over, baby. I want to see all of you."

Her lips part and I can *hear* the stuttered breath that leaves her, then slowly, she does as I asked. Her hips fold over, the jersey inching higher with her movements, and I watch with rapt attention.

She peeks at me over her shoulder, her bare ass up in the air, completely exposed to me, and I commit this moment to memory.

"Holy shit," I mutter, and she giggles, causing her ass to jiggle, and the desire to see my palm print on it hits me out of nowhere. I've never really been one for spanking, but right now, I want to see Rosie covered in my handprint so damn badly. "You're perfect."

"Thanks," she says quietly, squeezing her legs together. She's just as turned on as I am, and I love it.

"Have you ever played with your ass before, Ro?"

Her eyes widen slightly, but she nods. "A few times."

"Good. Do you have any toys?"

"Yes."

"Can you grab one?"

Another nod before she's sitting up and moving to her bedside table. I rip my shirt off over my head and undo my pants but leave my cock tucked inside of my underwear. I can't see at all what she's grabbing and am stunned when she returns with a little silver plug in her hand.

"Yes." The word comes out as a moan. "That one. *Please.*"

Her eyes fill with mischief as she resumes her position, giving me a full view of her asshole. For what feels like the tenth time in the last hour, I wish I wasn't on the road, and I wish I'd had more time with her last night so I could have explored her body properly.

Next time.

She rests her weight on one shoulder, then reaches between her legs. I see the plug peek through a few times as she uses it to rub against her clit. I can see it glistening with each passing stroke, then suddenly it's gone, and she reaches around herself, pressing it against her tight hole.

"Oh god," she moans as she begins to push it in, and I watch as her ass stretches around the toy.

"Talk to me, Ro. What's it feel like?"

"So good," she mumbles. "So, so good. But I bet your cock would feel even better."

"Has anyone ever fucked you there before?"

She shakes her head the best she can. "No. Never."

"Good. Because that ass is mine."

"All yours," she agrees, inching the toy in further.

When it's fully seated, I get my first real look at it. There's a little pink gem on the end, and it shimmers in the soft light of the room.

She looks gorgeous, absolutely fucking stunning.

"I wish I was there," I tell her.

"Me too." A soft moan leaves her when she shifts around. "I feel so full."

"Just think how it'll feel when my cock is in your cunt and you're wearing it."

She lets out another moan, and I palm my dick, pressing on it to relieve some of the ache that's building.

"Do you want to come?"

"Please."

"Put your hand on your clit, Ro. Get yourself off. Pretend I'm there and it's my hand fucking you."

She doesn't hesitate, just slips her hand between her legs and begins rubbing herself. I'm not surprised when just thirty seconds later, she's falling apart.

"Oh, fuck. *Ivan.* Yes, just like that."

I lied before. *This* is the most beautiful sight, Rosie with a plug in her ass and her hand on her pussy, calling out my name.

I reach into my pants and pull myself free, gripping my length and giving myself just three short strokes before I'm coming all over my lap as her shudders continue to rack through her. When I've drained the last of my cum, I sink back against the headboard, completely spent.

Rosie is still up on her knees, her eyes shut and looking every bit as tired as I am.

"Ro?" I say softly.

"Hmm?" She peels her eyes open and looks at me, giving me a lazy satisfied grin.

I laugh at how sleepy she looks. "Go to bed."

She nods, then pushes herself up, another noise of pleasure leaving her. She turns around, facing the camera once more, and I don't think I'll ever get over the sight of her wearing my number.

"How, um…" She chews on her lip. "How was that? For you, I mean. That was my first time…"

"Mine too," I tell her, "and I'm not sure it can get better."

Her eyes light up. "Really?"

"Really. You did so good, baby."

She smiles, then tucks a strand of hair behind her ear. "Thank you."

"Now, go to bed. You have an early morning tomorrow."

"Ugh, I know." She rolls her eyes. "I swear, when I open my own bakery, I'm not doing early mornings."

"You mentioned that before with…" I trail off, not wanting to remind her of when I tricked her with my identity. "Is that something you want to do soon?"

She looks startled a moment, then nods. "Yes. I'm taking classes to get my business degree."

"No shit? That's awesome."

"It's not a big deal. I still have a long time left before I graduate."

"Hey, no. Don't do that." I give her a hard look. "Don't sell yourself short. You're busting your ass at Scout's, you're streaming, and you're going to school? That's fucking amazing. Be proud of that."

"I… Thanks," she murmurs, her focus anywhere but at the screen.

"Ro?" She peers up at me with uncertain eyes. "I'm proud of you."

"So you don't think I'm an ungrateful moron?"

"What? No. Why would I think that?"

"Well, Scout and Stevie have done so much, letting me run that truck. Wouldn't that be me throwing it in their faces?"

"Do you *really* think they'd think that?"

She twists her lips back and forth a few times before finally shaking her head. "No."

"Yeah, I don't either. They'll support the hell out of you, even when you kick ass and steal all of Scout's customers. You're going to be amazing at it."

"Thank you." She smiles softly, then grabs her phone, bringing it closer, and I love how bright her eyes look in the light of her screen. "Hey, Fitz?"

"Hmm?"

"I wish you were here."

I sigh heavily. "Me too, Ro. Me too. Good night."

"Good night…Ivan."

With reluctance, I end the call. I take a quick shower to clean myself up, then crawl into bed alone, wishing like hell Rosie was here and not over a thousand miles away.

I can't wait for this road trip to be over.

CHAPTER 14

ROSIE

"Can I just say that the fact that we're all here is the best thing ever? I love afternoon games because it gives us a better chance at getting everyone here."

I glance over at Harper, who is grinning down the aisle at us.

She, Ryan, Hollis, Emilia, Scout, Stevie, and I are all sitting together. Even little Freddie and Macie are here, each sitting next to their mom. Hollis' new baby is at home with her grandma since she's too tiny for the rink just yet.

This isn't my first Comets game and I know it won't be my last, but it's my first time getting to sit with all the wives and girlfriends of the core group. It's so nice to be included in this, and tears are jumping to my eyes. I never, ever thought my crush on Fitz would land me here, sitting with all these badass women.

I blink them away, hoping nobody sees.

"It's about time we got all of our schedules to work out," Ryan says. "Between your booming prop business, my demanding YouTube schedule, Hollis being a kick-ass mom of two, Emilia keeping our idiots in line, Scout running her truck *and* her author career, Stevie being an overall badass, and Rosie doing her thing…"

"It's a wonder we ever hang out at all," Hollis finishes for her, bouncing her adorable daughter who is wearing the cutest headphones ever on her knee.

"I for one still can't believe we pulled Scout away from her laptop," Stevie says pointedly to her sister.

"Hey! I'm on a deadline!"

"You're *always* on a deadline."

Scout shrugs her comment off.

"I'm just glad Rosie and Fitz finally pulled their heads out of their asses and decided to get together." Stevie giggles at her own words.

"Hey!" I protest. "I'm sitting right here."

"I know, and I meant what I said."

"Um, Mom, you can't say ass, remember?"

"You're right, Macie. I meant I'm glad Rosie and Fitz decided to pull their heads out of their *jack*asses."

"Again, right here," I say.

She ignores me, and so does everyone else, but truthfully, I'm not mad about her words. I'm glad we're together too.

When Fitz finally got home from his road trip, the first thing he did was show up at my apartment. I questioned him as to how he got my address, but then I realized I didn't care and threw myself into his arms. He carried me right to the couch, dropped to his knees, and showed me just how much he missed me by eating me to orgasm twice before finally letting me ride his cock until he came inside of me.

We spent the rest of the night in my bed and have spent the last three weeks alternating between his place and mine. During his away games, we spend our nights on video chat. I used my plug again, and once he let me be the one to watch as he jacked himself to release. It was so hot and made me really understand his desire to just sit back and observe.

Of course, when we got off the video, I used my rabbit toy to get off…twice.

It's not all about the sex, though. I've spent more time talking to Fitz in the last three weeks than I have in the last year I've known him, and I learned his obsession with strawberries extends past donuts. Honestly, it's a little scary how much he loves them, but that's his problem, not mine.

He told me about his childhood and his parents and how supportive his mom is of his hockey career. I caught him on the phone with her one morning, and seeing him blush every time she called him "Baby Boy" was the cutest thing ever.

I'm so damn happy with him that I couldn't stop smiling even if I tried. I'm not usually a grumpy person by nature, but this happiness feels like something so much more.

He feels like something so much more.

He makes me feel seen and desired, and he's so damn

supportive of everything I do that sometimes I have to stop and stare at him, wondering what I did to deserve it all. Then I remember…I don't have to *do* anything to deserve it. I do deserve it, full stop.

It's such a weird feeling, and now that I've experienced it…I never want to let it go.

"Stop it," Stevie hisses, jabbing me with her elbow.

"Oof!" I grab my boob. "What was that for?"

"You're grinning like an idiot and it's scaring people. Especially that kid." She nods toward a little boy who is peering up at us, his eyes wide with fear.

I wave at him, and he hides behind his mother, who then turns around and shoots us a glare. The moment she turns back around, Stevie and I giggle like schoolgirls.

"This is so much fun," she says, and I nod. "By the way, I can't thank you enough for volunteering to let Macie come over after the game. She will not stop going on and on about wanting a pet, and I know Fitz has a cat. I tried to get Ryan to agree since she and Rhodes have pets, but…"

"Rhodes is…well, Rhodes?"

She laughs. "Yes. And Harper and Collin have so much creepy stuff around their house that I don't want her to get scared."

"That's fair." Harper runs her business out of her house. Pair her horror prop business with her obsession with all things horror, and it's safe to say their house is *not* kid friendly. "It's no problem at all. We're looking forward to it. Fitz even went out and bought snacks for the playdate."

"But not sugary snacks, right?"

"No, of course not."

It's a lie, a complete and total lie. In fact, I'm pretty sure sugar is all he bought.

She nods, seemingly satisfied with my answer, then shoots to her feet when the guys hit the ice for the last period.

I was surprised during the warmups when they all took turns skating over here. I was even more surprised when Fitz did the same. He skated right up and bumped his stick against the glass, then pointed at me, sending me a full smile, missing tooth and all.

I melted right there.

They're up three goals at the beginning of the period but refuse to take their foot off the gas, and by the end of the game, they add another three to the score sheet without giving anything else up. I don't think a single soul leaves the building as they announce the three stars of the game: Greer for his saves, Fitz for his assists, and Miller for all the goals he racked up.

"A natural freakin' hat trick? My man is the best! I need to change my panties."

"Scout!" Stevie glares at her younger sister, then slides her eyes toward her daughter, who is very much paying attention to what's being said.

"Pantyhose," Scout says in an attempt to cover her blunder. "I need to change my pantyhose."

Macie wrinkles her nose. "Why are you wearing pantyhose with jeans, Aunt Scout? Mom only makes me wear those with dresses on Easter or Christmas."

Scout mumbles something to her niece, then begins shuffling out of the aisle as the rest of the arena clears out. I stifle a laugh, following behind them closely.

Flashing our badges to the security team, we make our way through the back hallways to the parking garage where we're meeting the guys. One by one, they all come out of the arena, every player wearing a smile, still flying high from their incredible win.

"Jackass!" Macie yells, running from her mother's side and into Greer's arms. "You did so good! I mean, it would have been cool to get a shutout, but only letting in one goal is amazing."

He squeezes his girlfriend's daughter tightly. "Thanks, kid. I can always count on you to tell me my weak points."

"You're welcome," Macie says, not picking up on his sarcasm at all.

"Hey, Rosie," Greer says, lifting his hat and running his hand through his hair before placing the cap back where it belongs. "We appreciate you letting Macie hang out for a bit."

I wave him off. "No biggie, really. We're excited."

He leans into me and whispers, "Between you and me, if she starts driving you nuts and you put *Miracle* on, she'll be out within the first thirty minutes. She loves the movie, but she's seen it too many times. It's basically cinematic Benadryl at this point."

I nod, smirking at him. "Thanks for the tip."

"Fitz!" Macie yells, promptly abandoning us. She races up to him and bumps her fist against the one he's holding out. "Does Carl like mac and cheese? I can make her some."

"Um…" Fitz's eyes shoot to Stevie, who is shaking her head, then he looks back at Macie. "You know what? She doesn't, but *I* love mac and cheese."

"Really? I mean, it's not mac and cheese night, but I can whip some up for us if you're hungry."

He pats his stomach, the one I know for a fact is practically an eight-pack, and grins at her. "Oh, man. I am starving. I'd love that."

"Yes!" She bounces up and down on her heels, then skips to Fitz's truck.

I have a feeling we're in for a long night. Who knew a kid would have this much energy at this time of night?

"Hey, where's your mom's kiss, kid?"

Macie sighs dramatically but goes to her mother, wrapping her arms around her and squeezing her tightly. Stevie kisses the top of her head, then Greer steps up, accepting the hug Macie gives him. It's still so strange to see grumpy Greer in a dad role, but it suits him so much more than I ever expected.

"Be good for Rosie and Fitz, all right?" She nods. "And if you need *anything* at all or want to come home early, just call, okay? We'll come to get you like *that*." He snaps on the last word, just to emphasize it.

Macie giggles. "I will."

She gives him another hug, then heads back to the truck. When I look back at Stevie and Greer, both are staring after her like their whole heart is walking away.

We say our goodbyes, and they pile into Greer's fancy sports car, then peel out of the garage.

"Who wants a strawberry smoothie?" Fitz asks.

"Oooh! Me, me, me!" Macie says, opening her door. "But can I get mango instead?"

He gives me a look that says *Can you believe this kid?* "I'm not sure why you'd pass up strawberries, but sure."

I shrug, then climb in behind her.

Yeah, this is totally going to be a long night.

"Eight…nine…ten…eleven…twelve! Holy smokes!" Macie claps her hands together. "You can fit *twelve* sour worms in your gap? That's better than the four straws and the six Twizzlers."

Fitz grins proudly like he's just as excited about this as she is. He uses his tongue to pull them out, then chews them all at once and swallows. "Pretty awesome, right?"

"Best. Day. Ever."

They high-five, and I can't seem to wipe the smile off my face watching them. I'm pretty sure after this evening, Macie is going to tell everyone else to get lost and proclaim Fitz as her best friend, and honestly, I don't blame her. He's pretty amazing.

When we got back to Fitz's place, he patiently introduced her to Carl, who took a few minutes to warm up to the hyper kid, then quickly became attached to her. In fact, the cat is currently curled up inside Fitz's hoodie, which Macie is currently wearing. Another odd little thing I learned about the brown and white cat—she loves to sit inside hoods.

After introductions, Macie did make us some mac and cheese. She complained there were no hot dogs or baked beans to put in it but was happy with the results after Fitz let her crush up Cheetos and crumble them over the top.

It was surprisingly good.

Afterward, I whipped up a quick batch of peanut butter caramel cookies.

"Fu—"

"Fitz," I warn him.

He widens his eyes, mid-bite. "Frick," he amends. "These are amazing. When you open your own bakery, you *have* to put these on the menu!"

"You're going to open your own bakery?" Macie's eyes are wide too. "Can I come hang out there? Don't tell Aunt Scout I said this, but sometimes the donut truck gets boring, and sometimes I just want cookies instead of donuts."

"Of course you can come hang out with me," I tell

her. "But it probably won't be for a while. You'll be a teenager and way too cool for me."

"I'm too cool now, but I still like you."

Fitz lifts his hand for a high five, and Macie smacks her palm against his.

I grab my chest. "Ow. That one hurt."

"You still love us." The kid shrugs, then looks at Fitz. "What about Raisinets? How many of those will fit in your gap?"

His eyes widen, and he looks at me with panic in his expression.

"How about we put a movie in?" I suggest.

"Yes!" the kid shouts loudly. "Do you have any hockey movies?"

"Hello, hockey player here." He rolls his eyes. "Of course I do. Come on."

We get *Miracle* loaded up and gather enough pillows and blankets for about ten people, then snuggle up on the couch.

Turns out, Greer was right. We're not even thirty minutes into the movie, and Macie is passed out. And she's snoring—like a full-grown-man kind of snoring. It's cute until it's not anymore.

Luckily, we don't have to listen to it for long. Stevie and Greer show up at eight like we planned.

"Thanks again, man," Greer says to Fitz, lifting Macie into his arms. She doesn't even stir when he jostles her around. She's definitely out for the night, and I don't blame her. It was a big day for her between the game and hanging out with Carl. "We really needed those few hours alone."

"Any time you guys need a break, just let us know," Fitz tells him.

My heart stutters at his words.

Us. Let *us* know.

I love how easily it rolled off his tongue, like it was always meant to be there.

"We will. Good night." He looks at me, then back at Fitz before leaning in and not-so-quietly saying, "Don't do anything I wouldn't do."

I roll my eyes at him, and Fitz slams the door in his face. I hear Greer laugh on the other side.

"I was not aware that sound could come out of a child," Fitz says, shaking his head as he goes to the couch and begins cleaning up the mess of blankets we've made. "None of my nieces snore like that. It's new territory."

"Do you get to see them often?" I grab one of the extra blankets and put it inside the basket near the couch. For a guy, his place is surprisingly organized and well-decorated. I briefly wonder if his mother came and helped him. That would be a total Fitz thing.

He shrugs. "A few times a year. Not as much as I'd like, obviously. They live in Arizona, so I always make sure to get them tickets to games whenever we play there. Last season, I scored two goals with them in the crowd, and since we had a day off the next day, I got to go to their show-and-tell. It was awesome."

His whole face is lit up talking about them, and it's a side of him I haven't really gotten to see yet. I love it.

"Do you want kids?" The second I realize what I've just asked, I stop dead in my tracks, spinning to face him. "Oh my god, forget I asked that. It was totally out of line. I mean, we've only been dating for a month. That's like a one-year-mark kind of question. I have no business asking you questions like that. I mean, I'm nob—"

Fitz covers my mouth with his hand, his hazel eyes narrowed on me. "I swear, if you say something ridiculous like you're nobody, I will be forced to take you back to my room and spank your ass."

"But, like, in a sexy way, right? A sexy spanking?"

"Do you really think you'd deserve a sexy spanking after that?"

"Yes."

His eyes spark with lust, a smirk pulling one side of his mouth up. "You're…"

"Amazing? I know."

He laughs. "Something, Ro. You're something." Another smirk. "To answer your question, yes, I do want kids. But not for another few years."

I'm suddenly hit with so many images all at once. The one that sticks out the most is of me, Fitz, and a little girl with blonde hair and hazel eyes smiling up at us as we stand at the kitchen counter all wearing matching aprons and making cookies. Fitz boops the tip of her nose, leaving behind a speck of flour. She giggles, and it's the sweetest sound I've ever heard.

"What are you thinking about?" he asks.

"Us," I answer honestly. "Future us."

"Yeah?" I nod. "I like the sound of that."

Before I know what's happening, he grabs my hand, hauling me down the hall toward his room.

Only we don't make it. He presses me against the wall halfway there, then covers my mouth with his own. His tongue pushes past my lips, sliding against mine. He tastes like my peanut butter cookies, and I love it more than when he tastes like strawberry donuts. Those aren't mine, not really. But this? It's all me.

He grinds his hips against me, and I can feel his hardening cock against my leg, which tells me…

"We should really move this to the bedroom." I grab his hand and drag him the rest of the way.

The second he closes the door, I pounce. This time, it's me pressing him against the door and covering his mouth. He groans as our tongues tangle together, and he's so damn lost in the kiss I don't think he even realizes I have his belt buckle in my hand and I'm undoing it, or that I drag his zipper down. In fact, I don't think he realizes what's happening until I wrench my lips from his and fall to my knees.

"Oh, fuck…" He stares down at me with glassy eyes. "You look beautiful like that."

"Do I?" I tug his jeans down his legs, dragging his boxer briefs along with them. "Your cock is so perfect," I tell him when it springs free. "I've been thinking about sucking it all day."

A low growl rumbles out of his chest, and I love it so damn much my pussy throbs just from the sound alone. I lean forward and run my tongue along his shaft, from base to tip.

"Christ," he mutters, staring down at me. I know because I haven't taken my eyes off his the entire time.

I lick him again, then again, like he's a lollipop and I'm dying to know how many licks it takes to get him to explode.

"You're a terrible tease." He reaches for me, and I shake my head.

"Hands on the door, Fitz."

His eyes spark, and with one nod, he listens, flattening his palms against it, earning himself another lick for following directions. He lets out a low groan, and I smile against his cock.

"You're killing me," he says, but I know that's not true. He loves being teased like this as much as I love teasing him. The anticipation…the buildup…it's important to him.

I continue to run my tongue along his shaft, occasionally sucking the head of his cock into my mouth and applying enough pressure to drive him crazy. The longer I lick at him, the more *I* get impatient. I have no doubt in my mind that were I to reach my hand between my legs, I would find I'm soaking wet.

"Ro…" he whines, driving his hips toward me.

He needs more, and fuck it because so do I. This time when I run my tongue along him, I don't pull back.

Instead, I cover his cock with my mouth and pull him straight to the back of my throat.

"Fuckingshitohgod." It comes out as one word, and I smile when I hear his head hit the door.

I deep-throat him until I can't breathe, then pull back. I suck in a few breaths of air and then swallow him again. His hands are literally shaking against the door, and I know he wants to reach out and touch, so I grab his hand and bring it to my head.

"Finally," he grunts, tipping my head toward him. He holds my eyes with his own. "I'm going to fuck your mouth so hard, baby."

I nod, begging him to do his worst, and he does. He ruts into me, using my mouth and using me. He drives into me over and over, and I love every second of it.

"I want to come on your tits," he tells me, pulling out. "On the bed."

I shove up to my feet and rip my shirt off over my head, so glad I wore a front-clasp bra as I tug that off too. I lie back on my elbows as he stands over me, stroking himself. He never once takes his eyes off me as he grips his cock tighter and faster, fucking his fist as I wait for my reward.

The muscles in his neck jump as his entire body tenses, and just two strokes later, he coats my tits in his cum. I love every fucking second of it. I love when he marks me like this. It makes me feel like...well, *his*.

When he squeezes out the last of his orgasm, I reach down and run my finger through the mess he's made, then lick it off because I know it drives him wild, and honestly, it drives me wild too. His eyes light with a fire I've never seen before, and before I know what's happening, he yanks my leggings down along with my underwear, runs his fingers through the remnants of him, and then pushes them inside my already drenched pussy.

"Holy…" I whisper.

But he's not done. Of course he's not.

He drops to his knees, shoves my legs open wide, and presses his mouth to my clit while he continues to fuck me with his fingers. He gives my cunt two more strokes before sliding them out of me and down to the hole only I've played with so far.

I'm up on my elbows watching him, so I don't miss when he peers up at me, asking for permission.

"Do it," I tell him. "Stretch my ass with your fingers."

He growls against me, then slowly begins slipping his digit inside of me. It feels different than the plug but just as good. He works one finger in, then another, and quickly, I'm riding his hand, aching for more.

"You look fucking gorgeous with my fingers in your ass, Ro. I can't wait until it's my cock buried inside of you."

"I can't…either," I manage to get out, completely lost in this sensation, loving how full I feel with him inside me like this, already anticipating what it's going to feel like when it's his cock.

He sucks my clit back into his mouth as he works his

fingers in and out of my ass, and my orgasm hits me out of nowhere.

"Ivan!" I cry out his name as shudders make my entire body shake. I've never felt an orgasm like this before, and that's saying something because I've had quite a few of them since Fitz and I started seeing one another.

Is this normal? Will it always be like this? Better and better each time?

When the last of my trembling subsides, he slowly pulls his fingers from my ass, then gives my pussy one last kiss before crawling his way up my body. He peppers me with kisses, covering my body with his own.

"How the hell did I get so lucky?" he whispers against my lips.

I don't tell him I've been asking myself the same thing.

Because this thing with Fitz? It's real…and I never want it to change.

CHAPTER 15

"Move the puck, move the puck!" our special teams coach yells. "We want surprise. We don't want to be predictable."

I slide it against the ice toward Rhodes, who barely touches it before shooting it to Wright, who then feeds it to Miller. He looks for an opening, but when he doesn't find anything, he sends it my way. It's not even on my stick for a second before it's back to Miller, then in the back of the net.

"Yes!" Miller shouts, like this is a real game and not just practice.

"You got lucky," Greer grumbles, tugging his goalie mask off and setting it on top of his head as he reaches for his water bottle. He drenches himself with water, then shakes his head. "Let's go again."

We run the play again and score again. Then we switch it up, me taking Miller's spot. The same thing happens—the puck goes right into the back of the net.

Greer is obviously unhappy, but the rest of the team is feeling damn good about it.

"That's the winner," the goalie says on our way to the locker room. "If you guys can move it like that out on the ice, get someone in front of the net to screen the goalie and tip the puck in, you're fucking golden."

"Good thing too, because we've been shit on the PP lately. Don't get me wrong, our five-on-five is awesome and we're obviously winning games, but we need a PP as dangerous as our PK."

Miller snickers. "You said PP."

Everyone rolls their eyes, but there's no missing the way several guys smirk. We might all be adults and professional athletes, but we're also guys. We're going to laugh every time someone abbreviates power play to PP. It's inevitable.

"Fitzy Baby, are you and Ro coming over for Thanksgiving dinner?" Rhodes asks.

"At your house?" I don't even bother trying to mask the surprise in my voice. There's a reason his nickname is Beast, and it's not just his scar. He lives in a house up on a hill that's dark and spooky-looking and he *never* invites anyone over. I've been dying to ask Ryan if the dishes talk, but I'm sure she'd deny it even if it was true.

"Yeah. It's my turn to host. Ryan's excited about it, so I guess I am too."

I try not to laugh because based on the frown gracing his face, that's not even remotely true.

"We'll be there. Need us to bring anything?"

"Maybe a pie or some other dessert? I mean, I'm sure we'll have plenty, but then again…"

I understand what he's getting at. There's going to be an assload of hockey players in his house, so there's no such thing as too much food. I smile to myself thinking of last weekend when Macie was over for her playdate with Carl and she yelled at me for eating a whole box of mac and cheese myself.

"We can do that," I tell him, then I grab my phone from my cubby.

Me: I kind of just agreed to go to Rhodes' house for Thanksgiving. Is that okay?

Dots pop up on the screen almost immediately.

Rosie: Of course! Besides, Ryan stopped by earlier this morning and already asked. I told her yes.

Rosie: Now I'm realizing I should have checked with you first.

Rosie: We're bringing pie. And probably cookies.

• • •

Rosie: I have to run by the store and grab some ingredients after my shift at the truck. Want to come?

Me: Sure. Want me to pick you up?

Rosie: I'd love that. :)

I feel my own smile tug at my lips.

"What are you looking at? Porn?" Hayes drops down into the stall next to me, even though it's not his. He tries to peek over my shoulder. "Is it that hot lady you were watching on the plane that one night?"

I snap my head up to him.

How the hell...

He shrugs. "I saw you watching before I decided to catch some shut-eye. I have no idea what was going on, but that little red number she was wearing was nice." He bites his bottom lip and closes his eyes like he's conjuring up the image right here and now.

My phone creaks in my hand and I glance down, surprised to find my knuckles turning white around the device. I'm not bothered by strangers watching Rosie on her streams, but I really don't like the idea of Hayes watching her. It one hundred percent has to do with who he is—a womanizing little shit.

"Don't worry," he says. "I don't know what channel it

was or anything, so I'm not whacking off to the stuff you are."

I blink at him, trying to decide if I want to kill him or not. I think I'd do okay in jail, but I'd miss hockey a whole hell of a lot.

"What?" he asks.

"Nothing," I mutter. "Go away."

He sighs, then shoves up to stand. "You're no fun anymore. None of you guys are. You're all paired off, all falling in love and shit. I'm lonely over here, man."

"I'm not fall—"

His laughter cuts me off. "Don't even fucking try it, Fitz."

"Try what?"

"Denying you're falling in love with that thick woman from the donut truck."

"Rosie," I say through clenched teeth, my patience with him growing thin. "Her name is Rosie."

"Whatever. I'm just calling it like I see it. You're clearly into her."

"Well, yeah. We're dating."

"No, man." He shakes his head. "You're more than dating. You're in love with her."

I smash my brows together. "No."

"Yes," he insists. He dips his head toward Greer. "I saw that idiot fall in love with my own two eyes earlier this year, and you're acting just like he did: all smiley and always attached to your phone, always ditching me to hang with your girl. You're in love."

Do I smile a lot since I started dating Rosie? Yeah. She makes me happy. Am I attached to my phone? Sure, but that's because I always want to talk to her. And do I ditch Hayes? Yes, but to be fair, I've been trying to shake the kid for a while now. I like him just fine, but his idea of a good time and mine are two totally different things.

All that said, am I *in love* with Rosie? No. There's no way. We've only been dating a little over a month now. That's too soon, right?

When I don't say anything, he sighs and claps me on the shoulder. "You just go ahead and figure that one out for yourself. I'm going to go find someone else to hang with." He starts to cross the room. "Hey, Ford. I—"

"No," the new guy says, not even looking up at him. "I'm not hanging out with you."

Hayes drops his shoulders and hangs his head, mumbling and walking out looking completely dejected. I feel a little bad for him and promise to make time for him after Thanksgiving.

I work on stripping off my gear as the space starts to clear out, everyone either heading home or to the gym a few rooms over.

"You know he's right," Ford says quietly, startling me.

I turn around to find him staring right at me with sharp eyes. "Huh?"

"The kid—he's right. You're clearly in love with this Rosie girl."

"How would you know?"

He lifts a shoulder. "Because a man in love knows another man in love."

"You're in love?"

A faraway look crosses his features, a smile tugging at the corners of his lips. "Oh yeah. Tessa came out of nowhere at the start of the season, and now I can't get enough of her. I hate going on the road, hate leaving her. Hell, I think I'd even give up hockey if she asked me to."

I swallow roughly because *fuck me*. I've had those exact thoughts.

I used to be okay with the travel that comes with the game—it's fun seeing different cities and exploring—but now? Now it grates on me every time I have to say goodbye. I just want to be close to Rosie.

And hockey? I still love it, but I love being with her even more.

Ford laughs lowly, bringing my attention back to him. "You have that same look on your face I see in my own reflection, and I definitely love my woman." He shoves out of his stall, then tosses his bag over his shoulder. "See you at Thanksgiving," he calls out as he makes his way from the room, leaving me standing there all alone with nothing but my thoughts and the reality that...

He may be right.

I think I'm in love with Rosie.

"Remind me again why we're going to the grocery store on Thanksgiving?"

"Because we need flowers."

"For?"

"Um, our hosts." Rosie sends me an incredulous look. "Duh."

I smother a laugh. "Right. Flowers. Duh."

She narrows her eyes at me, then points to the door. "Hush up and open that for me."

"Yes, ma'am," I say, stepping in front of her so the automatic doors can swing open.

She brushes past me. "Thank you."

Wiping the grin off my face is impossible. She's ridiculous, and I fucking love it. I've had more fun with Rosie than I've ever had in my entire life. She's full of fire and wit, and hanging out with her is my new favorite pastime.

Ford was right—I can't get enough of her, and I'm not sure I ever will.

She leads us through the corner market to the back of the store where there's a small cooler full of several different kinds of flowers. I try not to watch her ass the entire time, but it's hard. She's wearing that orange dress again, and all I can think of is the last time she had it on, her sitting up on my counter pouring water all over her chest, then fingering herself. And of course, that leads me to remembering what it's like between her legs.

Pure fucking bliss.

I usually love Thanksgiving and the endless supply of

turkey and carbs, but right now, I'd be perfectly fine with going back to my apartment and having Rosie for dinner.

She taps her manicured finger against her chin. "I love daisies personally, but should we stick with something traditional like roses? They are fancier."

When I don't answer her, she peeks over at me.

"What?"

"Nothing," I tell her.

"It's something. You're smiling at me. What?"

I can't stop myself from gripping the faux fur jacket she's wearing and dragging her to me, and I really can't stop myself from slanting my mouth over hers, kissing her in a manner that's entirely inappropriate for the grocery store. I slip my hands around her waist, unabashedly trailing them lower until I'm cupping her ass and tugging her as close as possible.

She wraps her arms around my neck, holding me just as tightly as we make out like fools in front of the flowers.

"Um, pardon us." Someone clears their throat.

I pull away, but not before placing one last kiss on the tip of her nose, loving the look on her face as she stares up at me.

"We just need to... Holy shit. Roly-Poly Rosie?"

Her entire body stiffens as she slowly turns in my arms, facing the couple standing before us.

The guy is blond, his hair perfectly coifed with too much product. The woman hanging on his arm is tall—taller than him even—and lean with blonde hair that matches the shade of his. They're both dressed up, I'm assuming on their way somewhere for dinner, and she's looking back and forth between him and Rosie.

"Levi?" she says softly. I hate the way the name rolls off her tongue. It's...familiar, and it makes my stomach hurt.

"Roly-Poly, wow! I almost didn't recognize you." Before I realize what the guy is doing, he wraps his arms around *my* girlfriend and says, "You look great with that extra weight."

He pats her stomach, and I see red because *What in the actual fuck?*

I take a step toward him, ready to pummel this fucking guy, but before I can, the woman he's with steps between us. My momma would kick my ass if I laid a hand on a woman, so I step back, squeezing my fists so I don't forget my manners and deck the fucker anyway.

"Hi," she says, holding her hand out. "I'm Kitty. It's great to meet you."

Her smile is genuine, as if she's completely unbothered by what the twat she's with just said.

"Hi," Rosie says, shaking the outstretched hand. "We've actually met before."

"Oh?" Kitty shrugs. "I don't remember. Sorry."

"It's fine." Rosie waves her off, but I know her, and it's anything but fine. She's hurt by the words, but she's trying not to show it. "So, Levi, how's England treating you?"

"England? That's so last year," the douchebag says. "We're back in the States. We live here, actually."

"Here?" The word comes out a squeak. Rosie clears her throat. "Since when?"

"A few months now. Kitty got a job at some law firm."

"Partner, babe. I'm a partner at the firm."

"Yeah, partner, whatever." Levi shrugs. "How are you? I haven't seen you since… Gosh, how long has it been now?"

"Two and a half years," Rosie answers, and I hate that she knows exactly how long it's been. "Since you left."

"Really? Time flies. Are you still doing that baking thing?" The asshole looks over at me for the first time. "Hey, man. I'm Levi Kane. Rosie and I go way back."

He holds his hand out, and I want nothing fucking more than to smack it away, but I have a feeling that won't go over so well with anyone. So, I do the mature thing, and I grip his hand…*tight*. Like so fucking tight his hand turns white under mine.

"Ivan Fitzgerald."

His eyes narrow on me, and I don't miss the way he stretches his fingers out when I finally release my grip. "Fitzgerald, huh? Why does that sound familiar?"

"He plays for the Carolina Comets," Rosie explains, and I love the pride in her voice.

"No shit? Think you could hook us up with some tickets to a game?"

Is this guy fucking serious?

"I don't really care for hockey," Kitty says, turning her nose up. "It's entirely too violent."

She has no clue how violent I want to be right now, and I'm not even on the ice.

"That's fine. I can go with Brady." He turns to Rosie. "You remember him, right? From high school? You guys dated for a while."

That rigidness is back in her shoulders, and I hate it just as much as before.

"I remember him sleeping with everyone else after taking my virginity, yes."

Holy fuck. I remember her telling me about that guy. Well, not *me* me, but ShootsAndScores me.

This guy is hanging out with him? What a fucking tool.

Levi laughs at Rosie's response, clearly not giving a shit about the hurt in her voice, and says, "Yeah, but that was so long ago. No hard feelings anymore. You're over it."

I grit my teeth. There are definitely hard feelings there, and I hate that he's telling her to feel otherwise.

In fact, I just straight-up hate this guy. I don't know him, but I don't want to.

"Babe…" Kitty tugs on his arm. "We should really get going."

"Can't you see I'm talking with an old friend?" He rolls his eyes at her, then sends me a lopsided smile. "Women, right?"

My hands tingle with the urge to acquaint this fucker with my fist.

"Actually, we need to get going too," Rosie says. "Our dinner starts soon, and we don't want to be late."

"Yeah, I bet you're excited to get there and eat."

He pointedly looks at her stomach, and it's the last fucking straw. I step toward him, fists ready to fly, but I'm stopped once more.

This time, it's Rosie. She tugs on my jacket, and I glance down at her. She gives me a subtle headshake, and it takes everything in me to step back.

"We should get together sometime," Levi says, not at all picking up on the tension. "Maybe a double date or something."

"Yeah, sure," Rosie agrees, and I pray she's just saying it to pacify him. There is no way in hell I'll go anywhere with this guy—except maybe out to the alley so I can kill him and leave his body there all beaten and mangled.

I should be concerned with how satisfying that image is, but I'm not. This guy deserves it and so much more.

"It was great to meet you," the girlfriend says.

"Again, we've met before," Rosie tells her.

Kitty pouts. "I still don't remember." She shrugs, then reaches into the cooler and grabs a bouquet of roses. "These will do."

"Let me know about those tickets, Ivan. See ya later, Roly-Poly." Levi winks at her, and I want to grab a rusty spoon and scoop his eyes out. "Call me sometime."

Over my dead fucking body.

I watch the fucker until he disappears around the corner, then turn back to Rosie.

She's not looking at me. Her focus is solely on the cooler of flowers, but she doesn't have to be looking my way for me to know she's upset. That fucker got to her. I can see it in her body language, in the set of her shoulders and the tightness in her jaw.

She's hurt, and it makes *me* hurt, and makes me want to hurt Levi. I move to go find him, because there's no way I can possibly let him just walk away after that shit.

"I think daisies," Rosie says quietly, stopping me in my tracks. "What do you think?"

I hate the way she's looking up at me, with trepidation in her gaze, like she *needs* my approval. It's not her, not the woman I know—not the woman I *love*.

I can't answer her. I don't have it in me to tell her what to do. It's not my style. All I can do is reach around her and pick up the bouquet of daisies.

"Come on." I press a kiss to her cheek. "We don't want to be late."

We don't speak for the entire drive.

CHAPTER 16

ROSIE

Everything changed.

It's all messed up, and it's all Levi's fault. Running into my ex-best friend, the one I was once in love with, has me completely topsy-turvy. Nothing feels right, not the clothes I'm wearing or the food I'm eating or even sitting next to Fitz. Something is broken…and I think it might be me.

"Holy crap, Rosie. This pie is incredible." Scout moans as she stuffs another bite into her mouth. "Like, I could kiss you this is so good."

I force a smile her way, then say, "I'd let you," because that's what the Rosie they know would say.

The problem is, right now, I don't feel like that Rosie. I feel like the me of two years ago all over again, and I hate it.

Scout giggles, then digs into the slice of pie once more.

There are about twenty-five people crowded around three long tables that have been shoved together. It's easily the biggest Thanksgiving I've been part of. With just me and my parents, who were both only children too, we didn't have big holiday gatherings.

It's been chaotic between all the couples and kids running around. Macie is having a blast being spoiled by everyone, Freddie is basically being passed around the entire table, and Miller is setting up his karaoke machine.

Well, he's attempting to. He and Rhodes are currently fighting over it.

"No. Absolutely not. I didn't want you people here anyway. I have to draw the line somewhere," the grumpy defenseman says, his brows drawn tightly together, his hands slashing through the air with every word.

"Aw, come on. You don't mean that. You looooove us, especially me."

"I don't love anyone, especially not you."

"Hey!" Ryan yells at her husband, whose cheeks flame instantly.

"Except you. I love you. So fucking much." He glares over at Miller. "Maybe a little less right now, but still, so much."

Ryan grins, satisfied with his answer.

"Miller, do you have 'Monster Mash'? I'll totally sing that," Harper volunteers, rising from the table.

"Jesus." Collin shakes his head but stares after his wife with a dopey grin on his face.

"Or Queen! I'll do some Queen!" Hollis says, joining her sister.

"Please don't let her sing." Lowell covers baby

Freddie's ears. "She's a horrible singer and I don't want to subject our daughter to this."

"I heard that!"

"Shit," Lowell mutters. "I forgot about the new-mom super-hearing."

I tuck my lips together, trying not to laugh. It all feels so…normal, and I love every second of it.

Well, I *would* love every second of it if I wasn't so damn scared to look over at Fitz. We didn't speak the entire way here, and I hated every minute sitting in that old truck. It wasn't his fault it was awkward with us. It was all me. I didn't want to face him after what happened with Levi. I was embarrassed about the way I let him talk to me, especially in front of Fitz.

I swore—*swore*—I would never be that person again, but the second I saw my ex-best friend, I slipped right back into the old Rosie, the one with no spine, the one who let everyone walk all over her and never stood up for herself. I hated it in that moment, and I hate it now because I *still* feel like that old version of myself, and I don't know how to shake it.

"Are you finished?" Emilia asks, pointing to my still full plate. I've picked at a few things, but my appetite was completely gone after the grocery store.

"Yes, but I got this," I tell her, grabbing my plate and rising from the table. "In fact, hand me those plates too."

She tips her head. "Are you sure?"

"Of course. I could use a little break." I gesture toward the room where Harper and Hollis are currently sharing a microphone and belting out Shania Twain's "Man! I Feel Like a Woman!" at full volume while Miller has his own and is singing every word right along with them. It's easily the most obnoxious and endearing thing I've ever witnessed.

Emilia laughs. "This group is so exhausting sometimes."

"You're telling me." I roll my eyes playfully.

I grab the plate from her hands, then retrieve a few more as I make my way to the kitchen. I set them on the counter next to the others, then get to work on filling the sink with water and soap. I know they have a dishwasher, but I welcome the distraction.

I feel terrible because this is my first time being invited to something like this with all these incredible people, and I'm in a terrible mood. And to think I woke up this morning to Fitz's head between my legs, feeling like I was walking on air. Then it all came crashing down around me thanks to one little trip to the grocery store.

Maybe Fitz was right. Maybe we should have skipped the flowers.

I have no clue how long I stand at the sink scrubbing dishes before I realize I'm not alone. I *feel* the moment he walks into the room. There's a charge in the air and goose bumps pop up on my arms.

"I'll dry," he says, stepping up next to me.

We work in silence for several seconds, and each one that passes grows heavier and heavier. It's unbearable and I hate it. It's never been like this with us before, and I don't want it to be like this now.

I'm just about to say something when Fitz breaks the silence.

"So, that guy..."

"Levi," I provide.

"Yeah, that's one name for him," he mutters. "He was your best friend, wasn't he?"

I can hear the contempt in his voice. He doesn't like Levi, and I can understand why, but he doesn't know Levi like I do. He wasn't always awful. A lot of times, he was nice. He was always there when I needed him most, and he had my back when I moved out of my parents' place. He was *mine*.

"Yes, that was him."

"The same one who made you feel like shit about your body?"

I can't confirm that one out loud. It sounds so bad when he says it like that.

Don't get me wrong, I *hate* the way Levi makes me feel about myself, but what I hate even more is the judgmental tone in Fitz's voice, because it's not directed toward Levi.

It's directed toward me.

"He's a prick, Ro. You know that, right?"

My hands close tightly around the plate I'm holding, and I grind my teeth together. "Yeah, I'm aware."

"Are you? Because you just stood there and let him treat you like shit in front of everyone."

I drop the plate, not caring about the water that sloshes everywhere. I turn to him, crossing my arms over my chest. "You don't think I know he's awful, Fitz? I'm not stupid. I'm more than aware of the jabs he took at me. If you really think it would have helped anything or anyone for me to say something, you're wrong. It would have done nothing but make the situation worse and more awkward than it already was."

"Then you should have let *me* say something." He lets the towel he's holding drop to the counter. "Do you have any idea what that was like for me? Just standing there and letting some asswipe say those things about you?"

"Really?" I scoff, shaking my head. "You're worried about how *you* felt? Did you ever stop to think I was humiliated to hear him say those things in front of you? In front of the man I'm…I'm sleeping with."

Both of his brows shoot up. "The man you're sleeping with?" Now it's him who's shaking his head. "Is that what this is? Just sex?"

"What? No! Of course not."

"Then why didn't you let me say something to him? I wanted to punch that fucker. Hell, I *still* want to punch him. Why didn't you—"

"Because it's not your business!" I shout over him, well aware that we're not the only people in the house and there's no way we're not drawing everyone's attention.

Right now, I don't care.

"It's not your business, Fitz. It's mine."

"*You're* my business, Rosie. Don't you get that? I'm all in over here. Completely."

"Yes, you're so *in* that you lied to me for weeks and pretended to be someone else—that's how all in you are?"

He looks like I've punched him in the gut.

It's unfair. I know it's unfair.

I forgave him for that and we're beyond it, but right now, it's the only ammo I have. I don't want to have this conversation about Levi, but he's insisting on it, so I'm using everything I have in my arsenal.

"You're right," he says quietly. "I did that. I did that, and I fucking regret it. I wish I'd had the balls to approach you as me, but I didn't because I'm not brave like you. I'm not strong like you are. I'm not—"

"Did you ever stop to think I'm not brave? Did you ever stop to think maybe this is all a front and I'm just a shy, sheltered girl who doesn't know who she is? Did that ever occur to you?"

"No," he says matter-of-factly. "It didn't because I *know* you. That's not you."

"No, you know the me I want you to know. You don't know me like he does."

"So, what, then? All this"—he waves his hand over me—"it's all just a big façade? You're a fake?"

I shrug. "Maybe. Maybe not."

"No." He shakes his head, then takes a step toward me. "No. I refuse to believe that. That's not you. That's not—"

"Stop telling me who I am!"

He pauses, both his face and his shoulders falling.

I hate it. I hate it so much that I want to just run. I want to put as much distance between us as possible because I cannot stand to look at him like this.

"I'm sorry," he says. "I didn't mean to—"

"That's the thing, Fitz. You never mean to. You didn't mean to lie to me and lead me on. You didn't mean to watch my streams. You didn't mean to ditch me at Slapshots, but you did. You did all those things and they sucked."

He reaches for me, and I back up.

"Stop. Please."

"Okay." He holds his hands up and takes a few steps away. "Okay. I... Fuck." He pinches the bridge of his nose, then looks up at me. "Are you still in love with him?"

"Are you serious?" I counter, completely taken aback by his question. The fact that he even has to ask me that...it sucks.

"Yes, I'm serious."

I narrow my eyes. "I think you should go."

He opens his mouth like he's going to argue, but then he thinks better of it. "Okay."

We stand there in silence for I don't even know how long. I stare at the floor, and he stares at me. I know because I can *feel* it. I know what his eyes feel like on me. I've had them there plenty. Hell, I've *craved* them before.

But right now...right now, I want anything other

than this. I don't want us when I feel like I don't know who I am.

"We…" He clears his throat. "We rode together. Do you want a ride?"

I shake my head, still not looking at him. "I'll get one from someone else."

"Fine." It's all he says before he walks past me.

I *burn* to reach out to him. To touch him. To tell him to ignore me and I'm just in a weird headspace. To beg him to stay.

But I don't do any of that. Instead, I just let him walk by. He reaches for the door that leads out the back of the house and pauses with his hand on the knob.

"You know," he says in a low voice, "I think you might be right."

I lift my head, meeting his gaze. I swallow when I see the pain swirl in his hazel eyes because I know I'm the one causing all that hurt.

But can't he see that *I'm* in pain too? Reeling in a way I never thought I would?

I want him to comfort me, not accuse me of still being in love with Levi.

"I don't think I know you. Not right now. Because right now, this isn't the Rosie I know, and it's not the Rosie I *want* to know either. If you find her…if you find the woman I fell in love with, let me know."

He walks out the door, taking my heart right along with him.

263

CHAPTER 17

I haven't spoken to Rosie in two days, and I feel like my insides are on my outside. It's terrible, and if I never felt like this again, it would still be too soon.

The worst part is, I can't do anything to fix this. It's all on her.

I meant it when I told her I'm all in because I am. I love her. I love her more than anything or anyone in my life. I hope my mother never finds that out, but it's true.

That said, until she figures out what *she* wants, I can't do anything about it.

"You look like the shit my dog took on the floor this morning."

He's probably right. We just beat Calgary 2–0. I should feel good, should feel like I'm on cloud nine, but I don't. I feel like crap.

"When did you get a dog?" I ask Miller as he takes the spot beside me.

"I picked her up yesterday." He pulls his phone out

and flashes me a picture. "I have no idea what she is, definitely a mix of pit bull and something else, but isn't she gorgeous? I'm in love with her." He slides the phone back into his pocket. "I got her so Macie would like me best again. She's *so* obsessed with you after you let her have a playdate with Carl, and I refuse to be shown up by the likes of you."

I flash him my teeth, pushing my tongue through the hole there. "I still have this, you know, and she *loves* seeing how much of stuff I can fit in there."

He holds his arms out. "Punch me, then. Knock my tooth out. I'll fall right on that grenade."

I shake my head, grinning for the first time in days. "Shut up, Miller."

"Aw, you're just saying that because you're worried. Don't worry, Fitzy Baby, I'll always love you even if Macie doesn't."

"Leave him alone, Miller," Greer says from across the room.

The guy in question sighs, then rises to his feet. "Fine —but I'm only going because I have to go meet Scout. We're going shopping for toys and stuff for little Mooseknuckle."

"You cannot name your dog Mooseknuckle."

He scoffs. "Says the guy with the female cat named Carl."

He shakes his head like *I'm* the crazy one, then walks out of the room. I'd never tell him this, but I kind of miss him when he goes. He might just be the best distraction there is, mostly because it's easy to laugh at him.

"How you holding up, man?"

I drag my eyes across the room, unsurprised to find a scowling Greer looking my way. He shouldn't be scowling, not after that shutout win, but of course he is. He *always* is. That's just who he is.

I sigh, then drop back into my cubby. I could lie to him. I could tell him I'm fine and things will be fine, but I don't have it in me to lie.

"Not good, Greer. Not good at all."

He nods. "I get it."

"Do you? Your perfect girl is probably waiting for you to come home to your perfect life with your perfect daughter-to-be. Mine is…" I trail off, not willing to admit I have no clue what Rosie is doing. I wish I did, but I don't. I want to reach out to her so badly it's hard to concentrate on anything else. It's fucking weird living in this limbo.

Greer huffs out a laugh. "It's not perfect."

"No? You're telling me you two aren't madly in love, then?"

"Well, yeah, we are, but we aren't perfect—not by a long shot." He sighs. "We bicker daily. I'm a grumpy asshole, and she's stubborn to her core. Also, Macie can be annoying as hell sometimes because she's a kid and kids are the worst."

"I'm not sure you're allowed to say that now that you're dating a girl with a kid."

He shrugs, not caring. "Just being honest. Relationships aren't always easy. In fact, they kind of blow sometimes. Even when things are amazing, they don't stay that way. It's like hockey: it's just grinding and working hard every day, hoping the result is what you want."

I laugh sardonically. "Thanks for the relationship advice. It's just what I wanted from a guy who only started believing in love this year."

He narrows his eyes. "Well, maybe you'll like hearing it from a guy who almost lost everything he loves by letting his emotions get the better of him and nearly ruin everything."

"If you think *I'm* the one who did that, you're wrong. It wasn't me. It was her. She's the one who is all… I don't even know what she is."

"And you think she does? Someone from her past— someone who broke her heart once—just came back. She's probably going through some shit you can't understand. Maybe she just needs space to figure things out."

When I don't say anything, he goes back to knocking things around in his cubby. It's several tense minutes before he looks my way again, giving me a hard stare.

"What." It's not really a question, mostly because I'm over questions today. I just want him to say whatever the fuck he has to say, then leave me alone to wallow.

"You know she doesn't love him, right?"

I nod. "I know that."

That's the thing. I *do* know. I know she's over him. I know it's not him she loves.

But I'm not so sure she loves herself either.

"Okay. Then you know she loves you, right?"

I don't say anything because I don't know that. I want to believe she does, want to believe it so fucking badly, but it's hard to at the moment.

Greer sighs. "Just give her some time, man. Give her space. As much as it sucks, she needs that more than she needs you."

His words hit me right in the chest, the pain spreading throughout my body.

Ah, hell. Who am I kidding? That pain has been there for days, and with each minute that passes with me not knowing what Rosie is doing, it gets worse.

"Look," he says, grabbing his backpack and slinging it over his shoulder. "You're going to be fine. Things with Rosie will work out. I know they will."

"How can you be so sure?"

"Are you kidding me?" He sweeps his arm out wide. "Look at this damn team, man. We're dropping like flies, another one of us falling in love every damn day—even *me*. I never in my life thought I would be here, madly in love with a woman I sure as fuck don't deserve, but I am. Wright, Rhodes, Lowell, Smith, and Miller are too. All those relationships turned out fine, and if you let it, yours will too."

He walks over to me and pats my shoulder twice,

clearly uncomfortable with comforting me. It would make me laugh if I didn't feel like such shit right now.

"She'll come back to you. Just be patient."

I nod. "Thanks, Greer."

"Yeah, course. Any time."

He gives me a sad smile before taking off, leaving me alone in the locker room trying to figure out my life.

I'm glad he has faith it will all work out.

Me? I'm not so sure…and I'm not sure I'm ready to find out.

I've been sitting at my computer for the last hour staring at the black screen in front of me. I've managed to power it on twice before shutting it off each time.

Now, the blue light at the bottom of my monitor is taunting me, and it's taking everything I have not to yank it from the wall and chuck it out the window. I've been itching to see Rosie, and I know this is the only way I can see her. Another two days have passed without hearing from her, and we're now sitting at four days way too fucking many.

It's harder than I thought going without her. Sure, we haven't been together that long, but she's been in my life daily for a year now. Suddenly not seeing her…it feels wrong, like my entire universe has been flipped around and I don't know which way is up or down. I went from a fourteen-game point streak to nothing in back-to-back games, and I haven't had a strawberry since I dug into the strawberry pie she made for Thanksgiving, not even my usual after-game smoothie.

Everything is off and all wrong.

It's crazy how everything I thought was so boring about my life suddenly didn't feel boring anymore with her by my side, how all the things I didn't like about myself suddenly became my favorite things because they were her favorite things. She made me feel like I belonged, like I was good enough.

I fucking miss her, and I *need* to see her.

Even though I don't want to invade her privacy and want to respect her space, logging into my old account feels like the only option to see her. Besides, I just want to make sure she's okay, check in with her. There's no harm in that, right?

Meow.

I look over just in time to see Carl strut into my office. She's been avoiding me for the last few days too. Girls always stick together, right?

She makes her way across the room, surprising me when she rubs against my leg.

"All right. Come on," I tell her, bending down to pick her up.

Meow.

"I know." I scratch under her chin just like she likes. "I miss her too."

Meow.

"I wish I could see her."

Carl hops out of my arms and onto my keyboard.

"Hey!" I try to shoo her away, but she ignores me like she always does. "Get off there, you little shithead."

Suddenly the fans of the computer spin to life and the monitor turns on.

Meow.

I grab Carl, tucking her back into my lap, then hovering my finger over the sleep button on my keyboard.

Meow.

"Hush," I tell her. "I'll lock you in the pantry again." Though I'm sure she would love that since I bought her a fresh loaf of bread this morning. She'd be damn comfortable in there.

I go to click the button, but I'm stopped by the little paw that reaches out, swatting at my hand.

"Carl, I swear to god, I'm going to—"

The words die on my lips when I look down.

I'm possessed again. I have to be. That's the only reason for the mouse to be in my hand because I sure as hell don't remember grabbing it.

"Might as well," I mumble.

I click on the internet icon, then navigate to the site I promised Rosie I'd unsubscribe to. Technically, I did. I stopped following her account—but I didn't delete mine. It's not because I plan on using it again to watch other women, but just in case she and I ever want to experiment.

I log in, then hold my breath as I type in her username with one hand and hit go on the search bar.

This user cannot be found.

"What the…" I sit forward, reading the message again.

Nope. It still says the same thing.

"Maybe I typed it in wrong."

I hit backspace several times, then type it again: R-O-P-L-A-Y-I-N-G. I hit go and the page refreshes.

This user cannot be found.

It's wrong. It *has* to be. There's no way she can't be found unless…

"She deleted her account."

Meow.

I'm pretty sure Carl's latest vocalization translates to, *No shit, idiot. Now give me a treat.*

But why? Why did Rosie delete her account? And what does it mean? Is she done streaming? Is she done with…me?

Emotion claws at my throat with that thought. I don't want her to be done with me. I want her to figure out what she wants and I want her to want me, but more than that, I want Rosie to be happy. If that means she doesn't stream and she goes back to whoever she was before and tells me to get lost, I guess that's okay with me too.

But really…really, I hope she chooses me, because I damn sure choose her, and I'll choose her every day for the rest of my life if she'll let me.

I just need her to believe that too.

CHAPTER 18

ROSIE

For the second time in as many months, I didn't show up to work. This time, I ditched for an entire week.

I have no clue how, but I still have a job. Either Scout is way cooler than I've ever given her credit for, or she's really that hard up for a decent baker.

When I finally drag myself into the donut truck a few days after Thanksgiving, I walk right into chaos.

"Oh, hey!" Stevie says from her position on the floor. "Watch where you step. I dropped some sprinkles, and that damn replacement cold brew pitcher snapped on me." She shakes her head. "What are the odds, right?"

Pretty slim, but I'm not surprised things are all screwed up. That seems to be the theme in my life nowadays. When I went to get dressed this morning—the first time I changed out of my pajamas in days—I discovered a hole in the thigh of my favorite jeans, and when I went to put my hair up in my usual messy bun, my ponytail holder broke in half.

Everything is messed up.

"Do you need to run and grab some supplies?"

"No need," a voice says from behind me.

I turn to find Scout walking into the truck, two bags in each hand. They're filled with everything we'll need to get us through the day.

"Rosie, glad you could make it in." She raises a pointed brow.

I grimace, guilt eating at me instantly. "Hi."

"Here." She shoves a fresh container of sprinkles at me. "Refill these, then get to work on icing the strawberry donuts."

Just hearing the word *strawberry* has my stomach dropping to the floor. Oh, look—there it is right next to Stevie as she continues scrubbing up the mess.

"On it, boss." I drop my head as I shuffle past her. I wash my hands, then pull on my gloves and get started on my tasks. The three of us work quietly for the next few hours as we open the truck and work through the line that's stretched to the parking lot.

Finally, at ten, we get a break. Scout sets the *Be Right Back* sign on the front counter, then spins in my direction.

"We need to talk." Her voice is terse, and it immediately sets me on edge.

Here it comes. I'm getting fired.

"Grab a drink and meet me out front."

I nod and take all the time in the world pouring myself a fresh cold brew. I should really opt for water since I don't remember the last time I had any, but if I'm

275

getting fired, I'm going down with one last delicious drink in my hand, not water.

When I exit the truck, that sour feeling in my stomach worsens when I see Scout *and* Stevie sitting at the picnic table, each with a frown on her lips.

Yeah, I'm totally screwed.

I suck in a deep breath and shove my shoulders back, holding my head up high as I make my way over. I settle onto the bench across from them and fold my hands around my cup, holding on to it like an anchor.

"Before you say anything, I just wanted to tell you what an honor it's been working here. I appreciate this opportunity you've given me, and it has meant more to me than you'll ever know. The friends I've made...the people I've met..." I swallow back the lump in my throat because *people* includes *him*. "I'm grateful. So damn grateful. I'm sorry I've let you down, and I completely understand why we're having this meeting."

Scout and Stevie look over at one another with furrowed brows for several seconds before turning back to me.

"Do you?" Scout asks. "Do you understand why we're having this meeting?"

"Well, yeah. I'm getting fired."

Stevie's brows shoot up. "Is that what you think?"

"Yes?" It comes out as a question because I have no clue what's going on. "Am I not?"

"Um, no. We love you. We'd never fire you."

"But I…I ditched work for the last week. Aren't you mad about that?"

Scout shrugs. "Sometimes the things happening in our lives are more important than someone getting their donut fix in the morning."

Is she serious? I'm not fired?

"We actually wanted to talk to you about something we heard."

Now my stomach sinks for a whole different reason, because the only thing this could be about is…

"You want to open your own bakery."

I physically lean back because *What?*

"How did you hear about that?" I ask.

"Macie."

Oh god. When she was over at Fitz's meeting Carl, we talked about me opening my own bakery. I should have known she would say something to her mom.

"Oh. That."

"Yeah, that." Scout stretches a hand across the table and grabs mine, the one that's currently fiddling with the straw in my cup. She stills my panic fidgeting and gives my hand a squeeze. "Why didn't you tell us?"

I lift a shoulder. "I…I don't know. I was scared, I guess. You two have done so much for me and given me such an amazing opportunity… It just felt like I was throwing all that back in your face by wanting to start my own place."

Scout shakes her head. "No. Not even close. Rosie…" She sighs. "You're an incredible baker. *Way* better than me. This place, as much as I love it—it's not enough for you, and that's okay. I knew that after the first week I hired you. I knew you wouldn't stay forever, and I never expected you to. I want to see you flourish. I want to see you grow. And more than that, I want to be the first damn customer in whatever shop you open."

I blink back the tears stinging my eyes because I wasn't expecting that at all. "You do? You'd come to my bakery?"

"Yes, of course. Why wouldn't I? I mean, you don't get an ass that don't quit like mine by not eating delicious sweets."

I laugh. It feels so foreign after not doing it for days, but it's good. *So* good.

"And if you think for one second I won't be coming to get some of those delicious peanut butter caramel cookies you sent home with Greer and Macie, you're nuts. Those were easily the most amazing thing I've ever tasted. Greer got jealous of them because I kept moaning every time I ate one and he was very threatened by it."

"Why can I totally see that from him?"

Stevie shrugs. "Because it's such a Greer thing to do. He's annoying like that." She might roll her eyes, but the smile on her face says she finds it anything but annoying.

And just like that, all the laughter inside me dies because I had something like that before, but now…now I'm scared it's gone.

"Uh-oh." Scout squeezes my hand again. "Have you still not talked to Fitz?"

Just hearing his name has my heart hammering in my chest like I've just run a marathon. God, I miss him so much. I want to talk to him so badly, but I don't know where to start. I don't know how to explain what I'm feeling because I still don't know what I'm feeling.

I shake my head. "No. I don't know what to say."

"I mean, telling him you love him is usually a good start," she suggests.

I don't even bother trying to deny it because I do love Fitz. So damn much. That's one thing I'm absolutely certain of, and that's not my problem at all.

My problem is me.

I don't feel like I know who I am anymore, and I'm honestly not even sure I ever did. One run-in with Levi and I slipped right back into everything I promised I'd never be again. All it did was show me that even though I try so hard to act tough and badass, I'm still just a scared little girl who is afraid to stand up for herself. As much as I tried, I don't think I ever got rid of the old me, not with so many old wounds left open and unhealed.

"You do love him, right?" Scout asks.

"Yes. I love Fitz. Like *I'm madly in love with him and am going mildly crazy without him* kind of love him."

"Then…what's the problem?"

"Me," I reply honestly.

She gives me a sad smile. "I know how you feel."

"You do?"

She nods. "Yeah. I kind of went through the same thing with Miller. It was never that I didn't love him, but

I didn't love *me*. I didn't know who I was anymore. I'd been trying so hard and throwing myself into my work and everything else that I lost who I was somewhere along the way. Being with Miller woke me up to the fact that I was missing something, and it wasn't just him. I was missing *me*. Is that how you're feeling?"

"Yes. Yes, that's exactly it." I run my tongue over my drying lips. "That's how I feel. I've tried so hard over the last few years to make myself feel good and, honestly, I thought I was doing fine. With my photos and my streaming and going to school…those are all things I wanted to do, and all those things made me feel good. But now…now I don't know. Did I just do them because they were the exact opposite of what I was told to do, or did I do them because I really wanted to, you know?"

Neither of them says anything, and that's fine. I'm not sure I want them to say anything. I'm not sure what answer I'm looking for. Maybe I just need to vent a bit.

"Can I ask you something?" Stevie says after a few minutes of silence.

"I've just spilled my guts to you, so I guess."

"Why do you stream?"

"Excuse me?"

"Your streams, your late-night activities—why do you do it? I mean, don't get me wrong, I think you're badass for it, but *why*?"

"I…"

All my usual reasons are right there on the tip of my tongue, but for the first time, they don't feel right.

"I don't know," I say honestly. "I think maybe because I liked feeling seen. I liked feeling wanted. I liked feeling…free. And yes, it made me feel good—sexy. It made me feel like I was a bad bitch with a banging body people actually wanted to look at, and it certainly opened up a whole new side of me sexually. But more than that, it made me feel seen."

"How does Fitz make you feel?"

"Seen."

The answer is automatic like it's been right there in front of me the entire time. Fitz makes me feel seen, and I don't just mean because he enjoys watching me.

It's more than that. He listens to me. He values my opinion. He asks me questions about myself. He encourages me to make my own decisions. He makes me feel like an actual human and not just a missing piece of whatever puzzle he's trying to put together.

That's how my parents made me feel—like an obligation, something they *had* to do, which is probably why they had my whole life mapped out for me when I was still in the womb.

Then with Levi, it was the same way. He was the one who planted the seed of me moving out of my parents' place and ditching their college plans for me. He was the one who told me who was good enough for me, who told me what I liked and what I didn't. He was the one who kept me tethered to him just enough that I felt like we had an actual chance of being together when I was always just a backup plan for him.

Then he left, and for the first time in a long time, I was alone. So, I threw myself into anything and everything I could to make myself feel desired again. I changed my clothes, my hair, and hell, my entire attitude because it was what I *thought* everyone else wanted.

But it wasn't, and I don't even know if it's what *I* really wanted.

Maybe...maybe this whole time, what I needed was to give myself permission to love...well, myself.

"How did you fix it?" I ask Scout. "Because this is awful. I want to be with him *so* badly, but I also want..."

"To fix what's broken, and you know you can't fix it by burying yourself in him?"

I nod. "Exactly."

"As much as it sucks to hear...time. I took time for myself, and I figured out what I wanted. I figured out who I was. After I did what I needed, I went to him, and the rest worked itself out."

She says it like it's the easiest thing in the world, and perhaps it is.

"For what it's worth," Stevie says, "I think you're a lot closer to that than you give yourself credit for. I think maybe this thing with your ex-best friend coming back into your life has you all messed up. Maybe that's a chapter you need to end properly before you can move on to the next."

"Hey!" Scout scowls at her sister. "I'm the author— book metaphors are my thing." She looks over at me.

"But Stevie has a point. Talking with him might be a good place to start."

As much as I don't want to talk to Levi, they might be right.

"Thank you—both of you. I have no idea what I'd do without you in my life. You're kind of my best friends."

"Then next time, maybe tell your best friends you're thinking of ditching them for your own bakery?" Scout narrows her eyes but squeezes my hand to let me know she's only teasing.

I chuckle. "I will. Besides, it's not something that will happen for several years still. I have plenty of time left here to drive you crazy."

"And we wouldn't change that for anything." Stevie reaches across the table, grabs my other hand, and squeezes it. "Now, as much as we love you and want you here, you look like you haven't slept in days, so…"

"Go home and get proper rest?"

"Please. I don't need you scaring away all my customers. I need all the regulars I can get before my competition heats up." Scout winks at me. "And I'm heading out too. I have to take Mooseknuckle to the vet."

"Who is Mooseknuckle?"

"Oh! Our new dog." She pulls up her phone and shows me a picture of an adorable little gray puppy. "I let Miller name her."

I lift a brow. "You don't say."

I look over at Stevie, who is rolling her eyes at her sister.

She rises from the bench with a shrug. "Love does crazy things to you."

And don't I know it.

"So, what are you going to do?" Stevie asks as Scout heads for the truck.

"I think…" I sigh. "I think I need to have a talk with my former best friend."

"Roly-Poly Rosie!" I hear from across the room.

I turn in my chair to find Levi strutting into Cup of Joe's coffee shop like he owns the place. When he reaches the table, he tries to give me a hug, but I thwart his advances, moving away from his outstretched arms.

"Aw, come on, Roly." He laughs it off, taking the seat across from me. "You know you missed me."

The sad thing is, he's right. A small part of me *did* miss Levi. I missed all the fun we used to have as kids. All the mud pies we made, all the times we hung out in his treehouse, him tossing that damn football against the wall and me reading a romance novel I'd snuck from his mom's stash. I missed his parents, and I missed the way he used to make me laugh.

But even though I missed all that, there's so much more that I didn't miss at all. Honestly, it makes me wonder what the hell I was thinking when I thought I was in love with him.

"So, Roly, how ya been? I can't believe it's been so

many years. How are things?" He looks down at the plate in front of me, which is empty save for a few crumbs from my caramel apple pie. "I see you're as big a fan of sweets as ever. Scarfed that one down, huh?"

He laughs, but there's nothing funny about what he just said.

"I didn't really come here for pleasantries, Levi."

His thick brows inch closer together. "Then what did you want to meet for?"

"Honestly? I want to tell you I don't love you, and I never did."

"Um...okay? I—"

"No." I sit forward. "I'm going to do the talking here, understood?"

He sits up straight. His eyes are wide, and he nods once.

"Once upon a time, I thought you hung the moon and I was madly in love with you. You were my best friend, and you were a good guy—or so I thought. Now that I've had distance and time away from you, I realize how wrong I was about all of it. You didn't hang the moon, and I never loved you. If I had, I wouldn't have let you talk to me the way you do. I wouldn't have let you treat me like you always have, like I'm this poor helpless girl who needs you to tell her what to do. I wouldn't have let you talk down to me or let you tell me I'm fat." I scoff. "Between you and my parents, it's a wonder I ever got away from any of it. I was so okay with all of you running my life, telling me what to do, but I never stopped to think about what I wanted.

"So, over the last two years, I did what I wanted. I built a version of myself that I like. I did boudoir shots. I took sexy photos of myself. I wore clothes that fit me. I met people who made me laugh and accepted every part of me. I learned I'm a damn good baker and friend. And more than all that, I learned that I'm worthy of being respected. I'm worth more than all those expectations and opinions other people—people like you—shoved onto me. I'm beautiful just the way I am. I'm smart, I'm capable, and I'm fucking worthy of being *loved* for just being me. I don't need to bend or fold to meet anyone else's standards, least of all yours. The only person I ever needed permission from was myself, and right now, I give myself permission to tell you I don't want you in my life, and you have no hold over me anymore."

I sit back when I'm finished with my speech, feeling the weight I've been carrying around for far too long fall off my shoulders brick by brick. For the first time in a long time, I feel free.

Levi just stares at me.

Then stares some more.

Finally, after several minutes of us sitting in silence, he speaks.

"You know, when I ran into you on Thanksgiving, I thought to myself, *There's no way that's the same Rosie I've always known.* And it turns out, I was right. You're not that same person. You're a lot stronger than you used to be, and frankly, I'm proud of you."

"I don't need you to be proud of me."

He gives me that same dimpled smile I used to love, but this time, it doesn't have the same effect. "I know."

And he sounds…resigned, sounds okay, like he's fine with me telling him off.

"I don't think we would have made a good match." His voice is low and sad and nothing like I've ever heard from him before. "And you're right, I did treat you like shit. I did keep you around as a second choice. You didn't deserve that. You deserve someone who looks at *you* like *you* hung the moon—like that guy at the grocery store did. He's more than I could ever be to you. I might not have acted like it, but leaving you behind sucked. I can see now that was probably the best thing to ever happen to you."

"It was," I agree. "I know that now."

He gives me a small smile. "Good. I'm glad." He lets out a sigh, then pushes his chair back. "I think it's best if I go."

"Yeah, probably."

He stands and peers down at me. "You know, you'll always be my Roly-Poly Rosie, and I'll miss all the good times we had. And…I'm sorry. Truly."

With that, he tucks his hands into his pockets and exits the coffee shop and my life for the last time.

I've never felt better.

CHAPTER 19

I've been checking MyFans daily, hoping for a glimpse of Rosie, but her account is still deleted. There's a part of me that's glad she's not sharing herself with other people when she can't even share herself with me, but fuck do I miss her.

I haven't seen her in two weeks now. I've gone to Scout's Sweets a few times, but only when I have an advance warning that she isn't going to be there. It's not because I don't want to see her, but because I'm trying to respect her need to be alone.

If I'm being honest, it's getting harder and harder every day not to just show up at her apartment and demand she talk to me, but every day, I do it. I stay away, and I'll keep staying away until she's ready. The last thing I want to do is pressure her or tell her what she needs to do. She's had enough of that in her life, and she doesn't need it from me.

Besides, I trust Rosie. I trust that, eventually, she'll

find her way back to me, and I'm willing to wait as long as that takes.

"All right, boys."

Coach Heller claps twice to get our attention. We're facing an uphill battle in the third period for the I don't even know how many-eth time this season. We're getting entirely too comfortable giving up early goals, then forcing our way out of a hole. We need to fix our shit before we run ourselves into the ground one too many times and blow any chance we have at the Cup.

"We've been in this position before—too many damn times if you ask me, but that means we have proof that we can do this. Get the pucks in deep, go hard to the net, and win this fucking hockey game."

Everyone claps twice, then Coach leaves.

"Coach is right," Lowell chimes in. "We got this. It's not ideal, but we know we can do this. Rhodes, watch your edges. Wright, win those board battles. Miller, Hayes, Fitzy, let's get to the front of the net, screen the goalie a bit more."

"And shoot blocker side," Greer adds. "He's having a hard time on that side tonight. For fuck's sake, give me some good defense out there, will ya?"

We'd all laugh if it wasn't so true.

We have three minutes before we need to be on the ice, so I bend down and pull my skates back on, getting ready to head back out there and give it my fucking all.

"Hey." Rhodes digs his elbow into my side. "Dude, look."

I look up at where he's pointing. There's a TV in the corner of the room, and I'm shocked by what I see on the screen. The Zamboni is still out there giving the ice a clean, but that's not what draws my attention.

No, it's the person sitting *on* the Zamboni.

"Rosie."

"What's she doing?" Rhodes asks. "And what's that sign she's holding?"

I lean closer to get a better look.

Hey, #91, I'll trade you a kiss for a strawberry donut.

"I'm pretty sure that's for you," Wright comments.

"Aw, I think she likes you, man." Miller smacks my shoulder a few times.

"What the fuck is she wearing?" Ford asks.

"If that was my girl out there, there's no way I'd be standing around in a locker room with a bunch of smelly fuckers. I'd be running out there to claim my kiss."

Greer's words snap me out of my stupor, and before I know it, I'm racing out and straight down the tunnel to the ice. I don't have all my gear on, and my skates aren't laced up properly. Damn, I'm not even wearing a shirt, but I don't give a shit.

I need to see Rosie, and I need to see her *now*.

I stop just short of my skates hitting the ice. She's on

the other side, still holding that damn sign. I cup my hands around my mouth and yell out for her.

"Ro!"

She turns my way instantly, and the biggest grin I've ever seen from her spreads across her lips.

"Fitz!"

Then she's tugging at the belt over her lap and jumping off the machine.

"Hey! Ma'am! Ma'am! You can't do that!" the driver yells, but she doesn't care, and fuck, I don't either.

She slips and slides, nearly falling over too many times for my liking, so I hit the ice, skating to meet her halfway, not even caring how much trouble I'm going to get into for this. I don't have it in me to care. Not now, not when she's so damn close.

I hear the chatter around the arena get louder and louder as they try to figure out what's happening. A few loud whistles, a few cheers, and distantly, I hear my name being called from behind me, but I ignore that too.

I stride toward her, coming to a stop just a few feet away. I want to reach out and touch her so badly, but this is all on her terms. I want her to be the first to make a move.

"Rosie..."

"You know it's ridiculously cold out here? I mean, I kind of figured since it's ice and all, but man, I really didn't think it would be *this* cold. And good gravy, it's hard as hell to walk on ice. Not as bad as I thought, but still difficult. You know, I really thought those two things would be flipped, that it wouldn't be as cold as it is and that it'd be harder to walk, and I—"

"Ro." I tilt my head to the side. "As much as I love your rambling, what the hell are you doing? That's a big jump. Are you okay?"

She grins at me. "Isn't it obvious? I'm offering you a kiss for a donut." She ignores my worry, lifting her sign to show it to me. "I mean, I don't have the donut with me, but I totally promise to get you one—that is, if you kiss me, and I'm not even sure if that's something you want to do since I haven't seen you in weeks, but just in case you do, I—"

I cut her off with a kiss because I *know* it's the only way to shut her up.

And okay, it's also because I really, really want to fucking kiss her. Having her lips on mine…it's so much more than I remember. She tastes like strawberries and heaven and everything I ever fucking wanted. She tastes like mine, and there's no way in hell I'm ever going to let this woman go.

When I finally pull away, she's as out of breath as I am, and it has nothing to do with the short skate it took to get to her.

It's all Rosie.

"Hi," I say, brushing my nose against hers.

"Hi." She presses her mouth to mine again briefly.

"Looks like you owe me a strawberry donut."

"I guess I do."

I kiss her again because I can't help it.

This time, it's her who pulls away first.

"Fitz, I'm…god, I'm *so* sorry. I…I don't know what happened. Seeing Levi again… It made me feel so many different things I wasn't expecting. No!" She shakes her head. "No, not like that—not like you're thinking."

I realize my face must be conveying everything I feel because hearing her say *Levi* and *feelings* in the same sentence makes my stomach feel like I swallowed lead.

"Do you remember when you asked me if I loved him?"

Of course I remember. She didn't answer, and at first, that killed me, but I also knew there was no way she still loved him.

"I don't. I don't love him. Not at all, and I never did. I was just in love with the idea of him, the fairy tale of falling in love with your next-door neighbor, your best friend, that person who knows you better than anyone. But him…" She shakes her head. "He doesn't know me. He never knew me. Not like you do. He doesn't know what makes me tick. He doesn't know all the things I like and all the things I hate. He has no clue who I am, and I told him that. I met up with him and I told him off. You'd have been so proud of me."

I am proud of her. So fucking proud. And I'm about to tell her that, but she keeps going.

"You know me, Ivan. Hell, you knew me before *I* even knew me. You saw through every mask I ever wore. You see me. You've always seen me." She brings her hands to my face, cupping my cheeks in the same way I always cup hers. "So, to answer your question, I don't love him. I love *you*, Ivan. I've always loved you, and I always *will* love you. I just hope I'm not too late in saying it."

I don't say anything for several seconds, mostly because I'm not sure what I should say.

She loves me? Rosie Calhoun is in love with me?

"Hey, idiot! Tell her you love her too! We got a fucking game to play!"

I look over my shoulder to find my entire team standing on the bench, all staring at us. In fact, the entire sold-out arena is staring, including the other team and a few people from security. I forgot about all of them because all that matters in this moment is Rosie.

"Fitz?" she says softly. "Are you going to say anything? I mean, if you don't love me anymore, that's okay. I just—"

For the second time tonight, I cut her words off with a kiss, and this time, I do hear the cheers and shouts from the crowd.

When I pull away, she smiles. "I owe you two donuts now."

"I always get two donuts."

She sinks her teeth into her bottom lip, peering up at me with trepidation. "Does this also mean…"

"That I love you? Yeah, Ro, I love you. I think I've been in love with you for a long time now, since way before I ever found your channel. Actually, I think I might have fallen the first time I went to the donut truck and you made fun of me for getting strawberry donuts when there—"

"Are so many better options? I know. It's insane."

"Then how come you always taste like strawberries if you don't like them?"

A slow grin spreads across her lips, which I'm dying to kiss again. "After I realized you like them so much, I perhaps started wearing strawberry-flavored lip balm. You know, just in case." She winks, and it makes me laugh. "What? It totally worked."

I kiss her again because fuck it. The game has already been paused because we're standing on the ice way past what intermission is, so might as well.

"Can I ask you something?" I say when I pull away.

"Anything."

"Why'd you delete your MyFans account?"

Her eyes widen. "You looked for me?"

My cheeks heat. "Yeah. I…I missed you. I know you asked me not to watch you anymore and I haven't, but then you were gone and…it was the only way I could think to see you. Please don't be mad."

"I'm not mad. I missed you too. And I didn't delete my account, just put it on pause. I needed to figure out if I was doing it for the right reasons or not."

"And?"

"I was. I miss it. But I also think I'm going to be okay if I don't go back to it. Turns out, there's this guy who makes me feel all the things I was looking for by streaming."

"Yeah? What's he like?"

"Well, for starters, he's pretty hot. He has this toothless smile that's just so *cute*. He's kind and intelligent. He treats me with respect, and he lets me do whatever makes me happy. And, between you and me, he's a little *naughty* in the bedroom."

I grin. "Cute and naughty, huh? He sounds pretty cool."

She nods. "Oh yeah, he's definitely cool. And he does this thing with his tongue that I *really* like, so I figure I'll keep him around."

She waggles her brows, and I laugh.

"You're insane."

"Maybe, but you like me."

"No, Rosie. I *love* you."

She sighs. "I love you, too, Ivan."

And then, I kiss her again.

The Comets win the game, no thanks to me. I got benched, but I'm okay with it, because I also got the girl.

EPILOGUE

ROSIE

I became a headline.

That wasn't exactly my intention when I decided to win Fitz back, but it happened.

WOMAN DRESSED AS DONUT INTERRUPTS COMETS AND GETS BANNED FROM ARENA

I won't lie, I wasn't at all anticipating that repercussion when I decided to jump off the Zamboni, but it was worth getting escorted off the ice by security and told I wasn't allowed back for a year. Really, I'm lucky it was that short. They wanted it to be for life, but Fitz talked them down. I think he may have bribed them a bit, but he says I'm worth it.

I just wish I could have deferred my ban to a season when the Comets didn't make it all the way to the Stanley Cup Final. Unfortunately, I missed all the home games and had to watch them from Slapshots. All the wives and other girlfriends stood in solidarity next to me and gave up their spots to keep me company.

Now, at the tail end of Game Seven, we're all wearing our Playoff jackets and seated in the suite we reserved because this is an away game, and the boys are five minutes away from doing something they've worked their entire lives for—winning the Stanley Cup. The score is tied, and all we need to do is keep the puck out of our net and get another goal.

"Just five more minutes," Harper says. "They just need to hold on for five more minutes."

Stevie has her hands on her cheeks, eyes locked on the ice. "I think I might junk punch Greer if he lets another goal in."

"He'll totally be the jackass again if they don't win."

Stevie doesn't even have it in her to scold her daughter for her comments. Besides, I think both reactions might be warranted.

After Fitz and I made up, the Comets went on one hell of a heater. They were the first team to clinch a Playoff spot and even took home the Presidents' Trophy. Now let's just hope that old superstition of winning the Presidents' Trophy but not the Cup doesn't come back to bite them in the ass.

"My panties are wet, and not even for a good reason. It's pure sweat at this point," Ryan says, watching as Rhodes slams a guy into the boards. "Okay, now they're wet for a good reason."

I laugh, then return my attention to the ice. Fitz has the puck, and he passes it to Miller, who shoots it toward the net. Everyone gets out of their seat as the puck rolls off his blade and misses the net by a foot.

Before anyone has a chance to sit back down, he has it back, and this time, when he shoots, he doesn't miss. Everyone is jumping up and down, including all of us girls, cheering so damn loud there's no way I'm going to hear anything my professor says tomorrow.

As much as the opponent fights, they can't do it, and just three minutes later, the Carolina Comets are Stanley Cup champions for the second time in their franchise history.

We're escorted by security down to the ice, and before I know it, I'm being swooped up into Fitz's arms.

"I'm so—"

My words are cut off by the best kiss of my life, and that's saying something because I've been kissing Fitz every day for six months now.

"I love you, I love you, I love you," he says, punctuating each word with a kiss.

"I'm so proud of you!" I tell him.

He's worked tirelessly toward this over the last several months. Every day is hockey, hockey, hockey. Being here to see his dream come true…it's everything I didn't know I wanted.

"Thank you," he tells me, molding his hands to my face in that familiar way I've grown so damn used to.

"For what?"

"For being you. For being here. For being *mine*. I don't know how I got so damn lucky, but I promise to never, ever take it for granted. You mean everything to me, Ro, and I promise to spend the rest of my life proving that to you."

I grin up at him. "I think I'd like that very much."

"Yeah?"

I nod. "Yeah."

"Good. Because I love you. More than strawberries even."

I gasp playfully. "Well, I never."

He shakes his head. "You knew. You've always known."

And I do know. I always have.

Four and a half years ago, I realized I was madly in love with my best friend, the guy I grew up next door to and had known my entire life.

Three and a half years ago, I was ready to tell him I loved him. I just needed to find the right time. This was big, life-changing. I couldn't just spring it on him. It had to be *right*.

Three years ago, everything fell apart when he told me he'd met the love of *his* life and was moving out of the country and the lease on the apartment we shared wasn't going to be renewed.

Two and a half years ago, I vowed to make my life into my own.

Two years ago, I met a man, not knowing he was going to change everything.

After some heartbreak and uncertainty, I made him mine.

And as of tonight, I'm more in love with him than I've ever been.

This is everything I've been waiting for, and I'm never letting it go.

EPILOGUE

Winning the Cup was easily one of the best days of my life, but every time I look over at the woman beside me, I know one day it's going to pale in comparison to when I officially make her my wife.

I stroke my finger over the ring that's adorning her hand. I proposed a week ago, our first night in Spain before all the other Comets filtered in for our group vacation. We decided we needed a break after winning the Cup and settled on a trip to a place none of us have been before.

"Babe, can you get my back?" Rosie hands me a bottle of sunscreen, then turns around in her chair.

"Babe, can you get my back?" Miller mocks from across the way.

"Shut up, Miller," just about everyone says to him, including me.

Some things never change, like my love for Rosie. We moved in together just before the Playoffs, and Carl has been having a blast in the new place. I'm having a blast not being worried about her getting locked in the pantry and not worrying about seeing my eighty-year-old neighbor naked.

It's a win-win for us.

I uncap the sunscreen, squirt some into my hand, and begin rubbing down my gorgeous fiancée. I fiddle with the strings on her orange bikini, wishing so badly we were alone so I could pull her top off and show her just how much I love her in the midday sun.

Who the hell thought a group vacation was a good idea again?

"Man, I'm so glad we could all do this together," Miller says.

Oh, right. Him.

"I'm here with my favorite people and my favorite girl." He winks at Scout. "And I'm the proud owner of a new title: Stanley Cup Champion."

"You already had that title," I remind him, rubbing the lotion into Rosie's soft skin.

"You're right. *Two-time* Stanley Cup Champion." He takes a sip of his beer, then smacks his lips obnoxiously. "What a fucking life, huh?"

"It's pretty nice," Lowell agrees. "And as much as I love my kids, I'm so glad to have a break."

"I'll drink to that." Hollis clinks her drink against Lowell's beer. "Though I do miss them."

"I miss Macie," Greer complains, frowning down at his phone like he's trying to convince himself not to check in on her. "She'd love this. We could be building sandcastles right now."

"No way. She's too cool for us now." Stevie rolls her eyes. "If she were here, she'd probably be at the pool with those boys we saw earlier."

"Boys? Fuck no!" Greer gets up like he's going to go beat some kids up, and Stevie tugs him back down into his chair, patting his back.

"Chill out. She's safe at home with her grandpa. There is no way he or Ernesto would let any boys near her."

"Um, you're both nuts. If anyone is going to chase boys away, it's Macie herself. My niece can handle things just fine," Scout says.

"Quit whining about your kids. I miss my dogs." Collin juts his lip out. "They're probably doing awful without me."

"Um, based on the photo Grams sent me, I doubt that," Ryan says. "They're living their best life with Frodo and Poe."

"I really don't know how my mother is handling all those animals and the kids *and* still has time to hang out with your grandmother." Harper shakes her head.

"Because Mom is a badass," Hollis tells her sister. "Duh."

"Yeah, duh, Harper," Miller says.

"Shut up, Miller."

I don't even know who says it this time, but it still makes me laugh.

"Um, Fitz?"

"Hmm?"

"I don't think I need sunscreen on my ass."

"Huh?" I look down and—yep, my hand is totally inside her bikini bottoms. "Oops."

She giggles, then swings back around, settling back into her chair. I toss the sunscreen aside, then reach over and drag her closer to me because the foot of space between us is entirely too much.

I'm addicted to this woman, and it's an addiction I'll gladly let rule my life. There's no way I'll ever get enough of her, no matter how much time we spend together. I'm going to soak it all in now while I can before we get back to North Carolina and reality, where I'll be busy with hockey and she'll be busy with her second year of college.

She's kicking ass, and I'm not surprised. Scout's even been helping her as she tries to find a location for her bakery. It's still a few years off, but she says there's no harm in starting to plan now. Rosie no longer streams, and all the sexy pictures she takes are sent directly to me. I wouldn't have an issue if she still wanted to do it, but she says I'm giving her everything she ever wanted.

"Hey, Ro," I whisper to her.

"Yes, Ivan?"

"I love you, future wife."

She grins. "I love you more, future husband."

"Aww, that's so sweet I could—"

"SHUT UP, MILLER!"

Everyone laughs, shaking their heads at him. He's as

exhausting as ever and we had to physically restrain him from packing his karaoke machine, but we still love him.

"Hayes, what's up, man? Why the long face?" Smith asks while casually playing with Emilia's hair as she sits in his lap. "Strike out on Tinder again?"

Hayes, the only single one here, is staring down at the phone in his hand, looking completely dejected. It's several more seconds before he looks up, and I'm not at all expecting the next words that leave him.

"I just got off the phone with my agent. I'm not playing for the Comets next season."

"What? Where are you going?"

"Seattle." He swallows roughly. "I'm going to be playing for the Seattle Serpents."

THE END

OTHER TITLES BY TEAGAN HUNTER

CAROLINA COMETS SERIES

Puck Shy

Blind Pass

One-Timer

Sin Bin

Scoring Chance

Glove Save

Neutral Zone

ROOMMATE ROMPS SERIES

Loathe Thy Neighbor

Love Thy Neighbor

Crave Thy Neighbor

Tempt Thy Neighbor

SLICE SERIES

A Pizza My Heart

I Knead You Tonight

Doughn't Let Me Go

A Slice of Love

Cheesy on the Eyes

TEXTING SERIES

Let's Get Textual

I Wanna Text You Up

Can't Text This

Text Me Baby One More Time

INTERCONNECTED STANDALONES

We Are the Stars

If You Say So

HERE'S TO SERIES

Here's to Tomorrow

Here's to Yesterday

Here's to Forever: A Novella

Here's to Now

Want to be part of a fun reader group, gain access to exclusive content and giveaways, and get to know me more?

Join Teagan's Tidbits on Facebook!

ACKNOWLEDGMENTS

This book wouldn't be possible without the support of these amazing people:

My husband. Thank you for always being my number one supporter. I love you most.

Laurie. You're my favorite person.

My editing team, Caitlin, Judy, and Julia. Thank you for providing your amazing skills and whipping this book into shape.

All the Bloggers, Bookstagrammers, and BookTokers who keep posting and sharing my books. Your support means the world to me.

My Tidbits. I LOVE YOU.

YOU. Thanks for taking a shot on this book. I really hope you loved it.

With love and unwavering gratitude,

Teagan

TEAGAN HUNTER writes steamy romantic comedies with lots of sarcasm and a side of heart. She loves pizza, hockey, and romance novels, though not in that order. When not writing, you can find her watching entirely too many hours of *Supernatural*, *One Tree Hill*, or *New Girl*. She's mildly obsessed with Halloween and prefers cooler weather. She married her high school sweetheart, and they currently live in the PNW.

www.teaganhunterwrites.com